She could feel her body still trembling . . .

Somewhere out there — for the first time in their lives — her children were confused and frightened and she could do nothing to ease their fears. Tomorrow she would have to put aside all feelings of helplessness, of rage, and assume a cheerful, compliant role. It would be her first acting role since high school, and her performance had to be good enough to convince Seth, the most important audience of her life. She could do it, she had to. But could she keep it up? How long could a person pretend without going over the edge?

Jen Sawyer's worst nightmare has come true . . . Somewhere out there Seth is waiting — to claim her body, her mind, her soul. And the horror that had been visited on her twelve years before seems about to happen one more time . . .

NIGHTSHADE

Gloria Murphy

CORGI BOOKS

NIGHTSHADE

A CORGI BOOK   0 552   13277 2

First publication in Great Britain

PRINTING HISTORY

Corgi edition published 1989

Copyright © 1986 by Gloria Murphy

This book is set in Fournier

Corgi Books are published by Transworld Publishers Ltd., 61–63 Uxbridge Road, Ealing, London W5 5SA, in Australia by Transworld Publishers (Australia) Pty, Ltd., 15–23 Helles Avenue, Moorebank, NSW 2170, and in New Zealand by Transworld Publishers (N.Z.) Ltd., Cnr. Moselle and Waipareira Avenues, Henderson, Auckland.

Made and printed in Great Britain by
Cox & Wyman Ltd., Reading, Berks.

Dedicated with love to my parents
Elizabeth "Betty" Walter
and
Frank Walter

ACKNOWLEDGEMENTS

Many thanks to my agent, Alice Martell, and my editors, Rick Horgan and Rennie Browne.

And last but not least, my daughter, Laurie Gitelman, who — as always — went far beyond the call of duty. It was she who believed in and encouraged me and served as my reader, my critic, and my sounding board throughout.

CHAPTER ONE

THE POCKET WATCH HUNG from the rearview mirror. Seth reached for it, his hand trembling as he cupped the gold case. The face read 2:55. Only five minutes to go. He struggled to control the excitement that welled up in him. Not that he wasn't used to holding things in – he was, but usually the feelings he held in were the bad ones, the ones that made it seem as though he were impaled on sharp spikes. This sensation was completely different. It was good.

There wasn't a doubt in his mind that he had earned this moment. He had been methodical and patient, doing what was necessary, waiting until he was sure the time was right. Now his dream would finally be fulfilled. The images that had played tricks with his mind all these years, making him happy for only the few moments, would at last find substance. Now, when he reached out to touch, his dream wouldn't slip through his fingers and disappear.

His thoughts drifted further: he imagined Jennifer already beside him. He could feel her cool, smooth body like velvet beneath his hands. But this sensation wasn't one he had just conjured up; this was one that he remembered all too well. It tormented him at the very same time it gave him reason to live and breathe. Never again could he let her slip away from him. Soon he would have Jennifer *and* the children – and he would not let them go.

He leaned forward, opened the glove compartment, and carefully removed the articles of clothing, studying each one. First came the pink-and-white panties. He drew the silk material close to his face, savouring the delicious fragrance of Jennifer. Next came the girl's blue tailored blouse. He preferred to see little girls in frilly things, lacy dresses with full skirts and sashes. But it didn't matter. Soon he'd be able to shower the girl with all the fancy clothes he had picked out for her. Finally he lifted a green sweatshirt out of the compartment. There was a felt *W* sewn across the chest. The boy's. Funny how things tended to work out. When he was a kid, he'd have given everything he owned to have a school letter – to be recognized as an athlete, a jock. Now it seemed silly, childish. Other things were more important.

Seth never tired of going through their clothing; it was almost like handling a little piece of each of them. During his 'visits' he'd always wanted to take more mementos, but each time he stopped himself. He didn't want Jennifer to discover he'd been in the house. That was why he always took care never to disturb anything. He just walked around, browsing, touching . . . Soon it wouldn't make one bit of difference one way or another, Seth thought. Soon he'd have all of them in the flesh. What would he need with mementos?

The dismissal bell rang, and he snapped out of his reverie. He quickly returned the clothes to the glove compartment, snapped it shut, then, spotting a piece of lint on his good, navy corduroy jacket, flicked it away. It was important he look his best. Finally, he focused his eyes on the tan brick building across the street: Winfield, Massachusetts' newest elementary school. At any moment, children would burst through the double doors. Seth rubbed the palm of one hand against the back of the other and shifted nervously in his seat.

The first child raced out of the building, heading a stampede of arms, legs, and faces all looking strangely alike. He squinted his eyes, searching each face, his breath now coming in spurts. They had to be there, he knew; he'd followed them to the schoolyard that morning.

Then he spotted the girl leaning against the chain-link fence, and his breathing slowed. It was impossible to mistake her: how very much like Jennifer she looked, her straight, sturdy body giving the promise of more to come, her thick honey-blonde hair hooked behind her ears. Seth pulled his eyes back towards the doors. Only a few stragglers, then nothing. He didn't like the delay, but whatever it was, it was temporary. He could see the girl's eyes focused on the doors – waiting, just like him.

He adjusted the rearview mirror and caught his reflection. Deep blue eyes stared back at him. His pallid complexion seemed to exaggerate his finely chiselled features, making them look too large for his face. A twitch pulsed rhythmically at the corner of his mouth like a heartbeat. He stretched his lips, trying to stop it.

Finally, out of the corner of his eye, he spotted the boy. The child raced to meet his sister, shoving his arm into the sleeve of his windbreaker as he ran.

Together they jogged along the dirt path, heading in Seth's direction. They were the same height and colouring, tall for their age and pale except for their pink cheeks. The boy's dark blond straight hair touched the collar of his jacket. Seth frowned. He'd have to do something about that.

They had just turned right onto Albany Avenue and were getting close to the car. Seth ran his fingers over his mouth as if to fix his expression in place, then looked over at the gold watch: 3:07. He rolled down the window.

'Hold on there!' The children stopped short. 'Margo and Matthew Sawyer?' He had practised the crisp, professional tone of voice.

The girl smiled. Seth watched as the boy stepped backwards, yanking his sister by the hand. *Slow, easy, calm:* Seth recited the words in silent warning to himself. Then he smiled at the boy.

'Don't be afraid, son.'

He lifted his hands from the steering wheel, his palms pushing downwards in a calming gesture. His fingers were steady; he felt more sweetly alive than he could ever remember feeling.

'I'm from the Winfield police. Your mother asked me to come get you . . .' He took his wallet from his back pocket, flipped it open to an I.D. card and silver badge. He held it up out of the window.

The boy shifted his weight from one foot to another.

The word *stranger* couldn't have been clearer had he shouted it.

'Why'd she do that?' he asked finally.

'There's been an accident in front of the shopping centre at Four Corners . . . Now, don't you go worrying none. Your mother's going to be okay.'

The girl sucked in her breath. 'Are you sure she's not hurt?'

'She's going to be fine – just a few minor bumps and bruises. Mostly she's shaken up.'

'What happened?'

'Seems a pole was sitting a smidgen too close to the road for its own good. What happened is she sideswiped it with her car.' He paused a moment, then went on. 'The truth is, that's a pretty nasty intersection out that way. Let's be thankful nothing worse happened.'

'Where is she now?' asked the girl.

'Emergency Room at Memorial. The doctors wanted to take a few x-rays, to be on the safe side. But like I told you, she's going to be okay, nothing broken.' He smiled. 'Of course, the pole's another matter . . . Come along with me and you'll see her for yourselves.' He watched them look at each other, then went on. 'You know how mothers are – instead of worrying about themselves, they worry about their children. What will make her feel best of all is having you kids right there with her.'

Margo started towards the car; her brother pulled her back by the shoulders.

'How come you're not in uniform?' he asked.

Seth laughed, then stopped when he saw the boy's face redden.

'Good question, son. You see, in our unit we don't wear uniforms. You've heard of plainclothes detectives, haven't you?'

Matthew nodded, but he made no move towards the car. Seth balled his hands into fists on his lap.

'Wait,' Margo said slowly, turning toward her brother. 'Remember when mama told us she'd never send a stranger to pick us up unless she told him her special name for us? If she really sent him, he'll know the name.' She turned back toward Seth and folded her arms across her chest. 'Hey, mister,' she said, 'what does our mother call us?'

Seth smiled. 'It seems to me that the name she used was "snowflake". What she asked me to do was to fetch her snowflakes.' He held his breath, waiting for their response. They weren't dummies, these two. No, not by a long shot. He felt a surge of pride.

'Okay,' Matthew said finally.

Seth blew out the air trapped in his lungs as the boy grabbed his sister's hand, walked to the dark blue Ford, opened the back-seat door, and got in. Margo climbed in after him and slammed the door. Seth flipped a button in the front panel and the four doors locked simultaneously.

Seth felt a charge of energy shooting through him, as if his system, having been overloaded, had momentarily gone haywire. He lowered his head and took a few deep breaths to quiet himself. It wasn't over yet. *Slow, easy, calm* – now, more than ever, he had to remember everything Dandy had tried to teach him. Slowly he lifted his head, turned the ignition key, and gunned the motor.

As they sped away from the school, Matthew looked into the front seat and noticed the man's ill-fitting jacket, its sleeve hiked up to show the beginning of a tattoo outlined on his right forearm. His eyes moved to the pocket watch hanging in front of the windshield, now dangling from side to side. He remembered a show he and Margo had seen: a magician had singled out a boy from the audience and ordered him to concentrate on a large swinging pendulum. The boy's eyes had followed the sweeping movement. It made him sleepy, then sleepier, then sucked the control right out of him. He hopped along the floor like a rabbit and meowed like a cat and never remembered any of it when the hypnotist snapped his fingers to wake him. Matthew quickly pulled his eyes away from the swinging pocket watch.

He wondered why his mother was shopping at Four Corners during working hours. She never did that. Why hadn't he asked the man that? His eyes turned towards his sister, who was staring out of the front window. He wanted to grab hold of her and jump out of the car, but he knew it was too late for that. *What have we done?* His shaky fingers combed though his heavy, tousled hair. Even before the car swung onto Route 93, north from Winfield – the opposite direction from the hospital – he felt his insides constricting and a heavy lump forming in his throat.

Jen immersed the hair brushes in Barbicide solution where they would soak overnight. She switched off the overhead fluorescents and took one last quick look around the backroom beauty shop before closing the door and heading into the kitchen. Two cancellations: feeling as she did after doing her last comb-out, they couldn't have come at a better time. Even normally agreeable women tended to be demanding and fussy when it came to their hairdos, but Jen couldn't recall old Mrs Carey ever being agreeable. And if her blue rinsed hair wasn't fingerwaved to the starched perfection of the forties, she was impossible.

She glanced at the kitchen clock: 3:10. The twins would be home any minute; if she hurried she'd have time to change before they walked in. She looked around: the table hadn't even been cleared from breakfast and the sink was overflowing with dirty dishes. It was Margo's week. She sighed then took off her smock and tossed it into the washing machine. It was pretty close to full – again. But first the dishes.

When she was done, she headed to her room. As she passed Matthew's room, she stopped: games, a dozen model aeroplanes and a box of CB components were piled up in the corner. Clothes were strewn along the floor like a trail of bread crumbs. No wonder he couldn't find his letter sweatshirt. She picked up some socks, underwear, shirts and a cellophane Ring Ding wrapper then stopped dropping the armful in a heap on the floor. No way. Surely an eleven-year-old boy could be expected to keep his own room up to Board of Health standards. Matthew would do it, the moment he walked in the door. Or else.

She glanced at the alarm clock on his bedside stand: 3:30 already. Now, where *were* they?

CHAPTER TWO

SETH LOOKED IN THE REARVIEW MIRROR every second he wasn't looking at the road. From the moment the car climbed the ramp onto Route 93, two miles back, the boy had suspected. Maybe even before, but that's when Seth saw the colour drain out of his cheeks. Then his teeth clamped down and bit into his lower lip. He didn't ask any questions. He looked too scared to ask a question, almost like he didn't want to know.

The girl had been easy. From the very beginning she had swallowed the accident story hook, line, and sinker, and it was taking her longer to notice where they were headed. But Seth kept his eye on her, waiting. Finally he saw her look around the roadway, her neck craning from one position to another. The mouth opened, then dropped. Watching her expression, he could almost see where one nightmare ended and another began. She rolled her hand into a little ball and pounded it on the back of his seat.

'Where're we going?' she said.

'To see your mother.'

'This isn't the way to the hospital. Where are you taking us?'

Seth didn't answer right away, not wanting to get upset and say the wrong thing.

'We're going to my house,' he said finally.

Margo bolted back in her seat, then turned to look at her brother. His head jerked up, and his eyes met hers. He grabbed hold of her hand and – almost as if she had passed him a message in silent code – took up where she left off.

'Take us home. We want to go home right now.'

17

'Now, don't you two start getting all upset,' Seth warned. 'I told you before, and I meant it – there's no need to be frightened. Soon your mother's going to be with us and then this will all make sense to you.'

'What are you *talking* about?' Matthew asked.

Seth could feel the little bubble begin to pulse again at the corner of his mouth; he stretched his lips to work it out.

'That's all I can say now. You're going to have to be patient and wait. Your mother and I have a lot of explaining to do and once you understand, you'll feel different about all of this. But for now I want you to sit still and hush up and not make things hard on yourselves.'

Seth felt his muscles relax. He had handled it just right, firm but not too harsh. Sometimes you had no choice with kids, you had to use a heavy hand for their own good. He looked in the rearview mirror. They sat huddled close together, so close it was hard to tell where one body began and one ended. Like Siamese twins, Seth thought. He felt bad that he had to scare the children like this, but it was better not to say too much now. It would only confuse them, throw them into a worse state than they were in already.

Children needed special handling. Most people didn't recognize that, but he did. Their heads were already brimming over with phantoms – bogeymen and monsters lurking in the middle of the night under their beds or hiding discreetly behind a pile of clothes in the closet, just waiting to pounce. Better to withhold information from them until they were able to fully understand it. Seth was sure that in time the children would appreciate what he was doing. Some day they'd thank him for taking them away.

Jen pulled her blue sweatsuit from the closet. Quickly she slid out of her skirt and sweater and into the soft cotton warmers. She glanced in the full-length mirror and adjusted the folds at her waist, then looked up. She had green eyes and a sprinkling of freckles across her nose. Thick dark ash blonde hair tangled its way down to her shoulders; she lifted a brush from the bureau and ran the stiff bristles through the snarls.

In the mirror, she could still see a hint of that stagestruck girl she had been at sixteen. No disgruntled customers to deal with ... and no stacks of dirty dishes. In those days she would have laughed had anyone suggested she trade in her dream to study beauty culture. As it was, no one had. Even the school drama coach had encouraged her theatrical ambition.

Today, at thirty-two, she could still remember the standing ovation she'd received when she played Laura in *The Glass Menagerie*. Her mother, as usual, had stood cheering in front row centre. Jen had been good – there was no doubt about it. The proof was that, though there were many girls prettier than she, she had been cast in the lead role of every high school play. Not musicals, though. In musical productions she had volunteered for any job on the production crew she could get. She was one of those people who dared only lip-synch 'The Star-Spangled Banner' for fear of throwing the rest of the voices permanently off key.

Aside from rare moments like today, Jen seldom thought about those times. The truth was, she never regretted her unexpected career choice. Though enthusiasm sometimes pushed her to take on more than was reasonable, she also had a practical side – a side that enabled her to single out what was most important to her. It was this combination that helped her land feet first when a curve was tossed her way, even to make the most of the curve. And it was her practicality that had finally convinced her not to pursue acting.

Jen's father left her mother when Jen was less than a year old; years later, he was killed in an oil rigging accident in Alaska. Aside from seeing a dozen tattered pictures of a stranger in an album, she had no memories of a father. Maybe because of that, Jen and her mother were doubly close. When her mother suffered a stroke and died the year Jen graduated from high school, she was shattered. As much as she loved the theatre, she decided she wasn't willing to risk years of loneliness and struggling in a career that might never again bring her a role as satisfying as Laura. What she wanted even more was a family. After graduation, she moved fifty miles south to Ashley, and using money from the small insurance policy left by her mother, enrolled herself in the New Hampshire Beauty Academy.

The fact was, if things hadn't worked out as they had, she might never have met Jim. And though their time together was ended all too quickly, she wouldn't have traded that brief time with him for ten acting careers. Their marriage had been special, both of them able to laugh and cry over what many people hardly noticed.

Having grown up as only children, she and Jim had been eager to fill the house with a half-dozen kids and the noise and confusion that accompanies them. For the thousandth time she thought what a wonderful father Jim would have made. Like Jen, Margo and Matthew had never known a father, and as much as she liked to think that she could be all things to them – could make up for that loss – she knew how impossible it was. She took one last look at the girl in the mirror, hooked her hair behind her ears, then tossed the skirt and sweater onto the chair. As she turned, her eye caught the hand-carved lovebirds Jim's folks had sent; it was the only gift they'd ever sent that she liked. She lifted the lovebirds off the dresser top and for a moment ran her fingers over the sculpted surface, then put them down and headed for the parlour.

She looked out of the window, then ran around collecting the remnants of last night's newspaper. *Darn those kids – they know better.* She went to the pail in the kitchen, stuffed the papers in, then looked again at the clock: 3:45. The children always came straight home from school. They were late, nearly a half hour late, and for the very first time.

With the thought, her irritation subsided. She walked through the parlour again, onto the front porch, her eyes searching up and down Arden Road. No sign of them. She folded her arms across her chest, shivering as a cool breeze whipped against her. She looked over at the lawn chair still out on the porch. The weather was quickly turning cold; it was time to get the chair inside. She started towards it, stopped short, then looked again up and down the block.

This time she caught a glimpse of a boy rounding the corner, a baseball cap perched on his head. His head was down, eyes following the rock he had just kicked into the gutter. She ran down the steps and across the path. When she reached the sidewalk, she cupped her hands to her mouth.

'Danny!'

The boy looked up, then ran over to her.

'Hi, Mrs Sawyer. Where's Matt?'

'I was just about to ask you that. Have you seen him or Margo?'

'Not since school let out. Matt stayed after for a couple of minutes to see what he got on the math test.'

'So what's your excuse?'

'Huh?'

Jen leaned over and tipped the boy's hat back. 'Why so late?'

'Oh, me.' He looked down and dug his sneaker into the dirt at the edge of the sidewalk. 'I had to stay after. The teacher caught me chewing gum.'

'I see. Did anyone else stay after?'

'Nope, only me.'

'You're sure Matt left school? There wasn't a last-minute track practice?'

'No way. I would have known. You mean he never came home from school?'

Jen shook her head.

'He should have been home by now, Mrs Sawyer. Maybe he stopped off at somebody's house.'

Jen bit down on her lip. 'If you see either of them, Danny, tell them I'm looking for them. Tell them to get right home.'

'Sure, Mrs Sawyer. I'll tell 'em.'

Jen turned to go, then stopped and looked back at the boy.

'You'd better get a move on yourself. Your mother's probably wondering where you are.'

The boy pulled at the visor on his cap, bobbed his head up and down, then ran off down the street. Jen marched back into the house and headed for the kitchen. She pulled open a drawer and took out the address book. Danny was right.

More than likely they had stopped at a friend's house on the way home and lost track of the time. But it was so unlike them – Matthew in particular. Aside from misplacing clothes and needing to be reminded to clean up his bedroom, he was always so reliable.

He was only eleven years old though. Sometimes she forgot that.

Matthew wasn't sure just when the two-lane highway they turned onto had run out, but it had. They were now travelling on a narrow wooded road, the kind that had lots of twists and turns and not a single landmark to make one spot look any different from another. When had they got off Route 93? He knew he hadn't been asleep. In fact, he was trying his best to stay alert – to remember everything he saw, anything that might help him figure out where they were headed. His mind had been busy trying to think up a plan of escape. The trouble was, all the plans he could think of required his being fast on his feet, and though he and Margo were faster than most kids, his legs felt stiffer and weaker than he ever remembered them feeling.

He looked out the side window at the road: no houses, no cars, no people. It reminded him of the road mama took when they visited their grandparents. Almost every summer they'd load the car with suitcases, rubber tubes, and fishing gear and drive to New Hampshire. They'd sing songs and tell jokes the whole way. Even though mama had one of the worst singing voices he'd ever heard, that didn't stop her. Mama wasn't afraid or embarrassed to do anything she really felt like doing. That's what made her different from all the other mothers.

Thinking of her made Matthew's eyes fill up, but he kept them as wide open as he could. Margo hadn't cried once; he knew how hard she was trying not to, and he wasn't about to make it harder for her.

Margo was the first to notice the abandoned diner ahead. She squeezed Matthew's hand to get his attention and sat forward on the seat. The car slowed to a stop.

'I've got to go to the bathroom,' she announced.

'There's no bathrooms here.' The man pointed to the boarded-up building. 'You wait right where you are, honey, I'm going to make a phone call.' Next to the building stood an enclosed phone booth. Matthew thought it an odd place for a telephone; he wondered if anyone ever used it.

When the man turned around to face them, Matthew looked hard at his features for the first time: the straight nose, thin lips, blue eyes. A lock of dark blond hair fell to one side of his forehead.

'I'm going to call your mother so she won't be worrying about you.'

'I want to talk to her,' Margo said.

'Not now. You sit tight, honey. Before you know it, you'll be with her. Then you can do all the talking you want.'

The man was in the booth only a few minutes before he came out and folded the glass cage shut. He walked back to the car, unlocked the rear doors by the front panel, swung one door open, and beckoned to Margo.

'Okay, you come on out.'

She squirmed closer to her brother. 'Where're you taking me?'

'Didn't I hear you say you had to go? Come on out here and squat down beside the car. We've got a long ride ahead of us, and there won't be any place to stop. You don't want to go having an accident, do you?'

'I'll hold it till we find a real bathroom. I'm not going out here in front of everyone.'

'You'll do like I tell you.'

He put his hand on her arm and pulled her from the car; Matthew jumped out after her, surprised at how fast his legs were working. He pointed up a trail covered with dry, fallen leaves.

'Let her go up there in the woods. Behind a tree.'

The man followed the direction of his finger, then looked at him.

'Who's to say she won't go running off?'

Margo hadn't taken her eyes off him for a moment.

'I'd never run off without my brother.' She spoke clearly, slowly, as if trying to get an obvious point across.

Seth nodded. 'No, I suppose you wouldn't.'

Seth and Matthew stood next to the car while Margo climbed up the hill. Matthew saw the man's eyes follow her as she walked.

'Just like her mother, isn't she?' the man said. 'Shy and bashful. I like that in a woman – it's something to be admired and respected. Most women nowadays aren't like that. You'll learn that soon enough. Oh they *look* pure and innocent, but what's in their minds is something else altogether. Take it from me, son, stay away from that kind. They'll only make you feel dirty.' He reached over and gently put his arm around the boy's shoulder. 'I know it's not a nice thing to talk about, but it's something every boy should know. And it's just not a thing a mother knows how to teach.'

Matthew didn't answer, didn't pull away. It took every ounce of will power he had to keep himself from doing either.

Jen had called every last one of their friends, the school, the hospital – then, finally, the police. She had just hung up the phone, her hand still cradling the receiver, when it rang. She jumped, then quickly pulled the receiver back up to her ear.

'This is Seth,' the voice said.

'I'm sorry . . . what number are you trying to reach?'

'I hope you haven't called the police yet.'

Jen felt a blowing in her ears, blocking them. She waited a few moments for her hearing to clear, then spoke up.

'Who is this?'

'Seth.'

'Seth who?'

'Jennifer, I have the children . . . *our* children.'

Her fingers tightened around the receiver.

'Is this some kind of joke? If it is, it's not funny. Now, who *is* this?'

'Don't you remember? You must have known I'd be back some day.'

Her fingers squeezed the receiver so tightly they ached, but still she squeezed harder.

'Remember?' she cried. 'What are you talking about? Who *is* this?'

'The children's daddy.'

Jen dropped the receiver. She stepped back against the wall; her eyes were closed, but she could hear the words reach up to her from the receiver on the floor: 'Jennifer? Jennifer! Are you okay? Answer me.'

She pressed her fingers to her temples.

'Jennifer, come back to the phone. Talk to me!'

Why wouldn't the voice stop, why wouldn't it leave her alone?

'Jennifer, remember – I have the children.'

She opened her eyes and looked down, afraid she would see fragments of his face push through the tiny holes in the receiver. She sank down onto her knees beside it, staring at the receiver as if it were alive. After a few moments, she willed her arm to extend outwards, and lifted the receiver back to her ear.

'Why . . . why are you doing this?' she asked.

'I love you, I've never stopped. And the children – I love them, too. I want to take care of my family.'

'Please, oh please, don't do this. Please bring them back.'

Silence.

'Do you hear me? I want you to bring them back, right this minute.'

'Jennifer, raising your voice isn't going to help matters. Now, listen carefully. I'm taking them home, Jennifer. To their new home. With me.'

Jen swallowed hard. 'What do you want, tell me.' She listened to her voice as she spoke; it sounded as if someone else were saying the words for her.

'I want you to meet us. To be with us.'

'I'll come.' It was the unfamiliar voice speaking for her again. Surely her own voice would never agree to meet this man. Out of all the people in the world, never him.

'I don't want anyone knowing about this, Jennifer. Not a soul. And if you go against what I tell you, you'll wish you hadn't. I'll find out and I'll take them away – so far you'll never find them.'

The voice didn't answer him. Shouldn't it say something? She guessed not, because she heard him talk again.

'Jennifer, please understand. That's not what I want. I want only to make a home for you and the children. Now, I'm going to hang up. The children are getting restless, and I want to get them to the house.'

'Wait . . . don't go yet. Wait.'

'Don't worry, I'll call again tonight at nine. I want to give you time to pull yourself together. Think over what I've said, think it over carefully.'

She nodded her head. The voice stayed silent.

'And most of all, Jennifer, I want you to calm down, relax. There's no need to be frightened. Trust me.'

She heard the click, then the line went dead. She dropped the receiver into the cradle and dashed for the bathroom. Minutes later, she finally stopped retching. Her head still hung over the toilet bowl, but there was nothing left to come up. Slowly, stiffly, she rose to her feet – as if any jarring motion might again throw the machinery out of whack. She rinsed her mouth in the sink, then looked at her reflection in the mirror. Her image seemed to float, giving the peculiar sensation that she was watching someone else. Her body felt limp; she grabbed onto the edge of the sink to steady herself. A part of her life that had so long been buried now came back in waves as violent as the waves of nausea. A jumble of pictures all vied for her attention – each piece more frightening than the next.

The man who had raped her: the father of her children. Surely he could have no rights, no claims. She remembered an article she'd read about a bunch of men marching on Boston Commons, carrying signs: 'Unwed Fathers Have Rights Too'. Suddenly, she let out a high-pitched laugh. She pressed her hand over her mouth trying to hold back the hysteria.

Finally, she sank down onto the cold tile floor and crossed her legs Indian-fashion. She was a survivor – hadn't she proven it time and time again? She thought back to the childhood illnesses, to Margo's bronchial pneumonia. Then way back to Matthew's accident when he was only two. She could still imagine how it must have happened. Stubby determined little fingers stretching and pulling until the metal roller sprang free and the gate opened. A strong little body wriggling and squirming its way through a gap in another fence. And then his explorations ending – in the Larsons' swimming pool. By the time she found him, he was underwater; she didn't know how long. She dragged him out onto the flagstone patio. A circle gathered around them; voices whispered and moaned, but she wouldn't listen to what they said. No, she wouldn't listen. She moved quickly, without hesitation – somehow knowing but never sure how she knew. Squeezing, adjusting the head, then breathing, counting the seconds, the intervals – over and over again. When the ambulance got there, she was holding him in her arms and they were both crying.

She raised her head and pulled her thoughts back to the present. On Seth. She turned his name over in her mind; today was the first time she'd heard it. He would call again tonight, and she had to be ready. If she went along with what he wanted, the children would be safe – he wouldn't take them away where she'd never see them again. His words spun around in her mind like a record. Had she really heard them? Had someone really said that to her?

She jumped at the sound of the doorbell, then remembered her call to the police. She had to think of something to say, having already decided somewhere in the back of her mind that she couldn't risk crossing this man by involving the police. She didn't yet know what she *would* do once she joined him; her mind hadn't yet gotten that far. But first things first. Get to the children.

The bell was still ringing. She stood up, turned on the cold water, splashed some on her face and blotted it dry, then went to the door. She hesitated a moment before opening it, arranging her features to resemble a smile.

The man had thick, dark hair – almost black – with matching brows and a deep cleft in his chin. He flashed a badge in front of her.

'Lieutenant Thorne.' He waited a few moments for a response, then said, 'You called about a couple of missing kids?'

'I'm sorry I bothered you.' Her voice came out high-pitched; she took a deep breath before going on. 'It was a false alarm – I found them. I guess I panicked. You know how it is. You read the newspapers, and before you know it you start imagining all kinds of crazy things.'

Thorne nodded. 'Can I come inside? I'd like to ask you a few questions.'

Jen stared up at him, not moving an inch. She knew she should get rid of him immediately, but for some reason she wasn't ready to let him go. Once the door was closed, she'd be alone again with her fear.

She stepped back a few feet and let him walk in. She could feel his dark eyes studying her. She moved to the coffee table and began to straighten the pile of magazines; he took her elbow and led her to a chair.

'Relax a few minutes, will you? You look like you've been through the wringer.'

She sank down into the chair and looked up at him.

'You're right, of course. It really threw me. Kids are like that, they can scare the daylights out of you. Don't get me wrong, it's not that mine make a habit of doing things like this. I mean, usually they don't, they go by the house rules.' She laughed; it sounded off-pitch to her ears, but she went on. 'It's important to set guidelines, you know. When they're expected home, when they... uh.' Jen's mind suddenly went blank. She fought desperately to remember what she had been about to say.

Thorne took her hand. 'Say, you *are* shook up.'

Jen forced a smile. 'It's just taking me a while to get over the scare. That's all.'

He stared at her for a moment. Finally he broke the silence.

'Where did you find them?'

She had been looking down at her hands in her lap, but her head jerked up at his question.

'At one of their friend's houses.'

'When we spoke on the phone, it was my understanding that you had already checked out all their playmates. Am I right?'

She was making a mess of this. He didn't believe her – it was evident by the way he looked at her, and it was evident by his questions. She had to convince him. If she couldn't pull this off, how would she ever handle Seth? 'I'm afraid I forgot one of them. You see, there's a new boy on the block. Not too far from here.'

'You remembered after we spoke?'

'Yes. I guess I panicked or I would have thought of him right away.'

'I see.'

'Tell me, lieutenant, do you have children?'

The question caught him by surprise.

'No,' he said. 'I'm a bachelor.'

'I see.' She made it a point to speak slowly, keeping her voice calm and confident. 'You worry about kids sometimes when it's not even necessary, lieutenant. You sometimes tend to overreact. I guess it goes with the territory of parenting – single-parenting, at any rate. This time you've had the misfortune to catch an overreactor in full bloom. I'm sorry.'

'How long have you been a single parent, Mrs Sawyer?'

'Jen. And to answer your question, that's the only kind I've ever been. My husband died before the children were born.'

Thorne nodded. 'Jen, I see a lot of things in my work. I have no doubt that it can be rough trying to raise kids alone. Listen, why don't you let me talk to the kids, let them know how important it is not to pull a stunt like this? You'd be surprised, one word from a policeman can sometimes make more of a dent than a twenty-minute lecture from a parent.'

As Jen listened to his words, the reality of the situation

came back and hit her like a slap. If only it were that simple – oh, how she'd love to take him up on his offer. *I'm sorry, lieutenant, a talk of that kind wouldn't be possible at the moment. There's a minor difficulty. You see, they're not home. Do you understand? They're not here – they never came home!* She wanted to shout it at him: instead, she stood up.

'Thank you,' she said, 'but that won't be necessary. I'm afraid I've already delivered my lecture. They won't be doing this again. I really appreciate your concern, but I think what I need now is a hot bath to soothe my nerves.'

Thorne remained sitting. 'Are you sure there's nothing else you want to tell me? I'm a good listener.'

'What else could there be?'

Thorne strolled down the path with his hands in his pockets. He wasn't quite sure what to make of it. What was it about her? She wasn't beautiful, but there was something that made you want to keep looking – the pale face and pink cheeks and all that tousled hair falling over her shoulders. Fresh and natural, almost like a kid herself. Those big eyes seemed to suck you in . . . They reminded him of Carol's eyes. And just as it was with Carol, he wasn't sure what they were trying to tell him.

He opened the car door, sat in the driver's seat and took a pen and pad from the glove compartment. He still had to turn in a report. The fact was, most parents didn't know who the hell their kids hung out with these days. He looked back at the house, tapping the end of his pen against his chin. She didn't strike him as that kind of parent. In his eight years as a patrolman and four as detective, he had developed pretty sound instincts about people. No, this one wasn't irresponsible, and she certainly wasn't an overreactor – screw what she said. In spite of her concern on the phone, she hadn't been hysterical. She'd shown control, was using her head to check out all the possibilities.

He pushed the pad and pen back into the glove compartment, slammed it shut and turned the key in the ignition. As he approached the corner, Jen's face was still vivid in his mind. According to her, the kids were safe and sound. Yet he could have sworn there was real fear beneath all that composure she had come up with – more fear than she expressed earlier on the telephone. Why?

She had shifted from hyper to cool-and-controlled within seconds. He felt worn out, as if he'd been on a roller coaster for fifteen minutes nonstop. That first reaction of hers was one he'd seen many times over – the chattering, the jumpiness right after a crisis, the need to throw off some of that nervous energy. Even the hanging on to him as though she needed the security of a hand, any hand. That he could understand. What he couldn't understand was the sudden metamorphosis – the logical, calm demeanour coming to him right out of nowhere. That threw him. He thought about it, trying to figure it out. She was embarrassed and felt the need to put on an act – was that it? He sighed. No, that wasn't it. He was sure there was more.

CHAPTER THREE

THEY HAD COVERED SO MANY MILES since leaving school, Matthew had long given up any hope of retracing their route. He had, however, noticed several signs that showed they were in Maine. And he knew the man's name: he had told them it was Seth.

By the time the car stopped, it was already dark. Before turning off the motor, Seth released a button and the locks on the four doors flipped up. He carefully unwound the chain from the mirror and dropped the watch into his jacket pocket, then turned around facing them.

'Well, what do you think of it?' He gestured towards the tiny house.

They were parked at the end of a long gravel driveway stretching back a distance from the road. Matthew looked out the car window. He squinted his eyes to see the cabin; it reminded him of the houses he had built with his Lincoln Logs. Tall pine trees and thick brush surrounded the property like a fortress.

Margo made no pretence of looking at Seth's house.

'I'm not going in there,' she said. She slouched back in her seat and stared down at her feet.

'Sure you will, honey. You don't understand – this is where we're going to stay, you and your brother and your mama. And me.'

Margo held her position and didn't answer, as if by ignoring him she could make him go away. Seth turned from her, opened the driver's seat door and got out, then opened the back door. He leaned in towards her.

'Then I reckon I'll just have to carry you. Little girls like to be carted around, don't they? If you want, I can even throw you up on my shoulders. Piggyback.' He slid one hand under her legs and the other around her back. 'Come to daddy.'

Margo kicked her legs out from his grip and swung her arms forward to push him away.

'Don't you dare say that,' she shouted. 'You're not my father. Take your hands off me – leave me alone.'

Seth backed up as if her words had been blows. He slapped his hands over his ears and shut his eyes. His face twisted grotesquely, his fine features stretched out of shape as if they had turned into a rubber mask. The children stared at him, his panic spreading to them. Matthew grabbed with one hand for Margo and with the other for the door handle at his side. Then, just as his hand pushed down the lever to release the door, Seth's attention snapped back to them. He grabbed Margo's arm roughly, catching both children by surprise.

'You'll do what I tell you,' he yelled, his voice a high-pitched wail. A red welt was forming on Margo's arm.

'You're hurting me!'

Matthew grabbed at Seth's hand, trying to pry his fingers loose.

'Let her go,' he said. 'It's okay, she'll do what you tell her. Just please let her go.'

Seth looked at Matthew as though he wasn't quite sure who he was, then slowly released his grip. He pulled back, stood up, and turned his face from them.

Matthew put his arm around Margo.

'Please, Margo,' he whispered, 'you've got to go inside. It's going to be okay – you'll see. But for now we've got to do what he says. We can't get him angry.'

She looked into her brother's eyes, nodded, then followed him out of the car. The two of them stood next to Seth, awaiting his instructions.

'Well,' he said, 'it looks like we're all set to go in. I know you're anxious to take a look at the house.'

They followed him up the dirt path to the door, Matthew wondering if the man had already erased the past few minutes from his mind. Seth pulled a key ring from his pocket, then, picking one from the bunch, slid it into the lock and turned it. He pushed open the door, turned toward the children, and with a grand gesture Matthew had seen only in the movies, swung out his arm indicating for them to enter.

'Welcome home, children,' he said.

Jen rummaged through every drawer and coat pocket in the house without finding a single cigarette. She had given up smoking more than six months ago, thanks to the children. It had been murder, but with those four alert, accusing eyes there to monitor her, she had somehow managed it. Now those eyes were no longer there, and her nerves screamed for a smoke. It was only seven o'clock. He had told her he'd call at nine sharp with further instructions. Two whole hours.

The quietness she normally enjoyed when the children were asleep now seemed to isolate her from the rest of the world. The settling noises of the house that she usually found so familiar were making her jumpy. She sat down on the sofa and leaned back, her fingers pressed to her temples. She was the only one who knew the circumstances of the twins' birth. Her mind immediately corrected itself; she had *thought* she was the only one.

The doorbell rang, and she jumped to her feet. She wasn't expecting anyone, and the last thing she needed now was having to pretend everything was normal. She waited a few moments to collect herself. On the third ring, she opened the door a crack and looked out. Lieutentant Thorne stood on the doorstep holding a brown paper bag in one arm. He was not a tall man, yet his muscular frame seemed to dwarf the doorway. She fought the sudden urge to step forward, right into his arms. Instead she took a deep breath before she spoke and made her tone as formal as possible.

'What can I do for you, lieutenant?'

'Well, since you put it that way, I'll tell you what I had in mind. Being a single fellow, I have this tendency to exist on sandwiches – none of those good square meals you read about. It's not that I don't like a good meal as well as the next guy, but it somehow loses its appeal when you have to eat it by yourself. My thought was, maybe if I picked one up you'd share it with me. Look at it like you're doing me a favour.'

She looked down at her feet. 'Lieutenant, I—'

'Try Mike.'

She was again aware of his deep, soothing voice. She might as well look up.

'I don't mean to be rude,' she said, 'but I'm tired. As you know, I've had a harrowing day, and what I need most of all is peace and quiet. In other words, I need to be left alone.'

'Look, I know you've had a bad day, which is why I thought I'd try to see what I could do to pick it up a little. Now, you don't want to send me away like this, do you? It'd be a hell of a blow to my ego, and for that matter could quite possibly stunt my free spirit.' He held the bag forward like an offering. 'Barbecued spareribs, chicken wings, rice, and a bottle of wine. White wine with chicken wings, right?'

Jen didn't respond, and his expression sobered.

'You were pretty uptight this afternoon. I thought you might need to unwind.'

'I take it this is the usual fare given out by the Winfield police?'

He smiled for the first time. 'We've got an emergency slush fund for just such occasions.'

'I'm sorry, lieutenant – Mike. I really do appreciate the thought, but not this evening. I want to be alone.'

'The kids sleeping already?'

Jen, feeling her eyes sting, bit down on her lower lip. Then, afraid that one word out of her mouth might set her off, she answered his question with a nod.

'Did you eat yet?'

This time she shook her head no. Thorne pushed open the door, catching her off guard, and swept past her.

'Now, just a minute, Mike—'

'Hold on, don't take out the pistols, I'm getting out of here. I just wanted to leave this for you.' He set the bag on the coffee table.

'But what about—'

Thorne held up his hands to stop her. 'No problem, I'll grab a sandwich.' As he turned to go, the phone rang.

Jen stared at the instrument as though she had never seen a telephone before and wasn't quite sure what to do with it. Thorne followed her eyes to the ringing phone, then looked back at her.

'Okay, I give up. What are the house rules? Do we answer phones after seven p.m.?'

She walked over and lifted the receiver, not saying hello.

'Jennifer, is that you?' It took her a moment to recognize her father-in-law's monotone.

'Clarence?'

'Of course. How are you and the children? We miss you.'

'Yes.'

'Jennifer, are you okay?'

'I'm fine. Just fine.'

'You sound a little under the weather to me.'

'No, everything is fine.'

'Maybe you ought to be getting out more. Don't think I don't know how hard a job you have there, Jennifer. But all work and no play isn't good for anyone. I worry about you, dear. Now tell me, where are those two fine grandchildren of mine?'

'They went to bed early.'

'I see.' She could hear the disappointment in his voice. 'Well, sorry I missed them. It picks me up when I get to talk to those two.'

She wanted to change the subject but wasn't sure how to do it.

'How's Miriam?' she said finally.

His voice immediately lost what little zest it had.

'You know her, she's as well as can be expected. She's not well, Jennifer. Not able to take things in her stride like most women.' Jen sighed. To her, Miriam always seemed fit as a bull. 'Just a moment,' Clarence said, 'let me see if she's up to coming to the phone to say hello.'

The last thing Jen wanted was to talk to her mother-in-law, but before she could object he had already dropped the phone. She heard the whining, high-pitched voice in the background, then right in her ear.

'Jennifer?'

'Yes,' Jen said. 'How are you?'

'Not well, I'm afraid – the cold weather doesn't do much to help. I wouldn't wish my pain on anyone.'

Jen listened without responding as Miriam went on to describe in detail the various pains she wouldn't wish on anyone.

'Tell me,' she said finally, 'how is my grandson?'

Jen was used to her slighting Margo, but tonight it hit a raw nerve.

'*Both* children are fine,' she said.

'Are you making sure they don't go running out without their jackets? It may be only mid-October, but it's getting chilly already. Winter's coming early this year, you can tell.' Why did her every statement always sound to Jen like a condemnation?

'They're warm and they're fine.'

'No need to snap at me, Jennifer. After all, Jim would want me to check up on these things. And if we waited for your calls, we'd never know what was going on. For that matter, it wouldn't hurt for you to visit more often than once a year. Dad and I aren't getting any younger, you know.'

'And *you* know I can't be running off to New Hampshire at the drop of a hat. I do work for a living.' She put her hand to her forehead and shut her eyes. She hadn't meant to speak so harshly.

'If you ask me, it sounds like you're losing that unflappable attitude of yours. I've always said it, raising two children and running a business is just too much for any one person to handle.'

'The truth is, I think I'm coming down with a bug. I didn't mean to bark at you, but when your call came, I was just about to undress and crawl into bed.'

'Well, you take better care of yourself. No sense in spreading germs to the children. Drink some warm buttermilk, and fill yourself up with plenty of vitamin C. And for sake, don't take any of those over-the-counter drugs – they're poison. Dad and I will call again later this week to check in on you. Goodbye, now.'

Jen heard the click at the other end and set the receiver down wearily. Thorne stood with his hands in his pockets, studying her.

'Not your favourite person, I take it. Mother-in-law?'

She had never told anyone, but the truth was she didn't much like either of Jim's parents. She nodded.

He pointed towards the bag. 'Have something to eat and take your advice – crawl into bed. I'll get out of here.' He started towards the door, then turned back. 'Listen, do me a favour, will you?'

'What's that?'

'Call me at the station if you need anything. Even if it's just someone to talk to. Okay?'

'There is one thing . . . Mike.'

'What is it?'

'Would you happen to have a cigarette on you?' Thorne hesitated as if he were about to say something, then thought better of it. He pulled a pack of Marlboros from his shirt pocket, tapped the box and held them out to her. Jen managed to pull one out and put it up to her lips. He pulled a lighter from his pants pocket and lit the cigarette, watching her as she inhaled the smoke.

'Get yourself a good night's sleep.' He tossed the box of cigarettes on the table. 'You keep these.'

Just as he was about to close the door after himself, Jen called out to him.

'Mike!'

He turned back.

'Yes?' She didn't say anything. He waited, but still she said nothing. 'What is it, Jen?'

'The cigarettes,' she said. 'Thank you.'

The children sat across from each other at the table while Beth spooned the frankfurter slices and beans onto their plates.

'Eat up.' he told them. 'I don't want your mother think[ing]
I didn't care for you properly.'

'Is she really coming here?' Margo asked.

Seth nodded, leaned back against the small refrigerator an[d]
folded his arms across his chest.

'I wouldn't lie to you,' he said softly, 'she'll be here a[ll]
right.'

'Well, you lied to us about who you were and where yo[u]
were taking us. Maybe you're lying about mama comin[g]
too.'

'That's different. I had to do that so you'd come alon[g]
with me. Don't you understand? As long as there's goodnes[s]
behind the words, then a lie is not so bad. A lie is only evi[l]
when evil is the motivator – you know what I mean, th[e]
thing behind it.'

Margo studied his face. 'Who told you that?'

'Why, I heard it from . . . it's something I know, that's all[.]
Some things just come to you – you don't even have to pic[k]
up a book to know them, they're just all of a sudden tucke[d]
away in your head.'

'Why do you want us, anyway?' Matthew asked.

Seth rubbed the palm of one hand against the back of th[e]
other.

'I want to take care of you,' he said. 'I want to prote[ct]
you.'

'From what?'

'From all those people out there who might hurt you[.]
Seth sighed. 'You know, it's not as rosy out there as yo[u]
seem to think. There's people out there ready to harm you [if]
you're not careful. That's why it's so important for us t[o]
stick together, to be a real family.'

'But *we're* not your family,' Margo said.

Seth glared at her. 'What would you say if I told you th[at]
you were?'

'We wouldn't believe you. That's what.'

'Well, then, we'll just wait till your mother gets here an[d]
see what she has to say about that. You trust *her*, don't you?[']

Neither child answered him. Matthew stared at him, tryin[g]

o make sense out of what he was saying. The only relatives
_new of were his father's parents. Mama's had died before
_d Margo were even born. Why did this man insist he
was part of their family?

'Eat your food,' Seth said, changing the subject. Matthew
ished a frankfurter piece out of the runny beans and put it in
his mouth.

Once they were finished, Seth told Margo to do the dishes,
hen turned to Matthew.

'You come with me, son.'

Matthew followed him cautiously from the kitchen into the
ne big room adjoining it. Except for a worn sofa covered
vith a brown throw, a mahogany hutch, and three wooden
hairs standing in the back of the room under the window,
he room was bare. Seth pulled one of the chairs over in front
f the fireplace.

'Sit down right here,' he said.

'What are you going to do?'

'Nothing to be afraid of. You just sit still, and I'll be right
ack.'

Matthew lowered himself into the chair, watching over his
houlder as Seth opened the top drawer of the dark wood
abinet and lifted something out. When he returned to the
hair, he had a pair of electric clippers in his hand.

'What are you going to do?' Matthew asked again,
mping to his feet.

Seth put his hand on the boy's shoulder and gently pushed
im back down.

'I'm going to give that head of yours a clipping. No boy
ught to be walking around with all that long hair. You don't
ant to look like a little girl, do you?' He bent down and
lugged the cord into a double outlet on the floor.

'I don't want you doing that.' But even while he was
lking, Seth switched on the clippers. Matthew could hear
e buzzing next to his ear. 'No.' He wriggled away from the
ppliance. Seth shoved him down again, this time keeping
ne hand firmly on his shoulder.

'You stay put while I do what I have to. It's not going to

41

hurt a bit. You know, when I was a little boy, we'd line up once a month for a clipping like this, and everybody did what they were told without one bit of backtalk or else they'd be strapped into their chairs.'

Matthew, his hair falling and piling up on the bare floor, closed his eyes so he wouldn't have to look at it. He knew it would be stupid to fight more and make the man really angry. Besides, it was only a haircut – what was the big deal? He'd had dozens of haircuts. But never with clippers, and never against his will. This one made him feel the way he felt when someone took something from him that wasn't theirs and wouldn't give it back. Despite himself, he began to cry.

Margo watched from the kitchen, a dishrag held in her hand. When she saw Matthew's tears, she felt a cold rage seep into her and take hold. Her fist was squeezed so tightly around the rag that a small puddle of water formed on the tile floor. She decided right then and there: she would never tell her brother that she saw.

When the phone rang at nine o'clock, Jen grabbed the receiver on the first ring. This time, it had to be him.

'Hello.' Her voice sounded louder than she had intended.

'Jennifer?'

'Yes. Is this Seth?'

'Were you expecting someone else?'

'No, of course not. Seth, can I speak to the children?'

He sighed. 'I'm afraid I can't let you do that. By this time they ought to be fast asleep back at the house. Remember, he said, 'this has been a big day for them. For all of us.'

'They're alone?'

'Now, don't you go worrying about the children. They're fine. I'm taking good care of them, you can count on me for that. I gave them a good hot supper, and they're snuggled up in their beds warm and cozy. They've got two blankets apiece.'

Jen shivered. *Thank you, Seth, you would make my mother-in-law very happy.*

'I want to see them. You promised you'd let me come see them.'

'Of course I did. We want you here – we need you, don't you forget that for a minute. In fact, Jennifer, nothing will be right until you're here.'

Jen didn't answer him. Although she couldn't see his expression, she could hear in his voice how much he really meant everything he was saying.

'Are you there?' he asked.

'Of course. When can I come? I need to know where you are.'

'If I tell you that, how do I know you won't go calling other people into this, people who have no business butting into our affairs?'

'Seth . . .' She remembered reading somewhere that using a person's name when you talked to them made them feel important. 'I wouldn't do that, Seth. All I want is to be with the children. They're with you now. Why on earth would I make you angry or upset with me?'

'I really want to believe you. I don't want the children punished for your mistakes. Innocent children always end up paying the price for what their parents did. They're the ones who end up suffering the most.'

Jen nodded her head, forgetting he couldn't see her.

'Are you there?'

'Yes, I'm here. And I'm willing to do whatever you ask – don't you understand?'

He sighed and when he spoke his gentle voice held a note of sadness.

'Jennifer, I'm afraid it's you who don't understand. I want this to be your decision, not mine. I won't try to force you here against your will and then have you run out on me. I'm willing to wait as long as it takes, but once you come, it will be for keeps – no changing your mind. You see, I want this to be *right*.'

'But I do want to be with you, Seth. What I want more than anything is to be with all of my family.'

When he spoke again, she could hear a catch in his voice.

43

'Do you really mean that?' he whispered. 'I don't take kindly to lies.'

'Yes, I mean it. I've never meant anything more in my life.'

'In that case, you go to sleep now and get rested up. We'll all be together soon, I promise you. I'll call tomorrow morning at seven and give you directions.'

'Seven o'clock,' she said, her voice flat. Ten whole hours to get through.

'You'll meet me,' he went on, 'and I'll take you home to the children. And Jennifer, if anyone is with you, if you involve anyone else in this ... well, it hurts me to have to say this again, but what I'll do is go off with the children. You won't get another chance – I've given you too many already. Now, I don't mean to be hard. We all want you with us, the children miss you.'

Jen's heart skipped a beat at his words. She wanted to scream at him, but she said nothing and let him go on.

'I just have to warn you because people have lied to me before, and I could never stand for that again. Do you understand?'

What did he mean, he had given her too many chances already? Had he forgotten who he was talking to?

'Yes,' she said.

'Okay then, you get yourself a good night's sleep, and don't worry. Just leave everything in my hands. And one other thing, Jennifer.'

'Yes?'

'Thank you.'

'I don't understand.'

'You did a fine job with the children.'

'What do you mean?'

'The boy was real careful about not getting into a car with a stranger. You taught him good.'

CHAPTER FOUR

THE ENORMOUS WOOD-PANELLED BEDROOM took up half of the second floor. The two beds were set up on opposite sides of the room, both partially under the dormer that stretched across the front of the cabin. Though exhausted from the day's events, the children were unable to fall asleep. Seth had left their room hours ago.

After hovering over them and scrutinizing their washed hands and faces and freshly brushed teeth, he had got down on the floor and gestured to them.

'Kneel down beside me.'

Matthew took hold of Margo's hand and backed up against the wall.

'What for?'

'To pray, of course. Haven't you ever prayed?'

Matthew could remember bowing his head before meals at his grandparents', but nobody had got down on the floor. He shook his head.

'Well, you come here and kneel down. It's something your mother should have taught you, but since she hasn't I guess it's up to me.'

'Our mother taught us everything we need to know,' Margo said.

'Not if you don't know how to talk to the Lord, she hasn't. Come over here and kneel.'

Slowly the children walked up to him, then dropped down to their knees.

Seth folded his hands. 'Do what I do.' He waited until they complied, then said, 'Now close your eyes.'

'Why?' Margo asked. 'What are you going to do?'

45

'Nothing. You close your eyes because that's the way you talk to God. Then you can see him in your head. He'll be right there sitting inside you while you're talking.'

The children closed their eyes, keeping them open just enough to peek through at the bottoms without Seth noticing.

'I'll leave you alone now,' Seth said. 'You go ahead and talk to God.'

'What do you want us to talk about?' Margo asked.

'Anything you want. When you're like this, God can hear every word, and you can tell him anything you like. You can even ask for special things you've always wanted. It's almost like talking to Santa Claus, except that God really can do anything.'

'Can I ask him to let us go home?' Margo asked.

Seth stood up, eyes averted. Margo could tell that she had wounded him with her question.

'I'm not going to interfere with what you say,' he said. 'It's not up to me to do that. But I'll tell you one thing about God: He won't answer a prayer unless he thinks it's for a person's own good – something to make that person's life better. So asking for a thing like that would be foolish. You'd be better off saying your thank-yous for what you have.'

'How do you know what God's going to think?' Margo asked.

Seth paused before he answered.

'I don't,' he said.

'Then that's what we're going to talk about,' Margo said.

Seth switched off the light and closed the door. The children listened to his footsteps on the stairs.

'Dear God,' Margo whispered, 'please let us go home.'

Once they heard the front door slam shut and the car back down the driveway, they felt better. Even the locked door didn't bother them. Whatever Seth intended to do with them would at least be put off until the next day.

Now Matthew stood on a wooden stool looking through the tiny window set high in the wall. Two makeshift wooden slats extended in both directions on the outside, making each

f the four cubicles about six inches square. It was dark, and
most of the view was cut off by trees.

'We're out in the middle of nowhere,' he told Margo. It
was an expression he'd heard his mother use.

'Matthew, I'm sorry.'

He turned around to look at her. 'What for?'

'For getting us into this. It's my fault we even got in the
car. You didn't want to. I'm the one who fell for his story.'

Matthew jumped off the stool, walked over to her bed and
sat on the edge of it.

'It wasn't your fault, Margo. He did know mama's name
or us. When he told us that, I believed him too.'

'How do you think he knew?'

Matthew shook his head, remembering how Seth had
talked about being 'family'. He pushed the thought aside.

'The only thing that's important now is to find a way to
get out of here.'

Margo looked around the large bedroom with its one
wood-barred window and sighed.

'There's no way that I can see.'

'Maybe not now, but we can't give up. We'll get the
chance – and when we do, we've got to be ready.'

Margo rubbed her fingers lightly across the sore spot on
er arm, flinching as she remembered Seth's fingers digging
into her.

'Do you really think mama's coming?' she asked.

He didn't answer, just frowned and shrugged his
shoulders.

Margo looked at him, surprised.

'It almost seems like you don't want her to come.'

'He talks about her in a funny way,' Matthew said after a
long pause. 'It scares me. If she comes, she might be in even
more trouble than we are.' He stood up. 'We better go to
sleep, get some rest. If we ever get the chance to run away,
we'll need all our energy.'

He walked over to his bed and lay down. As he pulled the
blankets up to his chin, he thought about what he had just
said. Mama always knew what to do. *Wouldn't* she know how

to get them all out of here? But then he remembered the way the man had acted. He shivered. Would Mama really know what to do with someone like that?

'Matthew?' Margo's voice cut into his thoughts.

'What?'

'Your haircut doesn't look all that bad.'

He put his hand up to touch the short, stiff bristles standing up on his head. He rubbed the stubby edges back and forth, still not used to the feel.

'You look like one of those punk rockers.'

Margo felt good hearing her brother giggle. She was glad she had cheered him up. That's what mama would have done.

When Seth got back to the cabin, he'd listened outside the children's door: not a peep – they were fast asleep. Now he rolled over in his bed and stared up at the wood-beamed ceiling of his room. Since his talk with Jennifer, his excitement had built to a peak so intense that he felt he might rise up right off the bed. And no wonder: this was the highest point he had ever reached. His plan would work, now he knew it for certain. His life was shaping up at last; finally it was his turn to get the good things. It had taken so long that sometimes, as much as he hated to think that way, he wondered if God somehow had lost his name on the list and skipped over him.

The good things. That was all he ever wanted – just what he'd seen dished out to others – others who didn't know what to do with it or, for that matter, even knew they had it. Certainly they didn't appreciate it like he would. Not that he resented the others or ever meant any harm to come to them. It was just that when those people tried to shove you aside like vultures, snatching all the tasty morsels of life for themselves and squeezing the guts out of you in the process, you had to put them in their place, put the screws to them before they put the screws to you.

And the fact was, didn't he deserve more than they did? He thought back to last summer when he shot the doe. As much

48

as it hurt him to think about it, he couldn't help but feel proud of the way he'd handled the whole thing. He'd been out hunting that day and downed the animal with his first shot. He quickly made his way through the brush, only to discover a little fawn lying a few feet from the carcass. He hadn't known. There was no way he could have known from that distance, or he never would have shot the mother. But there he was, understanding with a certainty that could only be described as natural instinct what he had to do. And there he was, hurting like hell that he had to be the one to do it.

He looked down at the sad, gentle eyes looking up at him from the fawn's face. He even hesitated for a moment, though he knew he had no choice. What good was the little thing with its mother lying dead at his side? Didn't he know that better than anyone? He walked a distance back, set his sight for a spot between those eyes and pulled the trigger. The little fellow's head jerked, then slumped forward almost like he was falling asleep. It was almost beautiful, the way he lay there so peacefully next to the mother.

Seth still felt proud of himself for having the courage to do the right thing. Anybody else would have left the baby to fend for itself, to be pulled apart by larger animals until it was only bits and pieces rotting and stinking being picked at by the insects. He even dragged the two carcasses home with him to put to rest in his cellar vault. He wasn't about to leave them to the forest scavengers. He owed the mother and child that much.

But then he wasn't one to take his responsibilities lightly, that was for sure. Death wasn't the end, not by a long shot. He remembered back to his religious teachings: death was only the beginning. And if that were so, didn't he have an obligation when he took a life to continue to care for it?

Seth rolled back onto his stomach. He thought of his two children sleeping peacefully in the next room. He wasn't about to let any harm come to them, either. All he wanted was the chance to watch over and protect them from the hunters in the world who preyed off of other people and left them to rot. He felt his chest swell with pride, thinking of how the children would come to depend on him.

And Jennifer . . . he allowed himself to think of her angelic face. Hadn't he always been aware of his obligation to her right from the start? Finally he'd be able to live up to it and care for her like he had always intended. He never meant to desert her, but sometimes things got in the way, obstacles that had to be overcome before he could get on with what was important.

Jennifer would understand these things; he'd make her understand. She'd see why he took so long in coming, and she'd grow to love and respect him – so long as he was patient and didn't go off half-cocked. *Slow and easy . . . slow and easy . . .* He recited the magic phrase over and over as he drifted off to sleep.

'Lieutenant Thorne, please.'

'Sorry, ma'am. Lieutenant Thorne's not on duty 'til 9 a.m. Something I can do for you?'

Silence.

'Ma'am?'

'No, there's nothing.'

'Why don't you leave your name? I'll have him get back to you in the morning. Hello? Ma'am, you still there?'

Jen put down the receiver abruptly and flung her fist repeatedly against the wall. Finally she stopped pounding, sank down to the floor and burst into tears . . .

Twenty minutes later she sat up, wiping her eyes on the corner of the bedspread, and lit another cigarette. She glanced at the bedside clock: only eleven. She looked over at the two canvas suitcases beside her – all packed and ready to go – and wondered all over again whether she would be able to do this.

For the first time in many months, she was realizing the extent of her isolation. What with the pressure of earning a living and mothering the twins, she had built her own little refuge complete with a Do Not Enter sign. Of course there were girlfriends . . . thoughtful neighbours, but no one she felt close enough to turn to. Even men . . . Sure, there had been occasional dates through the years, but never anyone she'd felt strongly about . . . or anyone she could see as being the right kind of father to the children. Maybe it was her fault, maybe she had never really given them a chance.

She thought of Mike Thorne – she had just come so close to telling him. What would have happened if he were on duty, if she had talked to him? She sighed. But he wasn't . . . and she hadn't, and though there was a minute there . . . it was probably just as well. If only he was an insurance man or an accountant, anything but a cop. Cops had to answer to their superiors and follow procedures. Routine, they called it. And then, too, there was the possibility of some reporter catching wind of the kidnapping – which was what it was – and plastering it across the front pages of the newspapers for Seth to read. No, she couldn't risk that – a chill skimmed along her spine – but to think, she almost had.

She stood up, got in bed under the covers, then thought back to her mother-in-law and their conversation. It never ceased to amaze her how Jim could have grown up in that house. Though she and the children continued to visit each summer, she had never for one moment felt comfortable in the dreary surroundings. Each window, already half covered with the dark green blackout shades of the forties, was so heavily draped that hardly any sunlight could filter through.

Miriam was wary of over-the-counter drugs, but not the home-prepared remedies passed on to her by her family and kept carefully spelled out and indexed on six-by-nine cards in her file drawer. Though Miriam herself rarely woke before noon, Clarence was up and out at dawn leaving the children and Jen to manage for themselves, whispering and tiptoeing around to quickly dress, eat, and get outdoors. Each visit to her in-laws only confirmed Jen's opinion: it was nothing short of a miracle that such an environment could have produced her Jim.

Jen had been enrolled at the beauty academy when she met Jim. A new wing was being added, and Jim was the contractor. Six feet tall, blond, with blue eyes and a sense of humour that attracted most of the girls, he had singled Jen out from the beginning. But as much as she, too, was drawn to him, she wasn't so quick to open up to his advances. Though she didn't know it then, somewhere in her mind was the fear that what happened to her mother would happen to her. Not that her father's walking out had left her mother bitter – it hadn't. In fact, Jen could not recall ever hearing one complaint from her in all Jen's years of growing up. Nonetheless, a barrier was definitely there ... Somehow Jim was able to penetrate it, and within six months, they were married. And though Jen never took to his parents, it didn't really make a difference. Jim, who had a mind of his own, was not one to allow much interference in their private affairs.

The only reason Jen still continued her visits to them was because they thought they were Margo and Matthew's grandparents. She had become pregnant only one month after their son's car accident, and they took it for granted that she was carrying Jim's child. Even though she never out and out told the lie, the fact was that she had never told them anything different. Once the twins were born, of course, there was no turning back. And surely it wasn't a lie that had harmed anyone. It gave the Sawyers their one and only chance for grandchildren, and it gave Jen the obligation to keep in touch.

She turned over and punched the pillow, then lay her head back down. Beneath the covers she could feel her body still trembling. Somewhere out there – for the first time in their lives – her children were confused and frightened and she could do nothing to ease their fears. Tomorrow she would have to put aside all feelings of helplessness, of rage, and assume a cheeful, compliant role. It would be her first acting part since high school, and her performance had to be good enough to convince Seth, the most important audience of her life. She could do it, she had to. But could she keep it up? How long could a person pretend without going over the edge?

She closed her eyes and prayed, something she hadn'

one in years. Dear God, let them be safe tonight. Let them
all asleep and not remember their dreams. Tomorrow, I'll be
with them. Tomorrow.

Liar, liar – set your hair on fire! Liar, liar – set your hair on fire!
Louder and louder, the chorus of voices beat at Seth from the
outside. Then, relocated, they taunted and sang and
screeched inside his head until it wanted to split wide open
and spill out the contents. A hundred twisted hands reached
out to grab at him.

He kicked his way free from them all. His short wiry legs
raced across the length of the playground and into the
bushes, faster and faster. Still the voices followed; he
couldn't make them go away. He pressed his fists against his
ears. Feet pounded behind him, like horses galloping in his
shadow. A gust of hot, foul wind – their breath – whipped at
the back of his neck, stinging, burning.

Finally he could see the neat little house in the distance, his
mommy and daddy calling to him. They reached out their
arms; he could almost feel the gentleness of their hands
against his skin. With a burst of energy, he raced ahead as if
chains had been cut from him, setting him free. His eyes
closed, his face tilted upwards, his arms and legs worked
furiously to propel him forward. And then he was there. His
mother's long, graceful arms reached out to him; he hurled
his body over the edge—

His feet pedalled frantically, searching for ground. The
house, mommy, daddy, had all disappeared like a puff of
smoke. It had taken him too long to get there. He had not run
fast enough; they couldn't wait. From above the chorus of
voices jeered at him. Liar, Liar! He turned to look. The arms
hung down. Then, like globs of dough, they stretched longer
and longer, the hands getting closer and closer and—

Seth shot up in bed when he heard the piercing screams
ring out. It took him a moment to realize that the screams
were his own. He sat rigid, his eyes darting around the dark
room populated with dim shapes and shadows – unmoving,
but ready to lunge out at him at any moment. His eyes

probed each corner, looking for the hands; they would grab him if he didn't see them first. He clutched at the sides of his mattress to keep himself from falling down, and down; he kept his body pressed up against the headboard waiting for the feelings to subside. They always did. And though he would remember them all in the morning, he wouldn't be so frightened then. It was only in the dark of the night – when he slept, when he was tired enough to lose control – that it happened. It was then that he was stripped of his defences, leaving him unarmed to fend off the others.

The old worry came back to him. Would he someday be trapped in his nightmare unable to leave – unable to come back to reality? It was a fear that he had lived with as far back as he could remember. If only he didn't have to sleep, to let others take over. Then everything would be all right.

Matthew awakened when he heard the screams. He rolled over in his bed, remembering vaguely that he was up in the woods. He had heard animal cries like that before, when he stayed overnight at grandma's and grandpa's. He let his eyes close again; he was tired, and he didn't want to have to think about what he'd heard. Within seconds he rolled over and fell back to sleep.

CHAPTER FIVE

MARGO AND MATTHEW AWOKE IMMEDIATELY AT 6 A.M. with the first sound of the key rattling in the lock. When Seth opened the door, they were both up on their feet. They stared at him, waiting.

'Good morning.' Seth was wearing grey slacks and a white shirt underneath a crewneck pullover. He stood in the doorway, hands on hips, a sunny smile on his face. The children said nothing. Margo quickly grabbed a blanket from her bed and wrapped it around herself to cover up the cotton nightie he'd given her to wear to bed.

'I said good morning.'

'Good morning,' Matthew answered.

Seth looked over at Margo. She nodded, but he kept staring at her.

'Good morning,' she said finally.

'There's only two things I'm going to ask from you,' he told them. 'One is politeness and the other is respect. If you give me that, we'll get along just fine.' He clapped his hands together. 'Now I want you two to get dressed in the brand new things I bought for you.' He pointed towards the chair where he had laid out clothing the night before. 'I've got a hot breakfast waiting for you downstairs.'

Matthew walked over and lifted up his pants, shirt and underwear. Margo stood still, clutching at the edge of her blanket. Seth went to her and gently removed the cover.

'If you can't get dressed yourself, I'll help you.'

Margo ran to collect her clothes. 'I'll dress in the bathroom.'

She pushed past him and headed toward the hallway; Seth

leaned against the wall with his arms folded and watched Matthew climb into his new shirt and jeans.

The girl looked like a fairy princess in the yellow, lacy dress. Just like he had pictured when he'd seen the dress on the mannequin at the store. Once their beds were neatly made, the children followed Seth downstairs to the kitchen. Milk, toast and two bowls of oatmeal were set on the table. Seth sat across from the children watching them wolf down the food he'd prepared. It made him feel good to watch. It was like they were starting to depend on him, just a little. Oh, he wasn't dumb; he could see that they didn't trust him, particularly the girl, but he knew he'd be able eventually to overcome their feelings, especially when they found out who he was. Then they'd know this was their real home – they'd have no need to compete with him for God's favours. Kids could adapt to almost anything; he remembered Dandy saying that to him once.

'Today's going to be another big day for all of us,' Seth announced.

'Why?' Matthew asked.

'Today your mother's coming home. What do you think of that?'

Matthew felt his chest unclog as though a broom had come along and swept it clean. And then, as if a strong wind blew it all back, the fear returned.

'She wouldn't . . .' Matthew said, his statement sounding more like a question.

'Of course she will,' Seth answered. 'Don't you think she wants to be with her family? She's not the kind who would desert those she cares about. Most women maybe are like that now, that's the truth – but not your mother.'

Matthew knew that Seth was right, his mother would find some way to get to them. Still, the thought of her coming scared him somehow.

'When?' he asked.

Seth looked at him as though he didn't understand.

'When is she coming?'

'Soon. As a matter of fact, it's going to be sooner than expected.'

After breakfast, Seth scooted the kids back to their bedroom. He left a worn deck of cards on Margo's nightstand.

'I thought maybe you'd want something to do while you're waiting,' he said. Margo turned her face to the wall.

Seth put his hands in his pockets.

'I know this is a little hard on you now,' he said. 'I know you're not used to having a – well, a whole family. But you'll see, you're going to like it just fine.'

Seth closed the door and locked it. Before he left the house, he took twenty-five dollars in bills from the tin can in the drawer of the hutch. As his fingers stuffed the bills into his pants pocket, he felt a peculiar weightlessness as though gravity had left him to fend for himself. Though a feeling like this usually scared him, this time it didn't. In fact, he decided as he pulled the front door shut after himself, today he kind of liked it.

Before Jen shut the hatchback of the burgundy Toyota, she unsnapped the lock of the small valise. She carefully lifted the pile of underwear, unzipped the flowered toiletry bag and slid her hand in. She felt the cold metal of the revolver against her palm; just the touch made her jumpy. What made her think she'd be able to use it? Jim had once demonstrated the mechanics of it, but until now she had never so much as touched the gun. It had been their one argument: his insistence that she share his interest in guns and her refusal. Then, last night, she had taken it out of the locked desk drawer where it had been all these years, cleaned it and even loaded it. She zipped the bag again, placed the clothes over it and shut the suitcase, then got into the car.

She reread Seth's instructions: Route 93 to the New Hampshire border . . . exit at Ashley and onto Post Road. Having lived in Ashley, she was familiar with the area. He was to meet her at ten o'clock in front of a telephone booth next to an abandoned diner. The trip, he had said, would take no more than an hour. She tucked the instructions back into her purse and turned the ignition key.

Within ten minutes she was at Route 93. As she swung onto the ramp, the realization hit her: she was not only on the way to her children, she was also on the way to the man who had raped her twelve years earlier. It seemed still inconceivable to her that a stranger existed who was actually the children's biological father. She had pushed it out of her mind for so long: not thinking of her attacker in those terms, if at all. Now she knew it was time. She had to think about what happened or else she'd never get through the ordeal of coming face to face with him. More important, anything she could remember about this man – no matter how insignificant – might help her know how to handle him.

Jen forced her thoughts back to that evening. It was about one month after Jim's funeral. Instead of going directly home from work, she had driven out to the cemetery, something she had done often during the first two weeks following the accident. At first she had walked around like a zombie with a knot balled up tight inside her chest – solid, impenetrable. Even at the funeral she stood stiff and dry-eyed, her face never suggesting the pain and anger that made up the knot. It was only at the gravesite – with Jim – that she had learned to cry. As the weeks passed, she felt the knot loosening, and though she continued to mourn the loss of what Jim and she might have had, more and more often she felt her strength returning. That night, though, was different. It was only a little thing that set her off, but all at once – unexpectedly – the pain was back. She had spotted a young couple pedaling a tandem bicycle; from the back, it could have been her and Jim. Their own tandem bicycle had been a wedding present to each other, and they had used it often. Without even realizing what she was doing, she headed her car toward the cemetery.

A thin jacket shielded her from the light intermittent rainfall; the dense fog obscured her view of the gate. She lifted her hand, running it along the black metal bars, searching with her fingers for the bolt. Her fingers touched the thick horse-shoe-shaped piece and lifted it; with her free hand she swung open the gate. She padded along the soggy

ass, wind blowing softly against her hair. Her senses were
ert to the muted noises of the night. Moonlight occasionally
oke through the clouds; fireflies flickered on and off in the
arkness, allowing the briefest glimpse of the sleek, colour-
ss stones in her path. But even without the fireflies, her feet
ew the path: if she had squeezed her eyes shut, they would
ill have taken her to the exact spot where the small grey
adstone stood.

Before she saw it, she knew she was there. She sank down
to the wet, cool grass, soft spikelets crushing beneath her
re knees. She reached out, her hands rubbing the smooth
ne as if the movement of her fingers could make him
pear. The smoothness ended abruptly as her fingers felt
e edge where the marble had been cut. And as if she were
ind, she read the freshly carved inscription with her fingers:
mes B. Sawyer, loving husband, loving son, 1952–1974.

She felt a tingling, like a caress from the night blowing
tly against her neck. She sighed, then closed her eyes,
ting her arms fall to her sides. Thinking of Jim. She tilted
r head back, raindrops falling like petals against her face.
ddenly she felt it: the lightest of touches against her
easts. She sucked in her breath. Her hands flew to her chest
nd recoiled as though the fingers had been submerged in
lding water.

She opened her mouth to scream, but her vocal chords
re strangely paralysed – as though she were caught in a
ghtmare. She scratched and pulled at the arms, but now
ey squeezed her body like a vise, the fingers pulling at her
ouse. She struggled to turn, to face her assailant, but his
p immobilized her. As her struggles grew more frantic, his
ack gained momentum, her blows rolling off him like the
ndrops.

He lowered her down onto the soggy ground, then rolled
over. She could feel one hand groping clumsily at her
thing while the other grabbed for her breast. The rain had
up, and the moon briefly pushed its way through the
uds; she could see the shadow of his head as it moved
wn to her breast and his mouth opened wide. She gasped

59

for air, unable to breathe beneath his weight. And then, as his teeth sank in, she felt the excruciating pain. Before she blacked out, she tried to make out his face, but the features were blurred, indistinguishable, except for the fiery blue torches that were his eyes.

When she came to, she was alone. No pain, just numbness. She lay next to Jim's grave for what seemed like hours, unmoving, wanting only to be swallowed up by the earth. She never remembered how she got home that night. She stayed indoors for the next six weeks, not once leaving the apartment. Her co-worker and in-laws simply assumed that she was still grieving for Jim, and while they saw her sudden relapse as unfortunate, the consensus was that she was experiencing severe but normal depression following the death of a spouse.

The day she discovered she was pregnant was the day she began to take her life back into her own hands. After the initial panic and shock wore off, she decided she would have the baby. There was no way she could conceive of killing her own child. She and Jim had tried too hard to have one during their marriage, and now, more than ever before, she needed something outside herself to live for. When the twins were born – quite to her surprise, since she knew of no multiple births in her family – she made a fresh start. She left Ashley, moved to Massachusetts and used her savings to put a down payment on a house and set up her own business. To this day she had never regretted that decision – the children were the most important thing in her life.

Suddenly, as if a button in her head had been pushed, she could see their faces – frightened, waiting. She could feel the anger build up in her until she wanted to scream. How had this man known about the children, and how had he known where to find her? For that matter, how the hell did he even know her name? No longer a ghost from the past, he had a name – Seth, a living, breathing man who had simply walked into her life as if he belonged there, picked up her children and taken them away.

It had begun to drizzle; drops of water were running down

the windshield. She took one hand off the steering wheel and flipped on the wipers, then let the hand hang limp and shook it, trying to relax her muscles. She knew it was important that she be calm; anger would only cripple her. She had to be alert and self-possessed, to operate as if this horror were a scene out of a play.

Jen looked to her right; she was just leaving Massachusetts. The sign read: one mile to Exit 122, Ashley. She gripped the steering wheel with both hands and pressed down harder on the accelerator.

CHAPTER SIX

THORNE PICKED UP THE PHONE, dialled, waited, then hung up. It was the third time within a half hour he had tried to reach Jen. A message had been sitting on his desk that morning: a woman called the night before . . . she left no name. Maybe it had been she. He lifted his coffee mug and gulped down the strong, steamy brew, then looked at his watch. It was 9:45.

Henry Schroeder, sitting across from him, had quietly been keeping track of the calls and of Thorne's mounting irritation. He swivelled his heavy frame around to face him and ran his hand over his nearly bald head.

'Okay, you've got me curious. Who're you trying to call – your bookie?'

Thorne stifled a yawn, then shrugged. 'You can never get 'em when you need 'em.'

'Tell me something, Thorne, don't you sleep?'

'What's that supposed to mean?'

'Nothing, just that you look like hell.'

Thorne pulled out a cigarette from the pack on his desk and lit it.

'Thanks,' he said, not looking at Schroeder.

'Christ, look at those bags under your eyes. You're a young guy yet. By the time you hit my age – assuming you do, of course – you'll be a basket case.'

Thorne turned and smiled at him.

'I assume this lecture holds a punchline? A remedy to keep me young and fit like yourself?'

'Go ahead, be a wiseass. You ought to know by now, it takes more than that to shut my mouth.'

'Okay, Schroeder, what's on your mind?'

'You look worn out, Mike. You're a good-looking guy, you probably have more than your share of tail. But you bachelor have got to pace yourselves. You'll use up your fuel before you hit forty – which, I might add, is not that far off.'

Thorne smiled. 'Where have you been getting your information? If it's from Lucy,' he pointed to the computer sitting beside Schroeder's desk, 'you'd better have her circuit checked. The truth is, Henry – not that it's really any of you damn business, of course – the only woman in my life is a twenty-pound alley cat named Miranda.'

'You expect me to believe that?'

Thorne shrugged.

'Then maybe you're working too hard.'

'Now there you might have a point.'

'Well, dammit, why don't you do something about it You've got a cabin up in New Hampshire – when was the las time you got up there?'

Thorne thought about it, then nodded. 'Maybe you're righ A weekend spent fishing doesn't sound like such a bad idea He picked up the phone again and tried Jen's number. Still n answer. He rested his head on his palms, his elbows leaning o the desk. 'Listen Schroeder, do me a favour, will you?'

'Have a heart, Thorne. Look at the stack of work I've go sitting here.' He picked up a pile of request forms and shoo them. 'I hear you asking for favours, I know right off the ba it's not legitimate business. Your favours play games with m ulcers.'

Thorne wrote Jen's name and address on a piece of paper carried it over to Schroeder and held it in front of him.

'Get me some dope on her, will you?'

Schroeder read the paper, then sank down in his chair.

'The story about no women *was* just a lot of crap, then.'

'This is different, it's business.'

'Yeah. Well, who is she?'

'Just a widow with a couple of kids.'

'Where do you want me to look – FBI list, known sex offenders list?'

Thorne grinned. 'You can eliminate those.'

'What about the PTA roster?'

'Surely with your high-tech equipment, you have some methods available to get some routine information for me.'

'I give up. What are we looking for?'

Thorne crushed out his cigarette in the ashtray. 'Her background, her friends – male and female. We're looking to find out what makes the lady tick.'

'Jesus Christ, this isn't a computer dating service. Can't you do that kind of research on your own time?' He patted Lucy. 'What the hell ever happened to human contact? Are all you bachelors that scientific?'

'Aren't you the guy who just told me I'm overworked and ageing fast?'

Schroeder sighed, then plucked the piece of paper from Thorne's hand.

'All right, I'll have it for you by the end of the day.'

Seth knew how carefully he had to watch his pennies, but he wasn't sorry he'd spent all that money; it was worth it. He looked down and admired the twelve long-stemmed roses wrapped in green tissue paper lying on the seat beside him and smiled at the thought of giving them to Jennifer in just a few minutes. He'd expected her to mull over his offer for a while, and then, when she got to missing the kids, finally make a decision. He'd never expected she would want to start their life together so soon. But on the phone, she sounded like she meant it.

Of course, he wasn't naive: appearances could be deceiving, and he wasn't about to walk into any traps. He had prepared too well for too many years. It looked, though, as if his big dream of having a family of his own was about to come true, and he couldn't help feeling a certain amount of happiness – premature or not. He was especially gratified that Jennifer had stayed away from any relationships herself, just bringing up the kids, biding her time until he was ready. Now, more than ever, it was essential that he not forget the lessons he'd learned. He *must not* let his impatience or his temper get control of him. He would continue to go slow, let time run its course.

As her car pulled up, he checked his pocket watch: 9:50. She was ten minutes early. She got out of the car and leaned against it. He had parked some distance away, taking the dirt road overlooking the diner, and though it was next to impossible for her to spot him from where she was standing, he had a clear view of her. His eyes, however, couldn't see up or down the road for any distance; the twists and turns in it made that impossible. Before he went to her, he'd have to first check the area, make sure she had kept her word and come alone. It never hurt to take precautions. He squeezed his legs together and took several deep breaths trying to restrain his eagerness. He shook his head to clear it, to assure himself that he wasn't just imagining things, then looked back down at her standing there. It was Jennifer, all right, waiting more anxiously than he could ever have imagined.

He started the engine and let the car roll down the path. When he hit the road, he turned left, away from her, and rode a full five miles back in the direction she'd travelled. Seeing nothing out of the ordinary, he followed the main drag around until he reached the other end of Post Road, then turned in and drove the half mile back to where she was waiting. Pulling the watch from his pocket, he again looked at it. It was 10:05.

He got out of the car and stood in front of her.

'Hello, Jennifer.'

Jen stuffed her hands into her pockets. She didn't want him to see them shake. It startled her that he looked so familiar; she had obviously seen more of him when he attacked her than she had dared – or cared – to remember. She smiled.

'Seth?'

He nodded, returning her smile.

'Can we go to the children now?'

'Right away. First, I'll have to ditch your car.'

'I could follow you.'

Seth took her hand. She wanted to yank it away, but she let it lie limply in his. He led her to the passenger seat of her car and ran around to the other side, then took the keys from her.

'You won't be needing these,' he told her as he slid them in

66

he ignition. 'One car is enough.' He manoeuvred the Toyota onto the road and turned onto the path leading to the place he had parked earlier. They had only gone a short distance when he cut the motor.

Jen looked around at the woods, waiting to follow his lead. He leaned over, opened the glove compartment and pulled out the registration and insurance papers, then stuck his hand in his pocket and pulled out a screwdriver. As he did, his pocket watch dropped out onto the seat and rolled down beneath the cushions.

'Come on,' he said. She followed him out and watched as he walked to the back of the car, bent over, and carefully unscrewed the back licence plate. When that was done, he walked to the front of the car.

'Only one in Massachusetts,' Jen said.

Seth put the plate and registration under his arm, looked into the back seat to see if he'd forgotten anything: then, satisfied that he hadn't, pulled Jen's luggage from the back of the car.

'Let's go to the children,' he said.

She trailed after him down the steep hill that led back to the diner, twigs and shrubs scatching at her legs as she walked. When they got to his car, she looked down and, from beneath the cuffs of her pants, saw droplets of blood running down her ankles. She hadn't felt a thing.

Seth opened the door and dumped the bags in the back seat, then eagerly reached in front, pulled out a bouquet of roses and handed them to her. She stared at them, not at all sure what she should say. All she felt was revulsion.

'Take them, they're not going to bite. They're for you.'

Jen took them. 'Thank you, Seth. They're lovely.'

He reached back into the car and took out what looked to her like a wide headband.

'Don't be scared, this won't hurt,' he told her. 'I don't want to do this, but I have no choice. You understand, don't you?'

Jen nodded as he slipped the band over her head and adjusted it to cover her eyes. He put a pair of glasses or

67

sunglasses over the band, then led her into the car. She could hear him get in, then feel him beside her, looking at her.

'Are you comfortable, Jennifer?'

She nodded again, fighting the urge to scream. Here she was, blindfolded, being carted off to God knows where, with a bouquet of roses in her hand – roses from the man who had raped her twelve years before – and he wanted to know if she was *comfortable*. Shit. She tightened her fist around the thorny stems as she heard the four door locks snap.

Jen's muscles felt stiff and achy. She had been sitting in the same position now for more than two hours. She felt the car going at a fast, even pace; it was apparent that they were on a highway. Unless Seth had backtracked, which seemed unlikely, she assumed they were headed north. Her guess was Maine or Vermont.

Seth had not said one word since they left. Now and again she felt a rush of uneasiness, and though she couldn't see a thing, she was sure he was looking at her. For most of the trip, Jen kept her mind occupied trying to figure out Seth. The more she understood him, the better she'd be able to deal with him: it was that simple. But Seth himself was neither simple nor at all easy to understand. He apparently had a gentle side to him, a side that wanted to please people and make them like him. The violent side she knew all too well. The side triggered by – what? Frustration? Rage? Yes, but there was more to it than that. From her phone conversations with him, she felt that he believed what he said. To Seth, she and the children were his family. That meant, she suddenly realized, that in his mind he had to have turned what had happened in the graveyard into something totally different.

There were so many questions she wanted to ask, but she didn't want to rush at him with them. She had to earn his trust first, convince him they were on the same side. On the other hand, she didn't want to be distant or cold. The sooner she could get him talking, loosened up, the better.

'I'm getting tired,' she finally said. 'Are we almost there, Seth?'

'Not much further. Anxious to see the kids?'

She nodded. 'I miss them.'

'I have to admit, it doesn't take much for kids to rope you in. You forget how you ever got along without them.'

'What do you think of them, Seth?'

'They're smart as whips,' he said. 'No doubt about it, they've both got good heads on their shoulders. The girl is a little harder to handle, I'd say – kind of wants things her own way, not one for bending much.'

'Margo's always been like that. She's the type you have to earn your way in with before she's ready to listen to what you have to say.'

'The boy listens, though. He's on the quiet side – almost too softspoken and contained, maybe. You sort of aren't sure what's on his mind. Like maybe he's saying something different from what he's really thinking.'

'That's Matthew, all right. There's always something going on in his head. You can almost hear the ticking.'

'I suspect that comes from him needing to be the man of the family, so to speak, for all these years.'

Jen waited a moment before going on. 'I guess you *could* say that. Matthew has never been one to be hasty. He likes to mull things over for a while before he jumps into anything.'

Seth laughed. 'I could sure see that. He wasn't so quick to come with me when I stopped for them at the school.'

'But he *did* come. How did you ... I mean, how did you convince him and Margo it was okay?'

'I said I was from the police – showed them an I.D. and badge.'

Jen was silent.

'I told them you had an accident. Just a minor one, nothing to worry them too much.'

'I see.'

'It wasn't quite enough, though. The boy was still leery about coming along with me.'

'Oh?'

'It wasn't till I told them about you wanting your snowflakes that they came around.'

Jen drew back towards the door as if she had touched a ho
wire. Once, after watching a television programme o
children's safety, she had told them she'd never send
stranger to pick them up without telling the person her nam
for them – *snowflakes* would be the password. How could h
possibly have known? If he knew that, what other things di
he know? Jen shuddered at the thought that this man mig
have been watching her, observing her all these years. Sh
didn't speak for several minutes.

'Seth,' she finally said, 'you didn't tell them . . . you didn
let on who you are, did you?'

'What do you mean?'

'That you're their father.'

'Oh, I hinted around a little, but I didn't tell them in s
many words. I thought I ought to wait until you were wi
us. That way, they'll know for sure I'm not lying.'

'I see – I mean, I understand.' She had to think fast. 'But
do have a suggestion, Seth.'

'Oh?'

'Well, now, maybe it's none of my business. It's just that
know it's important to you for them to like you, to look up
you the way kids *should* look up to a father.'

He was quiet for a long moment.

'It is important,' he said finally. 'What's your suggestion?

'I think it would be better to wait a little while. Earn the
trust and respect first, let them get to know what kind
person you are before you tell them. That way they'll l
happy when they find out the truth. If you tell them too soo
it's likely to scare them – make them resent you.'

Seth was silent again. Jen took a deep breath and went on

'I don't want to try to tell you what to do, Seth. It's ju
that I know the kids so well. Maybe I can help you out wi
them.'

'I don't want to be waiting too long.' His voice rose. 'Yo
don't know what it's like – I've been waiting all my life. Ev
since I've been a kid, I've been waiting.'

At that moment, Jen felt the car swerve sharply to the le
she heard the blast of a horn coming from behind.

'Watch out!' she shouted.

The car's swerve back to the right knocked Jen up against the door – just moments before she heard a car whiz past on their left.

'I don't know what happened – what got into me,' he said, his voice trembling. 'I had no business taking my eyes off the road like that. You could have been hurt.'

'It's okay, Seth.' Jen reached out her hand and felt for his shoulder. 'It's my fault, I had no business bringing up a subject like that when you needed to pay attention to traffic.'

It was a few minutes before either of them spoke. Finally, Seth broke the silence.

'I'll do it your way,' he said. 'I won't tell the kids yet. But what I said before still goes – we're only putting off the inevitable. You have to understand, Jennifer, waiting is hard for me. It's not always something I'm able to do.'

CHAPTER SEVEN

DARK CLOUDS HOVERED OVER NORTHERN MASSACHUSETTS throughout the morning. By noon, torrential rains poured down, the wind blowing up bits of paper and leaves from the lawns.

Traces of light glowed from the windows on Arden Road in Winfield, giving the impression of warm, cozy kitchens with fresh-perked coffee hot on the stove and, perhaps, the buzzes and bells of a TV game show somewhere in the background.

Number Two Arden Road had no such signs of life. Claudia Wingrad trotted down the sidewalk, closed her soaking umbrella, and threw it into the back seat of her car. She was not used to being stood up for anything, let alone a hair appointment. 'Hell of a way to run a business,' she muttered as she manoeuvred her heavy frame back into the car.

The postman held his head down and cupped his hand over his eyes; a steady stream of water flowed down from his visor onto his nose and chin. He called out to Claudia: 'Count your blessings. Another month or so and this would be one heck of a blizzard.' Claudia just nodded and slammed her car door shut.

The postman slipped several envelopes – advertisements, mostly – and the November edition of *Modern Beauty Shop* into the mailbox. He peeked around the side of the house: no light coming from the back-room shop, either. Now that was peculiar. He turned and faced back into the wind, anxious to complete the last two streets of his route. A heavy gust of wind whistled through the air as it worked up momentum.

He grabbed onto his cap to keep it from flying off. A rumble of thunder rolled across the sky and exploded. Moments later lightning crackled overhead. Out of the corner of his eye, he saw the lawn chair on the Sawyer porch slam against the railing, then lift up and tumble down the front steps – where it collapsed upside down in the rosebush.

The sky was heavily overcast, but Jen still squinted when Seth took off the blindfold. She rubbed her eyes with her palms, then looked around. The log cabin was set back at least a hundred feet from the road, and there wasn't another house in sight. She turned back toward Seth.

'Can we go in?'

'Of course.' He got out and opened the door on her side. She stood up and flexed her legs and arms, trying to work out the kinks, still holding on to the roses. Seth lifted Jen's luggage from the back seat and carried it to the front step. As soon as he swung the door open, she stepped inside. She ran over to the fireplace and carefully placed her bouquet in a jar on the mantel, then turned to face him.

'Where are they?'

He pointed upstairs; her eyes followed his finger.

'Can we go up to them now, Seth?'

'Would you like to see them alone – maybe a few minutes by yourselves?'

'I would like that very much, Seth. Thank you.'

Seth led the way up.

'Ten minutes,' he told her. 'I'll be waiting by the door.'

Matthew and Margo, sprawled out on the floor when she walked in, leaped up to their feet the minute they saw her. As Seth closed the door behind them, Jen knelt down on the floor and scooped them into her arms. She tried to speak, but her voice had tears in it and then, as they hugged her, so did her eyes.

'Would you look at me?' she said laughing softly and wiping her eyes with her wrists. 'Anyone would think I hadn't seen you for a month, not a day. Just goes to show how mothers can be.'

Both children still clung to her.

'Mama,' Matthew said, his voice muffled against her shoulder, 'I wouldn't have gone with him, but he knew your name for us. I thought—'

'It's all right, Matthew. He told me.'

'How did he know?' Margo asked.

'I don't know yet, honey.'

Margo's hands were coiled into fists. 'Mama, he says he's family.'

Jen lifted Margo's chin and studied her face. Her little mouth was drawn into a tight line.

'The only family I see . . . is right here in this room.' As she said the words, Jen could see her daughter's features soften; she heard her sigh as if she'd been holding her breath. The thought of telling them the truth made Jen shudder.

'What does he want with us?' Matthew asked.

'I don't know that yet, either. But we're *together*. Right now that's what's important.'

'But how will we get out of here?'

Jen squeezed his arm. 'Can you ever remember a time when we all put our heads together and couldn't come up with something? Let's take one step at a time – fair enough?'

They both nodded.

Matthew drew back, and Jen lifted her hand to the stubby bristles on his head. His face turned beet-red. She smiled at him.

'Oh come on, now, it's not *that* bad. Besides, I give it two weeks – you hear me, young man? Two weeks and there'll be another whole new mop sitting on top of that head.'

The children laughed, and she hugged them again.

'And that sound, my darlings, is what I missed the most.'

They both hung on to her, now quiet. Finally Margo pulled away, looked up and put her hand to Jen's face.

'Are you scared, mama?'

Jen looked deep into her daughter's eyes, then nodded.

'But not half as scared as I was yesterday. Without you two.'

Seth was standing on the other side of the closed door. When he heard their laughter, he wished more than ever that he was inside. But he had offered her the time alone knowing it would please her and knowing she'd never work up the nerve to ask for it herself. Besides, even if he were there, they'd probably pretend he wasn't. You could be in the very same room with people and still be by yourself – hadn't he found that out years ago? He had to expect things like this, at least for a while. But knowing was one thing; how you felt about it was another.

He thought back to his conversation with Jennifer. He had almost smashed up the car, he had gotten himself that upset. And it wasn't her reasoning that finally made him agree to wait; he didn't buy it for a minute. Once she told the children who he was, they'd believe it and quickly come to accept him. What children wouldn't want a father? The truth was, Jennifer just wanted to put off telling them, and maybe it was her not being straight with him and his knowing it that had really upset him. If she had just told him the truth and given him time to think about it, he would have understood. Hadn't he figured it out himself and given in to her once he did?

After all, it wasn't easy for a mother like Jennifer to tell her kids a thing like that – not after all those lies and them believing their daddy was dead. But she should have trusted him enough to know that he'd be right at her side helping her explain. For all she knew, he might never have come back to claim them – what else could she have told them? No, she had done no wrong and he'd make sure the kids understood that.

But if waiting a little longer meant so much to her, then that's what he'd do. Maybe her real reason for waiting was silly, but in a way it was that very kind of reasoning that made him love her so much. Not many women gave a hang about how they looked in their children's eyes or, for that matter, that they might have done something to be ashamed of.

To Jen's surprise, Seth confiscated her luggage.

'Let's get rid of these,' he said, setting the suitcases down neatly in the hall closet. 'The only way to start fresh and new, Jennifer – take it from me – is to get rid of whatever reminds you of the past. It's like you've got to scrub away all that grease and grime so you can make room for the good to come in.' He stood with his hands on his hips, smiling at her. 'Now take that worried look off your face, I have no intention of letting you run around in the clothes on your back. Come upstairs and I'll show you what I bought to replace those old things.'

He took hold of her hand and led her up the steep steps to a large panelled room. In addition to the hall bathroom, a tiny bath was enclosed in the front corner partially under the eaves. The nylon quilt spread, draperies, and dressing-table skirt threw off splashes of lavender, blue, and hot pink, a combination she liked.

'It's lovely, Seth. Is this your room?'

He smiled, his cheeks turning pink. 'Thank you . . . I was hoping you'd like it.'

'You did this for me?'

He nodded happily and watched Jen's expression, then his face grew serious.

'I don't want you to worry though, Jennifer. I'm not about to push you into anything – just having you here with me is enough for now. I figure once you're ready to come to me, you will. Meantime I'll be bedding downstairs on the sofa.'

She hadn't even allowed herself to think about that – at least, she hadn't been aware of thinking about it. But with his words, she could feel a tiny ball slide its way out of her chest and dissolve. *Don't you know, Seth, that time will never come? Don't do this . . . please, don't fool yourself like this.* She stared at him, but said nothing.

'Go ahead.' He waved a hand toward the dresser. 'Take a look.'

She pulled out the drawer and began to leaf through the clothing.

'Did I forget anything?'

She looked at the lacy brassieres, bikini underpants, the sheer lavender nightgown with thin satin ropes at the shoulders. She lifted the soft sweaters: turtlenecks, cowlnecks, cardigans, all neatly folded, the tags still attached. She looked at one tag, size 36, her size. She picked up lipsticks, eyeshadow, liquid makeup and turned each of them over to read the labels on the bottom – quiet, pretty shades, the kind she liked. Then she lifted a sachet from the corner of the drawer. She held it to her nose and sniffed it, staring at Seth as she did.

'How did you know . . . ?' she asked.

Seth's answer was a sheepish grin.

Suddenly Jen felt naked, as if Seth knew all her secrets. Once again she asked herself how Seth could have acquired all this information about her. The possibilities only filled her with fear.

'Excuse me,' she said, walking quickly to the bathroom. Once there, she closed the door softly behind her. She leaned her weight against the corner wall, afraid her legs would crush right under her. She covered her hot face with her hands. After a few moments, she heard a light tapping. 'Jennifer?'

She didn't answer at first, she couldn't.

Again, 'Jennifer?'

A deep breath, then 'Yes?'

'Are you okay?'

'Yes. I'm fine.'

'Did I say something wrong? Something to upset you?'

She waited a few moments, then opened the door a crack and looked out at him. The eyes that she remembered as wild and piercing now looked bewildered.

'No, nothing you said, Seth, it's what you did. I'm just a little overwhelmed, I guess. I've never had so many lovely gifts. And all at once like this.'

'You're sure now? That's all it is?'

78

Jen forced a smile, then pushed open the door and took his hand in hers.

'Come on, Seth, let's go back. Let me see the rest.'

By four o'clock the storm that had rapidly moved north from Massachusetts reached the cabin. Within minutes, the already shadowy sky turned charcoal grey. Heavy winds lashed the trees and, with the first clash of thunder and lightning, the electricity in the cabin went off. Seth jumped up.

'Don't worry, this happens a lot up here.'

He ran to the kitchen and returned with four thick candles which he posted around the room. He struck a match and held it to each wick. Tiny flames flickered, then shot up, throwing shadows around the room.

'This looks like a bad one,' Jen said, peering out the window.

'I'm scared,' Margo said. She shivered as a particularly loud crash of thunder shook the cabin.

'It's a friendly storm, Margo,' Seth said. 'And it'll pass soon.'

She buried her face against her mother's shoulder.

'Come on, honey.' Jen was combing Margo's hair with her fingers. 'This isn't like you. Seth says storms like this come often around here – you'll notice that the cabin is still standing.'

Matthew sighed. 'Don't be a baby, Margo.'

'Be quiet,' she said.

'When we get storms around here, we get big ones,' Seth said. 'It usually throws out the power, but that's about all. Like I said, they're friendly.'

'Mama,' Margo said, 'can lightning come in through the windows?'

'Stop worrying honey. That's not going to happen.'

'That's dumb,' Matthew said.

Margo pointed her finger at her brother. 'You be quiet.'

Seth walked over to the china closet. He pulled out a long box, brought it back, and set it down on the floor.

'Come on,' he urged the children, 'let's play Monopoly.'

Margo pulled her face from her mother's shoulder and looked at Seth, then shook her head.

'Have you ever played?' he asked her.

'Sure – lots of times.'

'Then what's the problem? It'll be fun. Besides, it's a good way to forget the storm.'

She thought about it, then stood up. 'Okay, I guess.'

Seth waved Matthew over. 'You too.'

Both children sprawled out on the floor across from Seth.

'How about you, Jennifer,' Seth said, 'care to play?'

Jen shook her head. 'No thanks. I'll sit this one out.'

Seth shrugged. 'Okay, suit yourself.'

'I'll be the hat,' Margo said, plucking the metal piece from the box. Matthew chose the dog, and Seth the shoe. Seth counted out the money and put a stack in front of each of them.

'We're all set,' he said. 'Let's shake for first.'

After a dozen trips around the board, nearly every property was bought up, save for a few minor parcels of land and Park Place. Matthew owned Boardwalk. Deals were made, money exchanged hands, and soon the board was scattered with green houses and red hotels. Now, each roll of the dice was made with bated breath.

Although rain continued to beat at the cabin, the three heard only the rattle of the dice and the march of the silver pieces along the board. Jen watched from the sofa, her attention split between the Monopoly game and their own desperate situation.

Seth rolled the white cubes: nine. He counted out the spaces.

'Go to jail,' Matthew cried out.

Seth lifted the shoe and plonked it down.

'You going to pay fifty to get out?'

Seth shook his head. 'I'm staying right here where I can't land on you two.'

'That's not fair,' Margo protested.

Matthew looked at her. 'It is, too. Unless he gets doubles, he's got a right to stay there if he wants.'

'Oh, okay.' Margo sighed as she picked up the dice and threw them. She slowly counted out the spaces, then looked at Seth. 'Oh, no. How much?'

He grabbed up his deed and read the amount.

'You'll enjoy the St. Charles Hilton,' he said as Margo put the money in his palm. 'Strictly deluxe accommodation.'

On Seth's next turn he rolled three and stayed in jail.

Margo landed on Matthew's property. 'Not again.' She picked up the money and handed it to him. 'If someone doesn't land on me soon, I'll go broke.'

Matthew landed on Go and collected two hundred dollars.

Seth threw the dice and, this time, rolled doubles. He moved the six spaces onto his own property.

Seth and Matthew's fortunes swung back and forth, each landing on the other, each making as much money as they lost. Margo's pile of money continued to shrink. This time, she shook the dice with her eyes closed, letting them topple onto the board without even looking.

'Open your eyes, Margo,' Matthew said. 'You landed on Chance.'

'Whew!' She picked up the card. 'Oh, no.'

'What does it say?' Matthew asked.

'Pay twenty-five for each house and one hundred for each hotel.' She groaned. 'I'm going to have to sell.' She carefully removed the plastic pieces for her properties, adding up their worth as she went. Finally done, she was left with no houses, no hotels, most of her properties mortgaged, and three dollars in cash. The next time around she landed on Illinois Avenue – Seth's property.

'That's it – I'm bankrupted.'

'It's mine,' Seth shouted. Margo picked up her deeds and money and handed them over to him. 'Good try,' he said.

She shook her head and moved back leaving the board to him and Matthew. 'Can I be banker?'

Seth ignored her question and looked instead at Matthew.

'It's you and me now,' he said, giving Matthew a thoughtful look. 'It's funny how one way or another it always boils down to who's going to survive, you or the other guy.'

Matthew stared up at him.

'Only one can,' Seth said. 'Survive, that is.'

Something in Seth's voice brought Jen to attention. She slid down on the floor beside the children. 'Tell you what, Margo. You and I will be the readers of the cards. You take Community Chest, I'll take Chance.'

An enormous roll of thunder exploded and shook the cabin. Jen jumped.

After Seth unmortgaged Margo's property, Matthew picked up the dice and threw them, then slowly pushed his silver dog down the spaces.

'Missed you.'

Seth took his turn, landing on Pennsylvania Avenue.

'That's mine,' Matthew shouted. He picked up his deed. 'Pay up – you owe me fourteen hundred dollars!'

Seth counted out the money and shoved it into Matthew's hand. 'Like I said, only one can.'

This time Matthew ignored Seth's remark, anxious to take his turn. He landed on Park Place – the only property not yet owned.

'I'll buy it!' he said, as he bounced up and down on the floor. Picking up the money Seth had just given him he counted out the purchase price.

'Survive . . .' Seth mumbled the word under his breath so softly, Jen had to bend forwards to hear what he was saying.

'Maybe we ought to quit for now,' she said. 'Play something else.'

Matthew, who had just arranged the new Monopoly pair neatly in front of him, jerked his head toward his mother.

'We can't stop now.'

Jen could feel Seth's eyes bore into her.

'I don't give up till it's over,' Seth said. He snatched the dice from the board, knocking off some of the hotels in the process. Matthew carefully put them back in place as Seth threw the dice and again landed on the boy's property. Margo and Matthew cheered. Seth grabbed Matthew's deed from in front of him, read off the amount owed, then tossed the card back. He counted out the money and held it up to Matthew.

Matthew lifted his hand to take it, but Seth didn't let go. Matthew tugged; Seth hung onto the money.

'Come on, Seth, quit it.'

'The money, Seth,' Jen said.

Seth turned toward her, his eyes curious.

'The money – give Matthew the money.'

He slowly released his grip from the pile of bills: Matthew took it, setting it down carefully. He put two thousand dollars in the bank and took two hotels: one for Boardwalk, one for Park Place. Then he tossed the dice.

'Missed you again.'

Seth snatched the cubes from the board.

'I think maybe—' Jen began.

'No,' Seth said. 'It's not over.' Seth rolled five and moved his piece, landing on Chance. He reached out for the card but Jen put her hand out to stop him. She could feel his hand trembling beneath hers.

'Let me, Seth. Remember, I'm the Chance card-reader.'

He pulled his hand away as Jen lifted the orange card. She stared at it: Advance to Boardwalk.

'What does it say' Matthew asked.

'Read it,' Seth said.

Jen looked up at Seth and grinned at him.

'Seth, you've won second prize in a beauty contest. Collect ten dollars.' She could hear Seth let out a stream of air as though it had been trapped in his lungs, choking him.

Matthew turned towards her. 'It *can't* be.'

'Well it is,' Jen said. 'Take your turn now.'

'But Mama, that's not Chance, that's Commun—'

'Matthew!' Jen shouted. 'I'm surprised at you!'

Matthew slowly lifted the dice, then looked over the board at Seth, meeting the fiery eyes staring back at him. He flinched. Margo's eyes followed her brother's, and she pressed her hand onto his shoulder. Jen sucked in her breath waiting for Matthew to toss the dice. He cupped his hands together, shaking them up and down.

'Throw them,' Seth ordered.

Matthew dropped them, jumping as he did. He quickly looked at the numbers, at his silver dog, then at Seth.

'I landed on you,' he said.

Seth smiled.

Within ten minutes, Matthew had landed on Seth's property several times, his money dwindling with each throw of the dice. On the last turn, he extended his hand across the board.

'You win, Seth.'

Seth took his hand and shook it. 'Good game, son.'

The lights suddenly went on. The thunder and lightning had given way to soft, steady rain. The storm had passed.

For now.

CHAPTER EIGHT

STORM DAMAGE OF ONE KIND or another had kept Michael Thorne on the run all day. In addition to several minor automobile accidents and one serious one, a department store window had been shattered by a snapped-off tree branch, leaving the store owner convinced that his big-ticket items would all be carried off by looters. In his years on the Winfield police force, Thorne had yet to come across a single instance of looting. It wasn't until close to seven that he got back to the station, poured himself a cup of overbrewed coffee, and sank down into his desk chair.

The office help had already left for the day. He scanned the messages on his desk, most of which he tossed into the waste basket. The only thing that caught his attention was a skimpy report in a clean file folder.

> Jennifer Sawyer: S.S. No. 057-40-4377. Born May 15, 1954, Monsey, NH. Parents: Martha and Edward Greene, deceased. Married December 16, 1972, Ashley, NH to James B. Sawyer, deceased. Children: Margo and Matthew, born June 5, 1975. Massachusetts registered 1982 Burgundy Toyota Corolla Hatchback, Vehicle I.D. No. 2P34H999S2105, plate number ELM 811. Massachusetts licence to practice hairdressing. Obtained variance 1975 to operate a one-room beauty shop in residential zone, 2 Arden Road, Winfield, MA.

Thorne sighed. There it was: a concise life package tied up with numbers. It still amazed him how few people got by nowadays without some of their private business being programmed into a computer. Someday he'd have to run a check on himself to see what he'd find.

Born February 12, 1950, Leominster, MA. Parents: Sally and Kenneth Thorne. Heavy reputation as lady's man 1976 to 1980 – given up to settle down with feline, Miranda. Residence: 11 Westminster Avenue. Sally Thorne sneaks in to clean apartment monthly: covers tracks, hates cat; would prefer a daughter-in-law and some grandchildren.

What about prior to '76 . . . what about Carol? Would they have that, too?

He was only twenty-four then, a rookie no more than a month. He had met her on the street, outside a Seven-Eleven. Nineteen, no money, no I.D., no place to stay. Christ, she was scrawny – she couldn't have weighed more than a hundred. But he had been struck by those eyes: big green frightened eyes that were saying something, telling him that she needed help. He had always been a sucker for eyes like that.

He had let her sack out overnight at his place. He took the sofa. He smiled, remembering . . . overnight had turned into a week, then a month. Soon he wasn't sleeping on the sofa, and by that time he loved her more than he'd ever loved anything or anyone. She wouldn't marry him, though. 'Don't spoil it,' she'd say. 'No ties, no commitments.' She died of lymph cancer a year later. According to Carol, the doctors had only given her six months; he had given her the rest. It had been a long time ago, but Mike could never rid himself of the feeling that, if only he had known earlier, there might have been something . . .

He sat forward, dropping Jen's report on the desk and rubbed the balls of his palms over his eyes. He hadn't really expected to learn anything that would really help. He decided to take another shot at seeing her.

It was eight o'clock by the time he parked his car in front of the house, which was pitch dark. Though most people in

Winfield didn't bother to lock up their houses when they went out, usually a light or two was left burning. Thorne looked around the grounds and noticed the chair stuck in the rosebush. He walked over and pulled the chair out, folded it, and leaned it against the porch railing. As he headed back down the path, he noticed the mail sticking out of the box. He put his hands in his pockets and looked back at the cottage. Now where in the hell were they? Tomorrow he'd check just to make sure those kids were in school.

After Seth led the children in prayer, he left Jen alone with them to tuck them in. By nine o'clock, she had cleaned up the dinner dishes and joined Seth in the parlour, where he sat reading a book of short stories. She watched him read for a few moments, scolding herself for what she was thinking: that he was almost good-looking when his features were relaxed.

'Seth, I want to thank you for the clothes,' she said. 'I know I must have seemed ungrateful this afternoon but the truth is, everything is just happening so fast I haven't had a chance to catch my breath. On the other hand, it seems to me that you've had this planned out for quite some time. Am I right, Seth? Look at everything you've bought for the children and me.'

Seth put down the book and leaned forward in his straight-backed chair, elbows on knees, one hand cupping his chin.

'I never had anything new as a kid,' he said. 'That's why I want to make sure my family does. I don't expect it to mean as much to you or the kids as it does to me.'

'Surely you had something, Seth.'

'It doesn't really matter – look at me now.' He waved his arm out. 'A house, a car, a piece of land. Not doing so bad, am I? I'll bet you that would surprise a lot of people.'

'What people?'

'Oh, no one important. Just people who pass you by, sometimes so fast you don't catch their names or even remember their faces.'

'Then why would they even care?'

'Because people don't like to admit they've been wrong, made a misjudgment. Once they dump a kid in the trash, they expect him to come up smelling like it.'

'You're talking about yourself, aren't you? Your parents did that to you?'

He lifted his finger and shook it. 'But that's where they did me a favour – don't you see? Without even knowing they did it. You know, kids are smart, they learn fast. Just take a look at the kids in the ghettos. The tougher they have it, the faster they learn to fend for themselves.'

'That may be true, but—'

'But nothing. Getting dumped as a kid, getting knocked around helps teach you what to expect from people. From life, for that matter. You learn how to fight and grab what you want. How to get the chunk that has your name printed on it.'

Jen wondered if she and the children were the chunk he was talking about. And what did he mean, 'getting dumped'? She was quiet for a long moment, then decided to risk one more question.

'Seth, how did you find out? About me and the kids?'

Seth laughed and stood up.

'Come on, Jennifer, you want to know all the top secrets? They say secrets keep the spice in relationships. Now you wouldn't want me to go spoiling the mystery so quick, would you?'

Jen could feel her face heat up. She folded her hands on her knees.

'Seth, I don't like to be laughed at.'

His expression changed instantly. He lowered his head and slid his hands into his pockets.

'I wasn't laughing at you, Jennifer. I don't want to hurt your feelings – can't you see I want to try and please you every way I can? It's just that I can't tell you everything, not yet. I need a little time to get to trust you, to be sure you mean everything you say before I go pouring myself out, telling you all my secrets and looking like a—'

He stopped talking. His eyes darted from side to side while both his hands searched through his pockets.

'What's the matter, Seth?'

His only answer was a moan, like an animal in pain. He circled around the room, his head nodding and his hands flitting from front to back, pocket to pocket.

Jen jumped to her feet and stood right in front of him.

'Tell me, Seth. What are you looking for?'

He stared at her as if he had forgotten who she was. He put his hands to her chest and shoved her away, raced to the front door, threw it open and ran out to the car. Jen followed him as far as the doorway and watched as he crawled around the floor space, reaching and feeling beneath the seats. It wasn't until after he had pulled out the entire front seat that his frantic energy finally stopped. Shoulders slumped, he shuffled back into the house and sank down onto the sofa. His head fell forward and rested in his open palms.

Jen inched her way over to him, fearful that any sudden movement might set him off again. Obviously, what he had been searching for must have great importance. Jen wondered if it had anything to do with her.

'You can tell me, Seth. What *is* it?'

'He gave it to me, and now it's gone.'

'What's gone, Seth?'

'My watch.'

'Maybe you just misplaced it. Maybe you'll find it.'

She wanted to tell him that no loss was worth this agony, but she wasn't sure it was true. She tried to think if there were anything she owned that she could not bear to lose. There wasn't.

She slipped away from him and climbed the stairs. She wanted so much to look in on the children, but their door was locked. Instead she went to her room and fell onto her bed, closed her eyes and imagined herself inside the locked room. She stood in the doorway, adjusting her eyes to the moonlight filtering in through the bedroom window, moving closer to the beds where they both slept peacefully, arms outstretched. Matthew had thrown off the covers; they were wound in a ball at his feet. She bent down, gently untangled the blanket, then drew it up and tucked it under his chin. She bent over, her fingers touching the warm flushed cheek, kissing him softly. His breath moved lightly against her face . . .

She opened her eyes again, pushed herself up onto her elbows and looked around at the room – the room Seth had decorated for her. She fell back onto the bed, crossing her arms over her head. How long would she be able to stand never being sure how he might react from one moment to the next? She lay back down and closed her eyes, trying to remember everything she had ever read about prisoners and what they did to preserve their sanity.

Much later that night Seth, too, climbed the stairs and entered the room. Quietly he pulled up a chair beside Jen's bed, sat down and watched her. She had kicked off the covers in her sleep. He knew he had frightened her earlier, and just the thought of doing that made him feel sick inside. But of the things Dandy had given him – all of which Seth cherished – the watch was the most wonderful. And Dandy was the only person he had ever had, his whole life long.

Until now. He looked down at his Jennifer and reached out his hand, bringing it close to her and – without touching – tracing the curves of her face, her body. He drew the blanket up and tucked it under her chin. Quietly, carefully, he moved the chair back, closed the door and locked it. Tomorrow he'd do better. Tomorrow he wouldn't let the scary feelings take hold of him, even for a moment.

Since Clarence Sawyer's retirement from Northern Electric four years earlier, his morning ritual never varied. Waking at 6 a.m., he reached out for his wire-rim spectacles placed the night before in a soft leather holder on his bedside stand. Years ago Clarence had taken over the tiny back bedroom that once was Jim's. The move had been a relief both to him and his wife when it finally came.

After his morning shower, Clarence slowly climbed into

the clothes laid out neatly on the chair. Then, dressed in blue plaid flannel shirt and loose-fitting trousers belted a good two inches above his natural waistline, he tiptoed downstairs to prepare breakfast. He hoped Miriam would sleep till noon; she was more apt to be in better spirits when left to her own timetable. He switched on the kitchen radio and tuned in to WNOW, the local news station. Though his hearing was not quite what it used to be, he was careful to keep the volume down.

Just as he scooped his two-minute egg from the brown shell onto an unbuttered slice of toast, he heard the clang of the bell from upstairs. He lifted his eyes toward the ceiling and sighed: Miriam was up. He headed upstairs again, another ring of the bell beating at his eardrums, then opened her door.

'That's enough, Miriam. I'm right here – heard you the first time.'

'Well, I never know with you. Half the time you don't seem to hear a thing.'

'You're up early this morning.'

'It was a bad night – my joints felt like they were splitting in two. And once I finally did drop off, there you were, raising the roof, shuffling around the hallway and down those steps.'

'I tried my best to keep the noise down.'

'Trying isn't doing. You know how my head pounds when I don't get a full night's rest – my mind jumps around so, I think I'm about to go mad. It's a bad feeling, Clarence – one I hope you'll never have to experience.'

'Why don't you try to catch a little more rest? Go back to sleep for a few more hours.'

'You ought to know by now, once I'm up, there's no way I can just fall off again. I would think you'd be more careful to begin with. You don't want me ending up in a sanatorium like my poor mother, do you?'

'Why don't I bring up some of that avocado herbal mixture you like so well. That always seems to ease the pain.'

Miriam raised her palm to her forehead.

'That would be nice, Clarence.'

'I'll get right to it, then.'

'Now Clarence, you'll try to hurry, won't you? You know how you dawdle sometimes.'

Clarence forced a smile. 'I'll be back in just a few minutes, dear.'

Once he'd served Miriam her drink, fluffed her pillows and settled her back in, he came downstairs to eat his cold egg, then tidy the kitchen. Finally he went to the hall closet and lifted his wool jacket off the hook and slipped it on. He pulled his cap from the shelf overhead and adjusted it to his head, covering his thin, silver grey hair. He was ready to go out.

Early on in their marriage, Miriam had pestered Clarence about his daily outings, never able to understand how anyone could get even an ounce of pleasure from exercise. Before his retirement the ritual had been put off until evening hours, but never put aside even in the foulest weather. In fact, Clarence could not remember a day that he didn't pick himself up and go off alone. To stretch his legs – at least that's what Miriam believed he was doing.

Matthew couldn't see the faces in his dream. But even from such a distance he could see the shiny blade glowing in the darkness as the man knelt over her. When he heard the cry, he knew it was mama calling for help. He jumped up to run to her, but his legs felt heavy; his movements were slow and laboured as if he were running through soft, deep sand. Still he pushed – panting, straining – to run faster, to reach her before it was too late. As he got closer, her cries grew fainter and fainter. And then he could no longer hear them at all.

Finally he was there, standing over them. Their arms and legs were tangled together; the knife lay unnoticed at their side. The only sound he could hear now was their soft laughter.

'No, mama!'

He leapt on the man, his hands beating against the wide shoulders, then pushing with all his might, trying to tear them apart. The man wouldn't budge. Matthew looked down at his hand; the knife was squeezed tightly in his fist. And then as if the knife were alive, it guided his hand – forcing it forward. The sharp blade slid easily into the man's broad back. Blood squirted out; the man toppled over onto the ground. Matthew lifted his hands to his face: red droplets of blood were crawling on his hands, up his wrists, his arms . . .

Matthew bolted up in his bed, suddenly awake in the morning sun. His eyes darted back and forth around the room, trying to remember where he was. He lifted his hand, wiped his sweaty forehead, and looked over at Margo fast asleep, her hands balled up into fists on her chest. The blankets on her bed were all askew, as if she had been thrashing around. Matthew went quietly to her bed and pulled the covers back over her, then padded over to the window and climbed onto the stool to look out.

The trees were like rainbows, one colour blending into another. The sun was so strong that he could feel the warmth right through the window on his face. Today was Thursday. If he and Margo were home, they would be going to before-school track practice. But they weren't home, and they wouldn't be going. It would be the first practice they'd ever missed. He looked down at his hands, still trembling, remembering how, when he had been a few years younger, he would go into mama's room, climb into her bed and cuddle up. She'd always throw her warm puffy quilt over him and run her fingers through his hair. It always made him feel better.

Even if he wanted to do that now, though, he couldn't because her door was locked. He and Margo were locked in and mama was locked in, and nothing she said could change that. They were trapped here, all of them. They were all Seth's prisoners.

After going through her wardrobe, Jen decided on a cotton shirtwaist, the most conservative dress she could find in the closet. She slid it off the hanger and took it into the bathroom; by the time Seth unlocked her bedroom door at 7 a.m., she was ready and waiting.

Breakfast was on the table and the children were already eating when she walked into the kitchen. She leaned over to put her arms around them, noticing the dark circles under their eyes as she hugged them. She also noticed the lack of enthusiasm with which her hugs were returned. As she sat down, Seth slipped behind Margo's chair and tugged at her hair.

'What are you *doing?*' Margo asked.

'Just trying to get your attention,' he said with a grin.

'Well, you've got it. Now, what do you want?'

'Do you like picnics?'

She sighed. 'Sure. So what?'

'So I propose we have one this afternoon in the backyard.'

'A picnic is no good unless you go somewhere.'

'Says who? I bet the ants don't see it that way. To them, one place is as good as another.'

'It's too cold anyhow,' Margo said. 'Who has picnics in the middle of October?'

'We do.' He leapt onto his chair and cupped his hands to form a megaphone. 'Ladies and gentlemen! Your attention, puh-leeze. The Anthony family would like to make it known that they hold picnics year round. That's right, folks – summer, fall, winter, spring.'

The children stared at him.

'In addition,' he went on, 'I would like to clarify the definition of *picnic*. A picnic is defined as food of your choice. yes, you heard the man right. Hot dogs, candy, ice cream, cupcakes, popcorn, cookies – you name it, you get it. Just step right up and turn in your order.' He got down from the chair, grabbed a pen and paper from the countertop, and dropped them onto the table. Next, pulling a deep pot off the stove, he thrust it upside down on his head, the rim falling and covering his eyes, the handle sticking out like a horn from his head.

The words *Anthony family* were not lost on Jen. Even so, she found herself giggling at the sight of Seth with the pan over his head. Was it hysteria? She herself wasn't sure. All she knew was that something inside her had snapped. Unable to withstand the pressure any more, her body had sought relief in a spontaneous display of emotion. She laughed until tears came to her eyes, not certain herself if she were laughing or crying.

The children's stares shifted from Seth to their mother and back again as if the two adults were joined in a conspiracy. Finally Jen lifted the pen from the table.

'Why don't I go first?' She put the tip of the pen to her nose and furrowed her brows. 'How about a roast beef sandwich, french fries, and a chocolate shake?'

'Of course,' Seth said. 'A simple request.'

She wrote down her order and took the children's: hot dog and a chocolate shake for Margo, cheeseburger and a large Coke for Matthew, french fries and ice cream for both. Seth jumped down from the chair, grabbed the paper and stuffed it into his pocket.

'Consider it done,' he said in his normal tone of voice. 'As soon as you're finished with breakfast, I'll lock you back up in your room and go pick up your orders.'

Jen knew she had no reason to be startled, but she was.

'Of course, Seth,' she said, her voice flat. 'You do what you have to.'

'Well, what do you expect?' he asked, stung by the disappointment in her face. 'What is it you want from me? I can't very well leave you here on your own, *can I?*'

He led them upstairs and locked them in – first Jennifer, then the children. He could see by the expression on their faces that he couldn't leave them together; they wanted to talk about him behind his back. He always knew when people were doing that; he could tune the words in as clear as crystal, almost like he had a private CB hooked up in his head. But tuning in usually made him angry, and he didn't want anything to spoil the good time they were going to have at the picnic. Everyone was looking forward to it. He remembered the list and slid his hand into his pocket to make sure it was still there. Then he ran downstairs, pulled a few bills from the tin can and rushed out of the house to buy the food.

An hour later, the food he'd brought back was nearly gone. So was the gaiety he'd worked so hard to create. Oh, Jennifer made an effort, but Seth could tell her heart wasn't really in it. Couldn't she see he was doing everything in his power to make them all happy? He had even managed to make her laugh. It was the first time he'd ever seen her that way and if it was up to him, she'd be laughing and happy all the time. There was just one thing she had to accept first: she and the children would never leave him.

When the last bite was eaten, Seth shook out the blanket, folded it, and announced that he and Matthew would go out for a walk in the woods.

Jennifer stared at him. 'Why?'

'I want to get to know the boy, be with him alone for a while. And I'm not going to lock you and Margo in while we're gone.'

It made him feel good to see the smile return to her face.

CHAPTER NINE

HIGHLAND ELEMENTARY SCHOOL IN WINFIELD took up the entire block. The single-storey brick building was laid out in the shape of a horseshoe and opened onto a huge athletic field – three sides enclosed by bleachers, seating almost two thousand.

Michael Thorne stood on the sidelines watching the kids race around the track. All he could remember from grade school was a black tar playground, nothing like this. Certainly never a track team. He wondered how many tax dollars had gone into the playing field. Whatever it cost, the way he saw it the money was well spent.

He waited while the coach gave out instructions for the next meet. The kids paid strict attention, but once the whistle was blown they were off, racing for the locker room to change out of their gym clothes. Thorne jumped back just in time to keep his balance as they flew past him. He went to the dugout, where the coach was knotting the string of a burlap bag, and pointed to the children, now almost out of sight.

'You have a dangerous crew there. Do you make them take out liability insurance?'

The coach turned to him and smiled.

'I probably should.'

'I understand you've got a couple of star runners on your team,' Thorne said. 'The Sawyer twins, Margo and Matthew. Were they at practice today?'

'You on the staff here?'

Thorne pulled out his wallet and showed him his I.D.

'I don't understand,' the coach said. 'Is something wrong?'

'Not that I know of. Just checking to see if they're in school today. According to the office,' he gestured towards the building, 'they were absent yesterday. The secretary sent me out here to see if they showed up for today's practice.'

'You a truant officer?'

'No, nothing like that.'

'I see. Well, as a matter of fact, neither of them showed today. I figure they must be pretty sick.'

'Then it's unusual for them to skip a practice?'

'That's putting it mildly. Those two kids are my best runners – this is the first practice they've missed since I've been coaching here. And that'll be two years come December.'

'Hmmm . . . well, thanks for the information.'

Thorne turned to go.

'Just a second,' the coach said. 'There's no trouble, is there? We've got a meet coming up in two weeks – the biggest of the season. I don't like to think what our chances would be without those two.'

'Ah, no need to worry. They'll be here. I'm sure of it. Thanks again for your help.'

He stuck his hands in his pockets and headed back towards the car. If they *were* sick, they'd be home or in the hospital. He decided he'd check both.

Dressed in jeans and a heavy wool shirt that matched Seth's, Matthew followed Seth down the narrow basement stairs. The smell got worse as they descended, reminding Matthew of the time he'd found a dead woodchuck in the garage. Seth headed towards a workshop in the corner of the cellar. Matthew hung back near the steps, wanting to run back up where it was light, airy.

'Come on over here,' Seth said. 'I've got something to show you.'

Matthew watched him slide open the doors of a cabinet and pull out a gun.

'What's that for?'

'It's a hunting rifle, son. Did you ever go hunting?'

Matthew shook his head. The only person he ever knew

who hunted was grandpa, and mama had told him that his father used to when he was a boy. Though grandpa had offered to teach him to shoot, Matthew had never taken him up on the offer. Mama didn't much like the idea, and Matthew was sure he could never, ever shoot at anything.

'Well,' Seth said placing his hand gently on the boy's shoulder, 'you're in for a treat. I'm going to teach you how to use this gun.'

Seth pulled open the bulkhead, and Matthew followed him out into the fresh air. As they walked down the path leading to the back gate, he turned his head to see if his mother was watching from the window. She wasn't. He trailed behind Seth, hoping against hope that they wouldn't spot anything to kill.

As soon as Jen heard the bulkhead doors slam shut, she raced to the hall closet and pulled it open. The floor was bare. Margo ran after her.

'What are you looking for, mama?'

'My luggage. Seth put it in here yesterday, but it's gone.' She went through the rooms, looking in cabinets and closets, but found nothing.

'What about the cellar?'

'I suppose that's a possibility – come on.'

The minute Jen swung open the cellar door, the fumes stung her nostrils. She sucked in her breath.

'Yuck, it stinks down here.'

'Hold your nose, honey.' Jen ran her hand along the wall, feeling for the switch. Finally she found it and flipped the button, releasing a dim beam of light. 'Be careful now, these steps are steep. Follow me.'

'Why does it smell so bad, mama?'

'I don't know. Maybe a dead animal.'

'It's scary down here. I don't like it.'

'It's only a cellar, Margo.'

'Do you think there's rats down here?'

'Margo, if you're trying to make me nervous, you're doing a good job. Suppose we get down to business and start looking.'

Jen started on one side and Margo on the other. They

searched every shelf and cupboard big enough to conceal suitcases. Finally Jen threw up her hands.

'Let's go.'

They both took the stairs in a hurry. After the cellar door was shut Jen sank down onto the sofa.

'What's so important about the suitcases, mama?'

Jen pulled her over to sit beside her.

'I brought along Daddy's gun – the one we kept in the desk. I had it hidden in my toiletry bag.'

'A *gun*? Would you have shot Seth?'

Jen thought a minute about her answer, then said, 'I guess I would do whatever I had to – to get us out of here.'

Jen leaned her head back against the cushions, her mind on the missing luggage. Had Seth gone through it and found the gun, or had he just decided to get rid of traces of her past and dumped the bags? If he did know about the gun, all her efforts to gain his trust had been for nothing. She decided she'd have to proceed on the assumption that he hadn't found the gun. If she was wrong, she'd find out soon enough.

'What can we do now, mama?'

'I don't know yet, but we'll get out of here somehow.' In spite of her words, she no longer felt so confident. She hadn't seen one sign of a house or person since she got there. Seth didn't even have a mailbox; he probably picked up his mail at the post office. She wondered if anyone would be able to follow her trail. For that matter, did anyone even know they were missing?

She took hold of Margo's hands.

'There is something you can do,' she said.

'What?'

'I want you not to make Seth angry. I want him to think we all like him. Now, Margo, it's obvious how you feel about him – it shows all over your face. I want you to be friendlier. Nicer.'

'Why?'

'Because if he trusts us, we're more likely to get a chance to leave. He'll let down his guard. And when he does, we'll be ready. It's like acting – like the time you played the witch in *Snow White and the Seven Dwarfs*, remember?'

Margo nodded. 'You want me to pretend I'm nice.'

Jen hugged her. 'You don't have to pretend – you *are* nice. But I do want Seth to think you like him, and you're going to have to be nice to him to convince him of that. What do you say?'

Margo picked up her mother's hand and pumped it up and down.

'It's a deal,' she said solemnly.

They had been in the woods for more than an hour. To Matthew's relief, Seth had not shot at anything. For the past half hour he had been demonstrating to Matthew how to load and fire the gun. Now he put it into his hands.

'Go ahead, cock it like I showed you, then shoot it. Just remember what I told you about the kickback – spread your legs apart, get a firm foothold on the ground, and roll with the punches. That way you won't go flying backwards.'

'I don't want to, Seth.'

'Look, there's nothing to be afraid of. It's not going to hurt you. Trust me.'

Matthew cocked the gun and pointed it.

'Not so fast, son. Now, what did I tell you?'

Matthew looked at him, then spread his legs.

'That's more like it. Get that firm foothold on the ground so you'll keep your balance.'

The boy looked down at his feet, then back at Seth.

'Now put the butt underneath your shoulder.'

Matthew moved the gun into position.

'Now set your sight. Look through the telescopic scope – everything will be magnified.'

Matthew placed his eye to the scope sticking out from the top of the rifle.

'See those crossbars? Set your sight right through those bars, then shoot.'

Matthew stood stock-still, his eyes glued to the scope.

'Go ahead, pull the trigger.'

Still Matthew didn't move.

Seth sighed and pushed up his shirtsleeves.

'Here, let me show you.' He got in back of Matthew, crouched down and fastened his hands over the boy's, holding them firmly in place. Then he set the sight for a tree in the distance.

'You got a firm grip?'

Matthew nodded.

Seth pulled the trigger. Matthew jumped as the gun went off, the blast echoing in his eardrums.

'I told you,' Seth said. 'It's not a big deal. Didn't hurt you, did it?'

The boy handed the gun back to him.

'Thanks for teaching me, Seth.'

Seth grinned and swung his arm around Matthew's shoulders.

'That's okay, son. Maybe we ought to head back now, get back to your mother and sister. But don't you worry, we'll have another go at this real soon. Next time, maybe you'll land something – go home with a trophy.'

As they headed back towards the house, Matthew turned his face slightly toward the arm still draped over his shoulder. Seth had pushed up his long sleeves, and for the first time Matthew could make out the tattoo on his forearm. In heavy blue-grey ink there were eight letters: *Jennifer*.

Matthew tilted his head up.

'Seth, how long are you going to keep us here?'

Seth tightened his arm around the boy, looked down at him and smiled.

'Don't you worry, son, I'll never abandon you. Never.'

It had now been two years since Clarence had first started to visit the cemetery. Before then, except for the burial service itself, he couldn't bring himself to go near Jim's grave. It was a combination of things that kept him away. For one, he couldn't bear to think of his boy's body decaying beneath the soil. Ever since he was little, Clarence had been squeamish about such things.

A more serious problem was the guilt feelings he harboured whenever he thought about Jim. These feelings didn't come from any particular thing he'd done, but from the things he hadn't done when he had the chance. Like running interference when Miriam would pour castor oil all over the boy's food and make him finish every last bit, like it or not. Or her making him wear girl's knee-high stockings under his pants to keep his legs warm in school. More often than not, Clarence had backed down, not having the energy to go through a scene. The thing was, there were always those other things Clarence had to tend to. Those other responsibilities that he had kept secret from both of them.

And Jim surely was no match for Miriam: the woman was overpowering, used to getting her way about most things. Any other boy might have turned mean, resenting his mother for her domineering ways – and Clarence for his silence. But the fact was, Jim had turned out to be a fine boy anyway, and Clarence couldn't have been prouder the day he took Jennifer as his bride. She was a strong girl and, though Jim wasn't around to help out, she was doing right by his children. Even though Clarence didn't get to see them as much as he would have liked, their telephone conversations and summer visits kept him up to date on what was going on. He was grateful that Jennifer allowed him and the wife that much. Some girls in such circumstances became very possessive about the children and never let the grandparents set eyes on them again.

While he still couldn't see any purpose to his boy's early death and probably never would, no matter how much he thought about it, he could at least get pleasure out of knowing that some part of Jim still existed in his children. And though Clarence had made peace with himself and could now visit the gravesite, he still made it a point not to look down at the earth. No need to start thinking of the bugs and worms that fed on his son's body and get himself upset all over again.

After Clarence left the cemetery, he continued with his walk. There weren't many parts of Ashley that he hadn't travelled on foot at one time or another. Today he walked clear down Post Road. At one point, if he had turned his head to the right and looked up a bit, he might have spotted Jennifer's abandoned car sitting up in the woods. As it was, Clarence kept his attention on a red rose lying on the side of the road.

It was past four o'clock when Thorne got back to the department. Between assignments he'd managed to check with Memorial Hospital as well as the children's pediatrician, whose name he had copied that morning from their school records. Neither the hospital nor the doctor had any recent information about the Sawyer twins. He had also stopped at the house on Arden Road and checked the mailbox, this time stuffed to capacity. He took out the envelopes and magazine and deposited them on the shelf in the unlocked foyer, the entrance to the beauty shop.

Now he leaned back in the chair in his office and stared out of the window, not even noticing that Henry Schroeder had entered the room.

'Well, if it isn't Supercop.' Schroeder waited for a response. He got none, and went on. 'You see the printout I left on your desk yesterday? The one on that widow?'

Thorne nodded.

'I don't suppose it contained anything you could use, but then of course I don't know what the hell you're looking for.'

Thorne swung around in his chair and faced Schroeder.

'Two days ago this lady called reporting her two kids missing. Never came home from school. When I got there, she told me she found them. At a friend's house, a new kid on the block.'

'I'm listening.'

'There's no new kid on the block, I checked it out. And I never did get to see the kids.'

'So she lied to you about where they were. Are you saying she lied to you about finding them?'

'That's what I'm saying.'

'Why on earth should she?'

'She was scared, Schroeder, real scared. And the funny thing is, she was more scared after she supposedly found the kids than when she first reported them missing.'

'Hmmm . . . well, maybe the full impact didn't register till she located them. How many times do people hold up just fine during an emergency, only to fold up once it's over?'

'I went back there that night. On my own time.'

Schroeder leaned back in his chair.

'Ahh . . . now we're getting somewhere. There's more here than meets the eye. Is it fair to say your interest reaches beyond that of law, order, justice, duty, and other such pursuits?'

'Wait a minute—'

'No, you wait. Am I right or not? Level with me.'

Thorne looked at him. 'You're right, I guess. But that doesn't change the situation. She had more than a couple of hours to calm down by the time I got there, and when I showed up she was ready to jump right out of her skin.'

'Maybe you make her nervous. God knows, Thorne, I can relate to that – along with a few other people around here.'

Schroeder picked up a requisition form and started to feed it into the computer. Thorne went on with his story.

'Since that night, Tuesday, she's been missing. In fact, all three of them have been missing.'

'How do you figure that?'

'Her mail has been stacking up in the box and the kids haven't been to school in two days. I checked the hospital and the pediatrician and there's no report of their being sick.'

'Anyone report them missing?'

'No. I checked.'

Schroeder shrugged. 'So the lady overreacted to the situation, and she decided to take a few days off to mellow out. She packed up herself and the kids and went on a little trip. Maybe that's what you ought to do, Thorne. If you spend all your time looking for disaster where it isn't, neglecting your other cases, the chief's going to get down-right ornery.'

Thorne leaned back and folded his arms against his chest.

'You know something, Schroeder, you're about as much help as horseshit in a parade.'

Jen was relieved to see that Seth was in better spirits when they arrived back at the cabin. Matthew looked pale, but he must have handled the situation well.

Seth led them all up to the children's bedroom.

'I'll only be gone a little while,' he said. 'I have to mail a letter and do some food shopping. In the meantime, you'll have the chance to spend some time together.' The door closed, the bolt slid into place. They listened to his footsteps on the stairs, the front door slamming, the car engine starting.

Jen put her arms around the children.

'Come on, let's talk.'

She led them over to the bed.

Matthew said, 'What are we going to do?'

'This is only temporary, Matthew.'

'That's not what *he* thinks. I asked him. He thinks we're going to stay forever.'

'I know. But I want you to believe me, not him. We're going to get out of here.'

'Just saying it won't make it happen, mama. We need a plan to make it happen.'

'Until he trusts us, plans are useless.' She looked at the tiny barred window, the heavy oak door. 'There's nothing we can do locked in a room. What we have to do is get him to believe we want to be with him and stop locking us in when he's gone.'

'You and Margo could have run off today when we were in the woods,' Matthew said. 'He didn't lock you in then.'

'He had *you*, Matthew. You were with him. Seth may sometimes *seem* harmless, but he's not. He's dangerous. I could never leave while you were with him.'

'You should have taken the chance, mama. You could have brought back help.'

'No, Matthew, I won't listen to that kind of talk. I won't

leave here until both you and Margo are out – both of you, do you understand?'

She looked at Margo listening quietly and put her hand on her shoulder, then turned again towards her son.

'I didn't mean to get so upset,' she said. 'But you two are going to have to trust me. And the three of us are going to have to wait.'

That night, after the children had been tucked in, Jen went into the parlour and sat down on the sofa beside Seth.

'It was a good day,' he said. 'I really feel like I'm getting close to the boy, and at dinner tonight even Margo seemed friendly. Did you notice?'

Jen smiled. 'They're getting to know you, Seth, and I wouldn't be surprised to find they're starting to care about you, too. After all, you've been good to them.'

'Do you really think so?'

Jen nodded.

'Just you saying that means a lot to me, you know.' He leaned back. 'I want them to look up to me, to love me – but most of all, to need me. You and them are the only family I've ever had.'

Jen waited a moment, afraid she'd say the wrong thing, ask the wrong question.

'What about when you were young?' she said finally.

'I never even knew my parents. Not all parents are like you, Jennifer. Some don't care one bit about what happens to their kids.'

'Where did you grow up, Seth?'

'In a home. An orphanage.'

'That must have been rough. Children need a lot of love and attention, and—'

'I didn't say I didn't have that. There was someone – someone real special. He always cared about me, no matter what.'

'Who was he?'

'Dandy, my best friend.' He said the name softly, gently.

'Did he live in the home with you?'

'He visited me.' Jen could see the expression on his face soften as if he were seeing his friend at that moment. 'Every day, without fail, he'd come to see me. He gave me the watch.' He slid his hand into his pocket as if to take it out and show her.

Jen stared. Had Seth already erased from his memory the loss of the watch? She tried to head off a possible scene.

'You misplaced it, Seth, remember? But now I understand why it meant so much to you. Tell me, do you still keep in touch with him?'

Empty eyes stared at her. She pulled back a little, remembering last night.

'This is a beautiful cabin, Seth. I've always dreamed that one day, if I could ever afford it, I'd buy a place like this.'

Silence.

She waited a few moments, then tried again.

'Do you work, Seth?'

He looked at her, puzzled. She gestured around the room.

'The house, the car, the food, even the lovely clothes and flowers you bought me – all cost money. I'm just wondering how you manage to get along.'

'I do some odd carpentry jobs now and then.'

'Is that enough to make ends meet?'

'Why do you want to know?'

'I'm not trying to pry into your affairs, Seth. It's just that I have a hairdresser's licence. There's no reason I can't help out with the expenses. I wouldn't have to leave the house – the customers could come right here.'

'I don't want you working. Ever.' He reached out, took her hand and clasped it in his own. 'The others – they wouldn't understand.'

That night, Jen lay in her bed for hours, thinking. She had learned something about Seth's background: not much, just enough to know how much more there was to find out if she were ever to understand him. He hadn't had an easy time of it, growing up like that. She knew what it was like not having a father, but there was always her mother: a spunky, spirited woman who never tired of listening to every detail of every childhood catastrophe that came along. Or if she did mind, she never once let on. Jen couldn't even imagine what it would have been like never to have had her. A friend, no matter how close or loyal, was hardly a replacement for a parent.

Her thoughts turned back to their conversation about money; he certainly didn't seem concerned about it, almost as though he had more than enough. It didn't make sense. She found it hard enough to scrounge out a living for herself and the children, and she worked at it full time. How could an orphan with no steady income manage all this?

At the first sign of daylight, Matthew tiptoed to Margo's bed and nudged her shoulder.

'Get up,' he whispered.

She rolled over and stared at him, not yet fully awake. She rubbed her eyes with her fists, then pushed herself up into a sitting position.

'What's the matter?'

'I want to talk.'

She put her hands onto the mattress, hoisted herself onto the pillow and leaned her head back against the wall.

'Go ahead, talk. But you'd better keep it quiet or we'll wake Seth up.'

Matthew nodded. 'You know how you told me last night about you being nice to Seth – how mama asked you to?'

Margo nodded.

'Well, I was thinking . . .'

'Thinking what?'

'Suppose instead of Seth just taking *me* out in the woods, you asked if you could go along too. You could ask him to teach us about nature, couldn't you?'

'I guess, but why would I want to?'

'If you could get him to do that – if you could convince him to take both of us – then we might just be able to get out of here.'

'What's your plan?'

'Suppose that once we got way out in the woods, we both started to run.'

'We're fast, but not that fast,' Margo said. 'Seth is big – he's got long legs, he'd be able to catch us easy.'

'Not if we ran in different directions.'

'What do you mean?'

'If we run in opposite directions, he'd be able to chase only one of us. Sure, he'd catch that one, but by that time, the other would have a good head start. Then he'd be the one who didn't stand a chance. Remember: as big as he is, we can run for a longer distance than any grown-up.'

'Where would we run?'

'I'll go north,' Matthew pointed with his finger, 'and you'll go south. The one that doesn't get caught keeps on going no matter what. As soon as you or I meet up with someone, we tell him what's going on and he calls the police.'

'But what about the one who gets caught?'

'That's going to be me.'

'How do you know that?'

'Because I have it all planned out. First of all, you'll pretend you're scared – I'll give the signal when. Tell Seth you saw a snake behind a bush or something. As soon as he goes over to inspect, I'll start running and you stay right where you are.'

'And?'

'As soon as he starts to chase me, *you* start running – but in the other direction. He can't go after both of us.'

'But what about you?'

'I'll keep him running, dummy, you can count on that. I'm not going to try to get caught, you know.'

'But what will happen once he *does* catch you?'

Matthew shrugged his shoulders.

'What could he do to me?'

'What do you mean, Matthew? He can beat you up, for one.'

'So what? The important thing is that you can't stop, Margo. No matter what – even if you hear me yelling and screaming, you can't stop. You've got to promise to keep running.'

'I don't know. He could hurt you. He could *kill* you.'

'But that's not what he really wants, Margo. He doesn't want to kill us, he wants to *keep* us.'

Margo was quiet for a long moment.

'What about mama?' she said finally. 'Suppose he hurts her?'

'He won't be able to get near her – we'll be too far off in the woods. By the time he can drag me back to the cabin, you'll have already gotten help and be on the way back . . . Well, what do you think?'

Another long pause. 'I think yes. I think we should do it.'

Matthew grinned.

'But—'

'What?'

'I'm still afraid of what he'll do to you. You know, Seth's not like other people. When he gets mad, he's spooky.'

Matthew's expression turned grim.

'You can't let yourself be scared for me, Margo, because if you do, the plan's not going to work. Remember, no matter what, you can't stop running. And maybe . . .'

'Go on, what?'

'Maybe he's not as fast as we think. Maybe I can outrun him and then both of us will bring back help.'

Margo folded her arms across her chest and rolled her eyes.

'Oh, sure.'

'Well, it's not impossible.'

Margo started to say something, then hesitated.

'What's the matter?' Matthew asked.

Margo looked up at him. 'Oh, nothing. It's just that . . . well, I want you to be careful – that's all.'

Matthew smiled. 'Don't worry, Margo. Seth won't hurt me. He doesn't want to get mama upset.' He then turned and walked over to the closet, thinking about what might happen if he were wrong.

Seth had just about decided that Jennifer was right. Maybe this was the best way, letting them get to know him first. Matthew was loosening up, no doubt about it. And Margo was acting almost like he was her friend, smiling up at him and chattering on all through breakfast.

At this rate – the way things were happening so fast – it wouldn't be long before he'd be able to tell them the whole truth. He tried to picture the expressions on their faces when they found out. Soon they'd be calling him daddy.

'Seth?' Margo called out, startling him.

He looked up.

'Whatcha smiling about?'

He could feel his cheeks getting warm. 'Nothing . . . Just thinking.'

'Oh. Seth, do you know anything about nature?'

'What do you mean?'

'You know, nature. Birds, flowers, animals – things like that.'

'Sure, I do. I couldn't have lived in these woods all this time without learning something.'

'I don't know so much about it myself, but I love to walk in the woods. Once I went with my grandpa – he took me way out, real far, and we saw all kinds of birds and animals. Even a deer.'

He picked up his napkin and wiped his mouth.

'Well, what would you say to us going *way* out in the woods, too? I could teach you things just like your grandpa did. 'Course your grandpa doesn't live so far north—'

'How do you know that, Seth?' Jen broke in.

Seth was momentarily flustered. 'Well, I . . . I don't really. It's just that not many people live much farther north than this and I guess I was thinking he must live somewhere near where you used to live.'

The answer didn't completely satisfy Jen but she nodded anyway. Seth turned back to Margo.

'Well, what do you say? Would you like to go?'

Margo jumped off her chair. 'You mean it?'

'I sure do.'

'Matthew too? Can Matthew come too?'

Seth looked over at the boy and smiled.

'I don't see why not.'

Margo's eyes shone brightly. 'Can we go get ready now?'

'I don't know what the rush is. The woods aren't going anywhere, I promise.'

'Please, Seth. Please.'

He laughed. 'Okay, you go get dressed. I'll go downstairs and get the rifle.'

'Oh no, Seth, not that.' She ran up to him. 'I want to see the animals, I don't want to hurt them. Besides, I'm scared of guns. Please don't take it.'

'Okay, okay, don't you worry. We're not going to be shooting at anything.'

'Then you won't take the rifle?'

He shook his head.

'You two go get ready.' They raced upstairs and he followed. 'I'll be back in a while,' he said.

Seth locked their door, went to the cellar, and headed toward the workbench. He bent down, pulled open the bottom drawer and reached in, pulling out a long, flat wooden box. He unlocked the box and picked out one of the handguns, then, turning the little key, closed it and returned it to the drawer. He didn't like the idea of tricking the girl like this – actually, he hadn't lied, he *wasn't* taking the rifle. But he knew there was no way he could take the children out there without having the means to protect them. The girl didn't understand about animals. They could be fickle – one minute eating right out of your hand and the next sinking their teeth into you.

It didn't matter much, anyhow. If he needed to use the gun, she'd be mighty glad he'd been smart enough to bring it along. And if he didn't need it, she'd never know the difference. That's what it was like being a father, he guessed. As much as you wanted to treat kids fairly and never lie to them, you had to use your own good judgement. You had to stay in charge. This was all new to him, but he was catching on fast.

He took the rifle out of the cabinet and slid it under the

workbench – Jennifer would be alone, and though he was learning to trust her, there was no need to be careless. Not now, not when everything seemed to be going his way. He stuck the pistol in his belt under his jacket and headed upstairs. All he knew was that he never wanted that look to leave their faces – the way their eyes lit up this morning when they looked at him. He wanted it to last forever. He shook his head back and forth, as if to make sure it was all real. Everything was working out just like he had planned – he'd been right all along. Who said one person's dreams couldn't become another's?

Jen watched from the window as Matthew and Seth walked together, their steps closely in synch while Margo ran ahead, obviously delighted to be out in the fresh air. She smiled at the thought of her little actress. She was doing a good job of gaining Seth's trust.

And the nature walk would give Jen a chance to inspect the grounds, find out where they were. Though she could not see another house from any window and had never seen a car pass, she might spot something if she travelled down the road on foot. First she made a quick search for the car keys – not that she thought Seth would be foolish enough to leave them behind, but it was silly to close off any option without being certain. For an instant, she could picture Mike Thorne's face, shaking his head, his dark eyes scolding: *You mean to tell me you didn't even check for car keys?* She ran around the rooms, quickly checking drawers and all of Seth's pockets. No keys.

She figured she had a half hour – it would take them at least that long. That meant fifteen minutes each way: if she jogged, she could cover at least a mile. She wished she had pants to wear, but her dress would have to do.

She had gone over a mile without seeing a sign of life. She slowed to a walk, panting for breath: it had been years since she'd put herself through such a workout. She inched her way towards the edge of the circling mountain road and looked down. Far out in the distance, she could make out several small buildings – a tiny valley. The centre of town, it had to be. The place where Seth picked up groceries and mail.

She cupped her hands over her eyes and squinted – from where she stood, it looked to be at least three to four miles, but that was down the mountain. She considered the route, studying the steep, rocky incline and shook her head. Taking the road could be more than twice the distance, but the mountain was far too risky.

She gave herself a few minutes to rest before starting back, wondering what she would do with this information now that she had it. She wasn't really any closer to getting the kids out. First Seth would have to make his one mistake – give them the opportunity to escape. Then somehow they'd have to make it down to the valley. But in spite of all of the ifs, she felt better than she had since she arrived.

At least now she knew the way back to civilization.

CHAPTER TEN

MIRIAM SAWYER MADE HER WAY DOWNSTAIRS gripping the railing as though she were expecting her short, thick legs – wrapped in elasticized stockings – to give out. She headed for the wall-to-wall shelves in the kitchen. After due consideration, she picked out a jar labelled *Seaweed/Froth*. She carried the bottle to the sink, then poured the liquid into an eight-ounce glass. She spilled four vitamin tablets onto her palm and washed them down with her drink, smacking her lips loudly when she had drained the glass. She walked to the window and pulled aside the heavy curtains. The light hurt her eyes, and she squinted.

It was a bright, clear day, one of those days when people from Massachusetts flock to New Hampshire to see the colours, making a big to-do about leaves, of all things. Just as she turned from the window, Clarence walked in and headed towards the closet to hang up his jacket.

'It's a fine day out there,' he said. 'You ought to get a little of that air yourself.'

'Maybe I would if you got me a decent car. That old thing in the driveway hasn't sputtered to life in more than six months. What I'd like to know is when you're going to replace it with something that moves?'

Clarence came into the kitchen, took out two cups and poured tea, then set them down on the table.

'It's healthier to walk,' he said.

'Healthy, my foot. The problem with you is you're too stingy to spend the money. You had a good job for fifty years, now here you are retired with a comfortable pension and still you don't like to part with a nickel. You do know you can't take it with you, don't you?'

'Now there's nothing wrong with a man wanting to be careful with his dollars so he and his wife are secure in their old age.'

'What do you call *this*, Clarence? For godsake, time's running out to spend it.'

'Spending is one thing, wastefulness is another.'

'And cheapness is another. You're cheap, old man. Cheap.'

Clarence sipped his tea, not speaking. Finally Miriam pushed her empty cup towards him.

'Get me another cup – I'm feeling faint. All this arguing's no good for me.'

He stood up, lifted her cup and headed for the stove. Just as he slipped the used teabag into the cup, the telephone rang.

Miriam's eyes shot up towards the clock: twelve, on the dot.

'A phone that rings on the dot at noon, brings – at midnight – a full moon.' She chanted the words quietly, then looked up at Clarence. 'You best get that.'

He lifted the kettle and poured the boiling water in.

'For heaven's sake, Clarence, answer the phone.'

'Hold on, now, I'll get it.' He walked to the phone and lifted the receiver to his ear. 'Sawyer residence. Clarence here . . . No, I'm afraid not – what seems to be the problem? No, I'm afraid I can't . . . I sure will be.' He hung up.

'Well, Clarence, who was it?'

'A fellow from Massachusetts. Name's Thorne.'

'What did he want?'

Clarence sat down on the chair facing Miriam. His face seemed more creased than usual, ancient.

'He wanted to know if Jennifer and the children were here. Seems to be concerned about them – they haven't been home for three days. Wanted to know if he could drive up here and see us.'

They had been walking now for more than an hour, with Seth stopping often to point out birds and animals along the way – they had even seen a family of raccoons. Matthew figured they had gone at least a mile. He hadn't been able to concentrate on anything else but the plan; he had never wanted anything in his life as much as he wanted to be back home with his mother and sister. Margo had done her job perfectly. If he hadn't known better, he would have fallen for the act himself – she had gotten so excited about Seth taking them. He couldn't have pretended that much in a million years. Maybe girls were better at those things.

But the plan was *his* idea, and it was up to him to see that it worked. Margo had done her part: now it was time for him to do his. Every so often he saw her glance in his direction, looking for him to give the signal, but he wanted to make sure that they were too far away for Seth to get to mama and take his anger out on her. As scared as he was, he wasn't scared about the beating he knew he'd get from Seth. By that time, Margo would be on her way to bring back help, and that would be worth any beating.

'Isn't that something, Matthew?' Matthew jumped, startled by Seth's question. 'I know there's a lot to see out here, but you've got to pay attention to what I'm saying if you want to learn about things.'

'I'm sorry, Seth, I was—'

Seth put his arm on Matthew's shoulder.

'Take a look, son – over there. See the bird sitting up there on that oak tree?'

Matthew's eyes followed Seth's pointing finger to a rusty coloured bird mottled with black and grey. He nodded his head.

'That's a ruffed grouse. Some people call it a partridge – you know, like a partridge in a pear tree.'

Matthew nodded again.

'It's one of our finest game birds. It has a funny habit of striking its wings together real fast against the sides of its body. Makes a loud drumming noise.'

'That's weird, Seth.'

'Come on, I'll show you up closer.' Seth walked ahead and the children followed. 'Then we'll have to be getting back.'

Matthew knew it was time. He cleared his throat; sure enough, Margo turned to look at him. Seth was a few yards ahead, not paying attention to either one of them. As Matthew nodded his head to Margo, he could see her swallow hard as if she were working up the courage to do what she had to do. It took a few minutes, but then it happened – Margo let out a scream so convincing that Matthew actually jumped.

Seth rushed to her.

'What is it?'

'There, Seth . . . Look!'

'What did you see?'

Margo folded her arms up over her chest, her hands grabbing her shoulders.

'Over there, Seth. A snake – a big one. It slithered over there, behind the bushes.'

'Now, don't you worry. It's not going to be bothering you all the way over there.'

'But I'm scared, Seth. Suppose it comes out onto our path? I'm scared.'

'All right, I'll go see if it's still there. By now, it's probably a hundred yards from here – those things travel like lightning.'

He walked over to the tree, not hesitating even for a moment, then looked around the bush.

Matthew took one deep breath, then turned and ran, his sneakers making crackling sounds in the brush. Seth's head shot up; it took him only a second to catch on.

'Get back here!'

Matthew was by now fifty feet away.

'Stay where you are,' Seth told Margo, then sprinted after the boy.

Matthew could hear Seth's feet beating on the ground behind him – he could even hear him panting. Like in a nightmare, the feet were gaining ground, getting closer and closer, but in his nightmare his legs never worked. This time they were working fine, going faster and faster. On he went, snapping twigs in his path and scooting around bushes. And then he didn't hear the footsteps any longer. Had Seth stopped chasing him, had he given up that easily? Had he gone after Margo instead? No, that didn't make any sense. Seth wouldn't know in which direction she had run.

It was then that Matthew heard the shots: first one, then another. He slid to a stop and turned back, running even faster than he had before. He had to get to Margo – please, God, let him get to Margo . . .

Margo had been running for a few minutes when she heard the gun go off, but the instant she heard it, she stopped. She had promised Matthew she wouldn't – but she did. She didn't care about getting help, not now. She turned and ran back, faster than she had ever run in her life. She had to get to Matthew . . .

Seth stood in the clearing, waiting, his eyes darting back and forth from one direction to another. Then he heard the footsteps: she was there, the girl had come back. She slid to a stop.

'Matthew! Where's my brother?'

Seth held out his arms. 'Come on over here.'

She looked at the gun in his hand; with tiny, stiff steps, she came to him.

'Don't be afraid, your brother is fine. He'll be back.' He put his arms around her, trying to stop the sobs coming out of her. And then, almost before he could hear the footsteps, he saw the boy come racing out of the woods.

Seth led Margo by the hand to a boulder.

'You sit right here, honey. Looks like I've got to teach your brother a lesson, show him right from wrong. It's a daddy's duty to do things like this.'

He stood up, put the gun back into his belt, and walked over to where Matthew had stopped, his arms hanging stiffly at his sides. At first Seth thought about spanking the boy, pulling down his pants and reddening his bottom the way his own had been reddened when he misbehaved at the home. But then he realized that spanking him wouldn't be appropriate – not with his sister sitting right there watching. A couple of good hard knocks might hurt more than a spanking, but the pain inside wouldn't last nearly as long.

Seth lifted his hand up and swung; he could hear the crack of his knuckles against Matthew's face. The boy stood there, not moving, not making a sound, tears rolling down his cheeks. Seth knew that he was trying to be brave, and that was all well and good, but it didn't change what was. He whacked him again and again. He had to make sure the boy understood. It hurt him to do it; but what choice did he have? A child had to be disciplined; otherwise, there'd be no controlling him.

He swung his arm and hit Matthew again. This time, the boy fell.

CHAPTER ELEVEN

THE TWO BOYS PEDALLED THEIR BIKES up Post Road, the distance between them lengthening. Billy had just gotten his ten-speed racer last week for his twelfth birthday, and the newness had not yet worn off. Every day after school he took it out, being careful to be home before dark. He didn't want to get in hot water with his folks and risk getting grounded.

'Wait up,' he heard Tony call.

He turned his head and looked back at his friend who was a good two hundred feet behind. Tony's dirt bike with the thick wheels and tilted handlebars couldn't come close to keeping up with his racer. Billy shrugged his shoulders and braked to a stop, then threw his leg over the middle bar, jumped off, and waited. Up ahead he spotted a boarded-up shack. He turned his head again and cupped his hand over his mouth.

'Hurry up, Tony.'

He leaned against a tree and waited, still holding onto the handlebars of his bike. A few feet up he noticed a dirt road; he tried to see to the top, but couldn't – trees were blocking his view. Tony finally braked to a stop in front of him.

'It's about time,' Billy said. 'Let's take a ride up there.' He pointed toward the road.

'I don't want to – I'm dragging. Let's head back home and stop for a soda on the way.'

But Billy had already hopped onto his bike and was following the path, swaying back and forth as he pedalled up the hill.

'Just for a minute . . . let's see where it leads.'

'All right, but I'm not riding. This hill's too steep.'

Billy laughed, shifted into high gear and picked up speed. As soon as he made it over the first incline, he spotted the car.

'Hey, Tony,' he shouted. 'Come see what I found!'

The first thing Jen did when she returned to the cabin was to check the cellar for Seth's rifle. Seth had promised Margo he wouldn't take it. Not that Jen knew the first thing about firing a gun of that size. She didn't. Even the thought of holding it frightened her. But as it turned out, she wouldn't have to worry about it or firing it: she searched through every drawer and cabinet in the cellar, but couldn't find the rifle.

She had been standing at the back parlour window for almost thirty minutes when she saw Seth carry Margo through the gate. She ran to the kitchen and out the door.

'What happened?'

'Just an accident,' Seth said. 'The boy fell and the girl got all upset about it. No one was hurt.'

Jen spotted Matthew coming through the gate. 'My God! What happened?' She ran to him, but he avoided her eyes and swept past her into the house.

'I'm okay,' he muttered.

Seth carried Margo up to her room, deposited her on the bed, and walked outside the door, leaving Jen alone with her. Jen knelt at the child's bedside to talk to her: Margo turned her back, facing the wall.

'I'm tired,' she said.

Finally Jen left the room and watched as Seth locked the door. Without a word to her, he headed downstairs to the cellar. Jen took Matthew to the kitchen and with a damp cloth gently wiped the blood from his mouth and lips, which were puffed up to twice their normal size. Then she wrapped ice cubes in a dish towel and placed the towel over his black eye, now half closed.

'He *hit* you,' Jen said.

Matthew didn't look at her.

'No, I fell,'

Jen studied the bruises. There was no way they could have been caused by a fall.

'Tell me what happened, Matthew. Please.'

'I already told you, I fell. Just like Seth said.'

'Honey, I know there's more to it than that. If Seth did this to you, I want to know. He has no right—' She stopped.

Matthew looked up to his mother: her lips were pressed into two hard lines. He hung his head down again, staring at the floor.

'Mama, I'm tired, I want to go to my room.'

Jen ran her fingers through his hair and sighed.

'All right, if that's what you want. I'll have Seth come up and unlock the door.'

Once Matthew was in bed and Seth back downstairs, Jen sat in the parlour, tears stinging her eyes. She had never felt so useless, helpless. Everything was crashing down around her, broken pieces she couldn't put together. Neither of the children would talk to her: she was losing them as surely as she had lost Jim. They had counted on her to rescue them. So far what had she accomplished? Nothing that mattered. Seth was winning.

Suddenly her arms began to tremble, then her legs. Soon her entire body went into spasm. She crossed her arms up over her chest and hung onto her shoulders trying to control the tremors that seized her. Oh God, please let it stop . . .

Upstairs, Matthew stared up at the ceiling while Margo slept soundly across the room. When he looked through his injured eye, everything was fuzzy, distorted. As he lay there he tried with all his might to concentrate on running – to recapture the intense feeling of power, the high – but he couldn't call up the right feelings. Instead, he felt tears and sadness and pain rushing through his body, leaving no spot untouched. At first, no matter how hard he tried to push the pain aside, it stayed. Then a gust of heat began to fill his insides as if it were being pumped in, squeezing the pain out and turning his body rigid, as if it were about to catapult forward.

When he shut his eyes, he saw his mother's face. For once, it didn't make him feel good. To his horror, he wanted to hit out at *her*. He couldn't understand it – it scared him. Was it because he couldn't tell her the truth? She knew it anyhow, he was sure. He didn't see any reason to put what happened into words. And even if he did tell her, that would only make things worse than they already were. For the first time he could ever remember, his mother couldn't make everything better – she couldn't make things right like she always pretended she could. He felt a lump form in his throat, making it hard to swallow. He wondered if a lump in your throat could get so big that it choked you.

Seth was still in the basement. He needed more time to think, sift through his thoughts and get them in some kind of order. Every time he thought about Matthew, he felt worse. It hadn't been easy to hit him like that; it hurt Seth just thinking about it. But the almost unbearable part of the whole ordeal was knowing that the children had pretended about the way they felt. And there he was – a fool, believing they cared, believing they looked up to him.

He headed to the wall of shelving in the rear of the cellar. Reaching under the second shelf, he pulled down the latch, then slid the shelving to the right, exposing the small chamber. He held his breath. The smell inside was getting worse: he'd have to do something about it soon. He removed Jennifer's two canvas bags from the chamber, carried them to his workbench, and sat down on a stool, opening them both. One by one, he held each article of clothing and rubbed the soft material up against his face, sniffing Jennifer's scent. He never thought he'd need to do this once Jennifer was right here with him, but here he was, still handling her clothing and still getting a real sense of comfort from doing it.

He thought back through the last few days, trying to figure out where he'd gone wrong with the children. What did other daddies do? In all his life, he'd never really witnessed a father-and-child relationship; most of what he knew he got from television and movies. He thought back to his own childhood. Sure, he'd wanted a mother more than anything in the whole world. But the next best thing would have been a daddy. All his life hadn't he been busy storing up all his caring, holding it inside and waiting for someone to come to get it?

He lifted a flowered bag from the bottom of the suitcase and turned it around in his hands. Heavy. He slowly unzipped it. An electric current seemed to shoot through him as soon as he saw what was inside: he grabbed the sides of his head, pressing his palms against his temples.

Then he folded his arms on the workbench, dropping his head down onto them. So it wasn't just the children – it was her, too. All these days while he'd been knocking himself out, trying to make her love him, he hadn't stood a chance. All along she'd been pretending, scheming.

He lifted his head and stared up towards the ceiling. He couldn't give up – not now, not after all his wonderful plans. He'd just have to think; use that brain everyone had always told him was so sharp, and come up with another plan. He'd never go back to the way things were before he claimed his family – that much he knew for sure. If he were forced to do that, he might as well hang it all up; there would be no sense going on.

It was exactly 4:45 when Thorne pulled up in front of the charcoal grey clapboard colonial. Ashley had one of the liveliest road strips in the area, thanks to Fremont Park Raceway, but the Sawyers lived in a quiet backwoods area.

Thorne slammed the car door, followed the cobblestone path to the front entrance and rattled the brass door-knocker. Clarence led him into the tidy, dimly lit parlour and gestured toward a chair.

'Have a seat.'

Thorne waited for Sawyer to get comfortable before he began, not quite sure himself what he wanted to say. The last thing he wanted was to worry these people unnecessarily.

'Mr Sawyer, I'm concerned about your daughter-in-law and grandchildren.'

The old man nodded.

'So you said. Are you some kind of police officer, Mr Thorne?'

'Yes, a lieutenant – Winfield, Massachusetts. But this isn't exactly official business. I'm on my own time.'

'Then you're a friend of Jennifer's?'

Thorne looked down at his clasped hands.

'Not exactly. I only met her a few days ago.'

The older man sat forward on the sofa, speaking slowly, deliberately.

'Well, then, lieutenant, just why *are* you here? What has you so concerned?'

'Tuesday, about four o'clock, I got a call from Jen telling me that the children were missing. They hadn't come home from school, she said.'

Clarence stared at him.

'I don't understand, lieutenant. I only spoke to her Tuesday evening myself, and she told me everything was fine.'

'She told me that, too. Later on she said she'd found the children at a friend's house. But neither she nor the children have been home since that evening. I checked the school, and the kids have been absent since Tuesday. Your daughter-in-law was very upset when I saw her after the incident.'

'Well, that's understandable.'

'Yes, of course.' Thorne stood up and slid his hands into his pockets. 'But what I don't understand is why she dropped out of sight.'

'Maybe she went visiting. She's a very independent girl, that one.'

Thorne smiled, remembering.

'I thought perhaps you could give me an idea of who she might have gone to visit. The truth is, her disappearance has been bothering the hell out of me, and while I'm sure I'm making more out of this than it warrants, I'd feel a lot better if I could find out for myself that she and the children are all right.'

'Well, now . . . I just don't know. It's been a while since she lived up this way, and as far as her present friends, I can't say I know a single one of them. The girl hasn't got any family, excepting us – that is, the wife and myself.'

'What about when she lived in this area? Has she kept in touch with anyone?'

Clarence stood and hiked up the waistline of his pants.

'Now you just hold on here a minute while I go get the wife and see what she can tell you.' He shuffled upstairs. It was a good five minutes later before they both came down. By that time, Thorne was pacing.

'I'm sorry to bother you, Mrs Sawyer.' He noticed that she was dressed in robe and slippers. 'I hope I didn't get you up from a nap.'

'And if you did? Little we can do about it now. Suppose you say what's on your mind.'

'I was just explaining to your husband that I'm concerned about your daughter-in-law and her family. The children haven't been in school—'

'Yes, I know all that, but what I don't know is what you want from us. If I've told the girl once I've told her a hundred times, two children and a business are entirely too much for one person to handle.'

'Mrs Sawyer, could you give me the names of any friends she has in this area? Anyone she's kept in touch with?'

Miriam placed her finger to her lips.

'I can only think of one girl, a hairdresser she worked with. I have no idea if she'd kept in touch with her or not. Jennifer is a very antisocial-type personality. Keeps pretty much to herself. I've told her—'

'May I just have her name and address, please? I'll start there.'

Miriam sent Clarence to get a pencil and paper, then wrote out a name and address. She handed him the paper.

'When you get hold of my daughter-in-law, you tell her to give us a ring right away. Worrying is not healthy, lieutenant. Not for me. Bad things are apt to come out of it.'

She turned and without another word made her way back upstairs. Clarence followed Thorne to the door, speaking up for the first time since his wife had come down.

'Lieutenant, if there are any other questions – anything I can do – you just come right on over. Jennifer and the children mean a lot to us, and I want to do whatever I can to help.'

Thorne walked to his car, opened the door and sat in the driver's seat. He looked back at the house. Sawyer seemed nice enough, he guessed. He'd had no intention of scaring either of them, but it didn't seem to be a problem either way – the old man was about as emotional as a jellyfish, and his wife seemed too busy worrying about herself to be upset by anything else.

He unfolded the paper she had given him: *Karen Carter, The Beauty Nook.* Too late to go today; he'd hold off till morning. Right now he was going to get on up to his cottage, put on a pair of old jeans and treat himself to a roast beef sandwich, onion rings, and a couple of beers. Maybe the weekend wouldn't turn out so bad.

It wasn't until Seth came up from the basement that Jen realized she'd been sitting alone on the sofa for hours. The spasms had subsided. It was now six o'clock.

'What really happened out in the woods, Seth?'

'What I told you. Matthew—'

'I know what you told me. I don't believe it.'

'Does it make a difference?'

She looked down at her hands knotted up in her lap and said nothing.

Seth sat down beside her.

'Whenever I need to think things out, I go to my workshop. That's where I've been all afternoon. Thinking about us, about our future.

She felt her muscles tighten as if her body were readying itself for a needle to plunge into her. She looked up and met his eyes.

'I want us to get married,' he said.

'But how—'

'Let me finish. Naturally, we can't have a formal ceremony like you might want. But we can get joined in the eyes of

God, right here in this house. Right in front of the children. Think of it, Jennifer, how often do kids get the chance to see their own parents exchange vows?'

'Who . . . who would perform the ceremony?'

'We'd do it ourselves.' He put his hand over hers. 'It'll be more private, more special.'

She yanked her hand free of his.

'What if I say no?'

'Now I've been more than patient with you, Jennifer. I've done like you asked me to – waited to tell the children who I am. I've not forced my attentions on you.' He flung his hand out 'Don't you see? I've passed the test, but you aren't following through. I've waited for you to make the first move, to come to me, and you haven't. You've been shying away from your feelings, not facing up to what was meant to be ever since the first night I made love to you.'

Jen just stared at him, wondering if he could possibly believe what he was saying. Had he convinced himself that what he'd done to her in the graveyard had anything to with *love*? She wanted to scream. It was all she could do to restrain herself from digging her nails into his face.

'I've got to be firm, Jennifer. The children need both a mother and father, and you need someone to care for you. Don't play games with me – you've known that all along, haven't you? You must have. Why else would you have come?'

She couldn't answer his question – at least, not fully. Suddenly, her reasons for coming here seemed silly, naive. Had she really believed she could single-handedly get the children out of here?

Seth stood up, towering over her.

'I want you to pick the date for the ceremony. I'll give you a little time to think about it. But if you don't decide soon, I'll be forced to pick it myself. Now I don't mean to be hard with you, Jennifer.'

She remembered his saying those words to her on the phone – days ago. Everything that had happened since meant nothing. They were back to square one. No: square minus one was more like it. Now there was no opportunity to get help.

Seth took Jennifer to her bedroom early that night; he wanted some time to be alone. It hadn't been easy for him to be that firm with her even though he knew it was the right thing to do, the only thing to do. He had thought long and hard that afternoon, and now he knew what had gone wrong – and how to fix it.

If he wanted to be honest with himself, which he did, it wasn't all their fault. From the beginning he had allowed his love to override his good sense. Instead of taking control – leading the way – he'd been lenient, allowing them too much freedom, too many choices. He hadn't made his position clear: there were no choices. Though Jennifer was special, he couldn't afford to forget that she *was* a woman. Didn't all women need a firm hand at one time or another? And the children: how was he ever to expect them to love and respect him like their daddy when they didn't even know he *was* their daddy. The truth, now that he saw it, made so much sense that he wondered why it had taken him so long to come to it.

He went to the hall closet and pulled out the blanket, sheet, and pillow, then walked over to the sofa and made his bed. It had been a hard day for him, and he hoped sleep would come easily. He hoped this wouldn't be one of those nights when he was too ill at ease to let his mind roam free. Right now he just needed to forget.

CHAPTER TWELVE

MIKE THORNE'S COTTAGE SAT on the rim of Crystal Pond. In warm weather he liked to take his breakfast out onto the flagstone patio overlooking the water. A lot of memories were stored up there. Summers when he was a kid – boating, fishing, water skiing ... with his dad towing him along. His dad's death when he was twenty-one had hit him hard – they had been close, about as close as a father and son could be. When his mom signed over the deed to the cottage, she counted on his having a family to bring here someday. She didn't say so but his mother had a way about her – she didn't have to say so.

Today he sat in the large country kitchen sipping his coffee and scanning the Boston *Globe* he'd picked up the night before. The clock read 7:30 a.m. He wanted to get to Karen Carter's beauty shop before nine, before the Saturday customers trooped in to fix themselves for their big night out. He wondered if he weren't being a damned fool worrying like this. If Jen Sawyer *had* gone off for a week's vacation, she would surely decide he was one-hundred-percent nuts when she got back and found out he'd been pestering her in-laws and friends, sure that something was wrong. Still, something told him he wasn't wrong. Years of conducting routine police investigations had made him aware of patterns, and here the pattern didn't fit. He got up, put his coffee mug in the sink, and went upstairs to get dressed.

By 8:15 Thorne was standing outside the beauty shop. He didn't have long to wait before Karen drove up, parked in the side lot, and walked to the door. Thorne introduced himself and gave her a brief explanation of why he was there. She hesitated a moment, then invited him in.

'I don't have much time,' she said. 'My first customer is due in less than fifteen minutes.' He followed her into the back room and watched her take off her coat and hang it on a hook. She was small and dark-skinned, about Jen's age.

'I really don't know what I can do for you, lieutenant. Jen and I haven't seen each other much over the years. She usually drops by the shop once during the summer, on the way to her in-laws' place.'

'What do you know about her in-laws?'

'I really shouldn't say. I only met them once or twice and that was years ago. But I thought they were pretty strange. I don't think Jen ever took to them either – nothing she said, just an attitude. I think the only reason she kept on seeing them at all was because she felt it her duty, them being the kids' grandparents.'

'Do you know any of her friends? Anyone she might have gone to visit?'

Karen thought for a moment. 'I can't say that I do. I don't think Jen has much in the way of a social life – she's a hustler, always breaking her butt to make a few bucks and stay ahead of the game. I don't suppose it's easy. Christ, I have only one kid, and between myself and my husband we barely manage.'

'Did she have any male friends?'

'You mean boyfriends? If she did, she didn't mention them to me.' She turned around and started to stack a bunch of rollers and clips onto a tray.

'What about when she lived up here?'

'Are you kidding? She was wild about her husband. As far as she was concerned, other men didn't exist. When he was killed in that accident, it really threw her. It was funny, though . . . she seemed to come out of it after a while – you know, normal grieving and all – but then about a month later it was like it happened all over again. Talk about *depressed* – hell, I couldn't even get her to step outdoors. She cancelled all her customers, just sat by herself in that apartment, day after day.

I never saw anyone so devastated. Thank God she finally pulled out of it, when she found out she was pregnant.'

'She didn't know until after her husband's death?'

'Right. It was like the last thing he gave her – and for her it was the right thing. For some women, just the thought of bringing up a kid alone would have scared the daylights out of them. But no question, it was the pregnancy that snapped her back. And just nine months after Jim's death, the twins were born. It was June 5 – I remember because it was the day before my son's second birthday.'

Thorne sat and listened as she rattled on.

'And they were the two cutest little things you ever saw. You know, bald and scrawny like plucked chickens – needed to be in an incubator, and all – but I'll tell you one thing, to her those kids were everything. I don't think I've ever known anyone who took to motherhood the way she did.'

'Why did she leave Ashley?'

Karen sat down on a stool and began to fold towels.

'She said she wanted to make a new start, but I also think she resented Jim's mother breathing down her neck. She's a very domineering woman, and Jen's the type who needs her own space – real independent. Christ, I'd be scared out of my wits going off alone like that with two children depending on me. But leave it to Jen – from what I can see, she's made out okay. A house of her own, a little shop, and a couple of real bright kids who worship the ground she walks on.'

'But you don't think she has any close friends? Is involved with anyone?'

Karen shrugged. 'Like I said, we don't keep in that close touch. But from what I can see, her life revolves strictly around those kids.'

A bell sounded from the front of the shop and Karen jumped up.

'There's my customer, I've got to get going. I don't know if I've been any help to you, but I sure as hell hope you find Jen. Tell her to call me when you do.'

*   *   *

Thorne drove away, replaying the conversation in his head. On the face of it, the information seemed useless. But one thing she'd said kept sticking in his mind. He stopped off at the nearest phone booth, checked the directory, and dialled the number.

'The Beauty Nook.'

'Karen, it's me again, Mike Thorne. I have just one more question.'

'Okay, but make it fast. I've got a lady sitting here with a wet head.'

'Do you remember how much the twins weighed at birth?'

She laughed. 'You guys are something else. You tell me how that information is going to help you locate Jen, and I'll give you a shampoo and manicure on the house.'

'Do you remember?'

'No, not really. That's something you only remember about your own kids. But they were smaller than normal, I do know that. Like I told you, they had to be kept in an incubator for a while. From what I gather, most twins are pretty small at birth.'

Thorne thanked her, put the receiver down and stood for a moment at the booth. It seemed to him that she was right – about twins usually being small. But he was also pretty sure he remembered hearing that twins usually came early, twenty to thirty days early. Karen had told him Jen's twins were born just nine months after her husband's death. Of course, she might not have meant nine months literally, just a figure of speech. For a moment he considered calling her back to clarify the point, but then he thought better of it. He had already bugged her enough.

He decided he'd stop by the local police station to check the records, find out when Jim's accident took place. It was probably a waste of time. Even if he was right, what possible relevance could it have? He pulled out more change from his pocket, deposited it in the slot, called Massachusetts information, then dialled Schroeder's home phone.

'Henry, this is Mike.' He listened as Schroeder yawned in his ear.

'It's nine o'clock on a Saturday, Mike. If this is a friendly call, your timing stinks.'

'Sorry I woke you.'

'I thought you left town for the weekend.'

'I did, but I need a favour.'

'You in trouble, Mike?'

'Nothing like that. It's business.'

'Jesus, Mike, this is my day off.'

'It'll take you an hour, the most.'

'What is it?'

'Go to the station and put a bulletin on the teletype – Code C, interstate. See if you can pick up a line on Jen Sawyer's car. There's always the possibility of an accident.'

'The chief will be pissed.'

'Come on, Schroeder, he'll never know.'

Schroeder sighed. 'And where will you be?'

'Right now I'm going to grab a bite. I'll call you at the station . . . say in about an hour?'

Schroeder didn't answer.

'Listen, Henry, if you were here, I'd buy you breakfast too.'

'You're a real sweetheart, Thorne.'

'You'll do it?'

'Call me at the station – one hour. One minute later, I'll be gone.'

At ten o'clock, Schroeder answered Thorne's call on the first ring.

'Mike, I've got something for you. We found the car. No plate, but the I.D. number matches.'

Thorne's hand tightened over the receiver.

'Where?'

'You're almost sitting on it.'

'Can you make that a little clearer for me?'

'Jen Sawyer's car has been picked up by the Ashley, New Hampshire police. Abandoned.'

Jen had slept so little that she woke in the morning feeling almost as tired as the night before. She forced herself out of bed – washed, dressed, and was ready when Seth arrived at the door. Last night she had served the children a late supper of soup and sandwiches on trays in their room, but neither was hungry. They were visibly relieved when she took the uneaten food out and allowed them to go back to sleep.

At breakfast she felt uncomfortable with them, without being sure whether the problem was caused by them, or herself, or both. Were their eyes guarded when she looked at them, or was it just her imagination? She kept watching their expressions, trying to read what was going on in their minds, but she couldn't. Maybe the truth was that she didn't want to know. And every time she looked at Matthew's bruised face, she winced.

'Does it hurt?' she asked.

He shook his head and took a bite of his toast. Jen wondered if he were telling the truth. She felt a sudden urgency to get the children alone with her, knowing from past experience that it would help if they could get their feelings out in the open. But *would* they? She didn't think so. This was hardly a simple case of misunderstanding or hurt feelings. What could she possibly say to renew their hope and confidence? Right now she needed someone to renew her own.

Her thoughts returned, as they had over and over since last night, to Seth's ultimatum. Of course the marriage would only be a charade, but what would it do to the children? What could she tell them as Seth and she walked hand in hand to his bedroom? *Don't let this fool you, it doesn't mean a thing.* Then it came to her: Seth was not so crazy after all – or maybe, that's what crazy was. The real charade was the preacher who stood up and spoke the familiar words, put society's seal of approval on a marriage between two people. Seth's proposed ceremony would not be a charade. For all intents and purposes, she would be Seth's wife. At least that's how Seth and the children would view it. Worst of all, given enough time, someday she might view it that way, too. She pictured herself growing old with Seth while the children grew sick and bitter . . .

But that wouldn't happen. She wouldn't let it happen. A part of her knew that she'd do *anything* to stop Seth.

All the way to the Ashley police department, Thorne ran through his conversations with Jen. For the first time since last Tuesday, he admitted to himself that his instincts had been right from the very beginning. She had lied to him; those kids had never come home. But would she really have been foolish enough to try to get them back herself? He pulled in the station parking lot and hurried inside.

Within ten minutes, he was seated across from Chief Rizzano, trying to make him understand what he was doing there. Once he'd told his story, Rizzano folded his hands over his potbelly and leaned back in his swivel chair.

'Let me get this straight now. Is this an official investigation?'

Thorne shook his head. 'I'm on my own time.'

'You guys must love your work.'

Thorne laid his hands down on the chief's desk. 'Where did you find the car?'

'Post Road – a few miles from here. A young boy spotted it.'

'What have you done about it?'

'Look, hotshot detective, you want to work overtime, that's up to you. But don't come around here poking your nose in, checking up on our procedures. We checked the area where we found the car and we checked the car itself. There's no sign of foul play.' He shrugged his shoulders. 'I don't know the statistics on juvenile crime in Massachusetts, but from what I hear, you probably have more of it than we do. Some kids out on the town, looking for something to do, decide to go joyriding. They pick up a car, jump it, ride it around for a while, then ditch it. And if you're right and it's this lady's car, I'd say you ought to be home sniffing around your own juveniles.'

Thorne paused for a moment, mustering the control to sound civil. There was no point in getting this guy riled up, he'd just get himself thrown out on his ass.

'Listen. Do you mind if I search the car myself?'

'Help yourself. If this is how Massachusetts police like to spend their weekends, far be it from me to spoil your fun.'

Thorne stood up.

'Can I have the name and address of the boy who reported it and the exact location where you picked it up?'

The chief sighed, looked down at the report on his desk, then tore a piece of paper off a pad and copied the information. He handed it to Thorne.

'Before you go, give my guy the name and address of the owner of the car.' He gestured toward the outer office.

Thorne nodded, walked to the door, then turned.

'One more thing, chief.'

Rizzano ran his finger aside of his long beaked nose. 'You're starting to get to me. Tell me, Thorne, do you have the same effect on your own chief?' He didn't wait for an answer. 'Okay, what now?'

'I'd like authorization to go into your files.'

'Why?'

'I'm interested in an accident that took place up this area in 1974. The guy—'

Rizzano stood up and raised his arm to stop him.

'Do me a favour, don't fill me in on the details. I only work half a day today – any more mysteries I'll watch on television. Go ahead, have yourself a good time.' The chief shouted into the other room. 'Myers, give our brother from Massachusetts access to whatever records he wants. And then get *rid* of him.'

Within fifteen minutes, Thorne was holding the file on Jim Sawyer's accident. He had learned two things, neither of which gave him any clue as to where Jen and the children were. Number one: Considering the date of Jim Sawyer's death, September 3, 1974 – a little more than nine months before the twins' birth – it was unlikely that he was the father of the children. Number two: Sawyer's car had rammed through a string of guardrails and catapulted over a cliff. The accident had been reported by a passerby named Seth Anthony.

CHAPTER THIRTEEN

SENSING JEN'S DESIRE to be alone with the children, Seth deliberately kept them apart, not for one moment allowing them the opportunity to talk in private.

Though the children responded when Jen spoke to them, the responses were cool and abrupt, as if they were rationing each word. She felt more tired than she could ever remember as she watched Seth doing the things she normally would have done: tending to the children, entertaining them. All day she watched – when they were outdoors, from the chair at the window; when they were indoors, from the sofa in the parlour. Her children were turning into people she no longer knew – Matthew sullen, Margo docile. Margo followed Seth and Matthew followed them both, always keeping his eye on his sister. Jen felt like a stranger, just looking on.

It was as though she were watching them being pulled away and she could do nothing about it. All the power rested with Seth – and it was power the children were responding to. She realized, of course, that the children would never respond to Seth with anything approximating affection, that their hearts were permanently barred to him. But the thought gave her scant comfort. If Seth did not yet control their hearts, he had come very close to controlling their minds. The children had come to learn that it was far easier to go along with Seth than to oppose him.

After dinner, Seth insisted that Margo sit with him. With only a trace of reluctance, she climbed onto his lap. He leafed through a book of short stories, chose one to his liking, and began to read. As Jen watched, she could almost see a frame around them as if they were sitting in a box: Seth the puppeteer and Margo the dummy perched on his knee, with Seth tugging the strings. Matthew sat on the floor at their feet, his eyes narrowed, his body stiff, ready for attack.

Jen watched – horrified, fascinated – as Seth's fingers stroked Margo's forehead and Margo laid her head against his shoulder. Jen noticed the vacant look in Margo's eyes, as if she weren't even there, as if she had entered some inner world. He pushed her long golden hair aside and with his fingers drew invisible circles on the back of her neck.

Jen jumped from the sofa.

'Margo, Matthew, I want you to go to your room.'

Margo sat like a rag doll, not moving. Seth continued to read, not looking up from the page.

'Margo!' Jen shouted. 'Did you hear me?'

Margo lifted her head from Seth's shoulder. Jen lunged forward, grabbed her arm and pulled her off his lap. 'Go to your room!'

Both children ran upstairs. Seth stood up and lay the open book face down on the table.

'What's the matter, Jennifer?'

'I won't have you doing this to the children!'

'Doing what? Being a father to them?'

'You're trying to take them from me.'

'That's not true, Jennifer. No one can separate a mother from her children – excepting, of course, the mother herself.'

Jen lowered her voice; she could feel it shake as the words came out.

'You beat him. You beat up Matthew, *didn't you?*'

'I did what I had to. I have a responsibility to the children.'

'To beat them?'

'To teach them. And that's what I'm doing. Look at them. You can see with your own eyes that it's working – they treat me with respect, they follow me around like they want to be with me, they care about me.'

'They're scared of you.'

'Sometimes that goes hand in hand with respect, Jennifer. There's nothing wrong with children being fearful of punishment – why else would they choose right over wrong?'

Jen stared at him.

'What I think is, you're feeling a little jealous – seeing what's happening right before your eyes. The kids need a father, they know it and they're ready to accept me, but you're not. Way down deep you're still blaming me for taking so long to come to you. The kids forgive me – why can't you? Maybe we ought to be asking them what they think of us getting married, being a real family.'

With one arm he pulled her closer to him. He reached his hand to the neckline of her blouse and pulled it open; a button popped off and flew across the room. His eyes stared into hers as he slid his hand beneath her bra and clutched her breast in his hand.

'Remember, Jennifer – remember how it was?'

She lifted her arm and swung it, her hand snapping across his cheek.

'Leave me alone,' she shouted. 'Don't you touch me.'

She watched as his expression changed from surprise to anger to . . . what was it? She couldn't be sure. He moved toward her slowly, reaching out. She backed away until she felt the wall behind her, then sank to the floor, her head bent, tears sliding down her face.

'Please, Seth . . . please don't.'

He stood over her for a moment, watching, then bent to his knees beside her.

'I want you to be my wife, Jennifer. I've wanted that for so long, I can't remember a time when you weren't in my dreams. Even when you were married to Jim—'

She lifted her head and stared at him.

'You knew Jim?'

He nodded.

'How?'

'That's not important. What is important is that you're mine now, not his. He didn't deserve you. I did. All my life people have been taking and taking and taking. For once, I took back.' Seth lifted his hand again and this time his touch was gentle as he ran the back of his knuckles along her face. Jen squeezed her eyes shut and bit down on her lip so hard she tasted blood. Seth's hand felt like a tentacle – a slithery tentacle beckoning her forward.

'When, Jennifer? When will you set the date?'

'Tomorrow,' she whispered. 'Give me till tomorrow.'

That night after Seth had locked her in the bedroom, Jen ran over every alternative in her mind. For the hundredth time she thought of the sharp knives in the kitchen drawers. But for the hundredth time, she rejected the idea. She could never overpower Seth, not unless he was sleeping. And when he *was* sleeping, her door was locked.

Seth had given her an ultimatum. If it was the last thing she ever did in her whole life, she had to think of a way to get them out of there. She had to come up with a plan . . .

Matthew, lying in his bed, held up his fingers and counted – this was their fifth day here. Sunday. He was still sleepy, his muscles felt loose and relaxed even if his mind wasn't. He wished he could just stay in bed. As soon as everyone got up and bad things started to happen, the ache would come back and the anger would start up again, making his belly feel like someone was inside, tying knots.

He thought about last night. From their doorway right over the open staircase, he and Margo had watched mama standing up to Seth. They couldn't hear everything, but they could see everything, and they saw what he started to do to her. It was the first time in his life that Matthew had ever wanted to kill a person. It kind of surprised him that he felt no guilt.

Matthew had always felt like mama's protector. He knew it was silly, but that was how he felt. Even though she was tough and could do almost anything herself, there were some things she always asked him to do – little things like putting in window screens, lifting heavy boxes, opening jars. He'd never admitted it to anyone before, not even to himself, but doing those silly jobs made him feel important. He wondered now if she hadn't just asked him to do those things because she knew it made him feel good. Or maybe because she really wanted a grown-up man around to take care of her. Right now, she needed someone strong to protect her, and all he could feel was furious because he couldn't.

He heard Margo roll over in her bed and turned his head.

'Margo . . . you up?'

'Uh-huh.'

'Today is Sunday.'

'Who cares?'

Matthew got out of his bed, padded over to hers, and sat down.

'It wasn't your fault,' he said. It was the first mention of their attempted escape.

Margo sighed. 'If it wasn't for me stopping, breaking my promise, we wouldn't still be here.'

'I came back too, Margo.'

'But I was the one who was supposed to keep running.'

Matthew was silent. He walked over to the window and looked out, clenching his fists at the same time.

'You know, Margo, sometimes I hate him so much that I think I could do anything – anything – to make him stop. When he made mama cry like that, I, well, I—'

Margo cut him off. 'Oh, Matthew, I'm so tired of fighting. I've even taught myself how to stop feeling. I just imagine I'm in another place – maybe at the beach or at the lake – and then I stay in that place until Seth goes away. I don't even feel like the same person any more.'

Matthew said nothing. Instead, he continued to stare out of the window, clenching his fists even tighter than before.

When Seth came for Jen, she was dressed. She asked him into the room.

'Thursday,' she said. 'Thursday we'll be married.'

Seth smiled. 'You won't be sorry, Jennifer.'

'There is one thing . . .'

'Whatever you want.'

'We'll wait to tell the children who you are.' Seth started to protest but she rushed on. 'Just until Friday, the day after we consummate our marriage. Then we'll tell them – together.'

'If that's what you want, that's how it'll be.' Seth put his hand on her head and gently rubbed a lock of hair between his fingers. 'Now there's one thing *I* want.' Jen waited.

'I want to tell the children today – about the marriage. I want them to have something to look forward to.'

'It would be better if—'

'I insist, Jennifer.'

Seth had them dress in their best outfits to attend Sunday services in the parlour; the children and Jen sat in the straight-back wooden chairs Seth had lined up facing a high table serving as his podium. He opened the Bible to a passage and read. As his voice droned on, Matthew fidgeted with his stiff-collared shirt. Margo sat still, her eyes empty. Although Jen tried to get the children's attention, neither of them looked her way. Finally done, Seth cleared his throat and looked straight at the children.

'Your mother and I will exchange marriage vows on Thursday.'

Now Matthew's eyes swung toward his mother's. She met his stare silently, begging him to understand, to trust her, but she saw no emotion except anger. Margo gave no indication that she'd even heard the announcement.

'At that time,' Seth said, 'you will be my children and I will expect all of the love, respect and loyalty that such a position warrants.' He paused for effect. 'And I swear on this Bible,' he said, placing his right hand on the book, 'that I will care for and protect you with my life.'

Jen felt as though the air were being sucked out of the room. As soon as Seth finished the service with silent prayer, she took a deep breath and stood up, the creak of the chair a welcome relief to her ears.

'I'll make breakfast,' she announced.

She rushed into the kitchen and busied herself while Seth led the children upstairs to change their clothing.

'You children don't know how lucky you are,' she heard him say. 'I never had a daddy to take me places or do things with, and until now you haven't had one either. But just you wait and see – you're going to love it.'

Over my dead body, she thought, as she cracked the eggs against the countertop and dropped them into the bowl. She moved quickly, feeling as though she had been given a second wind. Finally, she had a plan – a way of defeating Seth.

Jen poured the scrambled eggs onto the platter and scraped the frying pan, then looked into the parlour. They hadn't come down yet. She tiptoed upstairs and, from the top step, peeked in. Matthew, already in jeans, stood staring out of the window. Margo was sitting on Seth's lap while he gently manipulated her limp arms into the sleeves of her knitted pullover. If Jen didn't know better, she'd have sworn that Margo was sleeping. She crept back downstairs.

'Breakfast is on the table,' she shouted. 'Come and get it.'

The day before, Thorne had inspected Jen's car, then the area where it was abandoned. He'd followed the narrow path leading to the shack, finding only a single shrivelled rose lying at the edge of the road.

Now he parked at the address Rizzano had given him, got out of the car, and headed towards a young boy kneeling on the driveway, screwing a wicker basket onto his rear bike fender.

'Billy Hutton?' he asked.

The boy looked up.

'Yeah, that's me.'

'Nice bike you have there.'

The boy grinned, showing wire braces on his teeth.

'It's a ten-speed.' He pointed to the speedometer on the handlebars. 'It hit thirty-five miles per hour yesterday.'

'Not bad. Listen, I understand you're the guy who reported the red Toyota abandoned on Post Road.'

The boy stood up, wiping his hands on the sides of his jeans as he did.

'Yeah. Me and my friend found it.'

'That's quite a distance for kids your age to be travelling. Must be a good ten miles from here.'

Billy cleared his throat.

'You a cop?' he asked.

Thorne pulled out his wallet, opened it and showed him his I.D.

'I'm investigating a case and I want to ask you a few questions.'

'Does the car have something to do with the case?'

'It looks that way.'

'Listen lieutenant . . . you won't have to tell my folks I was the one who found the car, will you?'

'I see no reason to – providing, that is, that you're willing to cooperate with me.'

'Sure. What do you want to know?'

'Did you or your friend search the car?'

'Well, we did look around some. We weren't sure at first if someone had just parked it there or what. But then when we saw the missing licence plates, we figured someone just went off and left it.'

'Did you find anything?'

'No, nothing.'

Thorne studied the boy's face.

'You know,' he said, 'if you did find something and took it, but gave it to me now, there'd be no problem. On the other hand, withholding evidence from a law officer is a serious offence. If I thought for a minute you were holding out on me, I *would* have to discuss it with your folks.'

Billy looked toward the house, then back again at Thorne.

'If I found something – now, I'm not saying I did or anything – but *if* I did, could I get in trouble? You know, like arrested for stealing?'

Thorne lifted his hand and placed it on the boy's shoulder.

'I'll tell you what, son. You give me what you found and I'll walk away from here like nothing happened. I won't even put it in my report. But if I find out later that you weren't dealing square with me, I promise you there'll be hell to pay. It's your choice. I don't suppose your folks would be too pleased to learn you were riding around on the other side of town. I'd say if you were my kid, I might even go so far as to ground you for a couple of weeks.' He gestured towards the bike. 'A kid with a beauty like that ought to behave more responsibly.'

The boy's eyes followed Thorne's to his bike. Slowly, he slid his hand into his pocket and pulled out a gold pocket watch attached to a heavy chain. He handed it to him.

'I swear, lieutenant. That's all there was.'

Thorne turned to go, then stopped, looking back at the boy.

'Thanks. And from here on you stay closer to home, okay?'

Thorne had travelled less than a block when he pulled over to the shoulder of the road, took the watch from his pocket, and examined it. He turned it over; then, holding it up to the light and tilting it back, he read the tiny letters and numbers engraved on the back: *N.E. 50. 1950?* He ran his thumb over the smooth, rich surface. Solid gold, he'd be willing to bet.

His brow creased. How on earth could this watch help him find Jen? He ran the initials over and over in his mind, but couldn't make any connection. He rubbed his eyes. He was plugging away, one step at a time, but where was it getting him? Right now, only tired. Aside from suspecting that another man was the father of her children – which, on reflection, didn't mean a hell of a lot – he didn't know one important thing about her.

He thought back to his conversation with Karen. According to her, there was no other man in Jen's life at that time – yet how could that be? She couldn't exactly get pregnant all by herself. He decided to back up. Maybe he'd gone too fast, missed something significant. First he had to be certain that his suspicions were correct; then he'd try to fit pieces together.

Thorne stopped at the first phone booth and dialled the Ashley police. The officer told him Rizzano was off duty. He quickly leafed through the directory, deposited some change, and dialled the chief's home phone. On the fifth ring, it was answered by a voice he immediately recognized as Rizzano's.

'Chief, this is Mike Thorne.'

'Shit, Thorne. What do you want now? Check the calendar, today is Sunday – you know, day of rest. Unlike you, I don't play policeman seven days a week.'

'This is important.'

'Tell me, Thorne – just what kind of interest do you have in this lady? What'd she do, stand you up or something?'

'Don't make fun of me, chief. I'm sensitive.'

For the first time, Thorne heard Rizzano laugh. It was a good sound – straight from the gut, the kind you wanted to join in with even when you didn't know the joke.

'Okay, Thorne, I'm game. What is it you want?'

'I want you to call the local hospital for me. Have someone look into Jennifer Sawyer's obstetrics file from June, 1975 and get the name listed as father of the children. Second, find out the duration of the pregancy.'

'Last I heard, they go nine months.'

'I want to know if she delivered early.'

'How does this help you find the girl?'

'I don't know.'

Rizzano sighed. 'Call me back in fifteen minutes.'

'I really appreciate—'

'Save the sentiments. And Thorne, if there's anything else you want to know, say it now because I don't want to hear from you again today.'

'For now, that's it.' Thorne put down the receiver and waited the fifteen minutes, then called back.

The chief answered this time on the first ring.

'Okay,' he said, 'the father was listed as James B. Sawyer and the children were born on June 5, 1975, 26 days premature. According to her records, their estimated due date was July 1 – twins weren't expected. From what they tell me, birth should occur approximately thirty-eight weeks from conception.'

'Thanks.'

'Hey, Thorne, you going home today?'

'Now don't tell me you're going to miss me? Oh, one other thing . . .'

'What?'

'There was a pocket watch found in the car. I picked it up from the boy.'

'I see. Okay, turn it in up your way. The Winfield police have already been notified. Sometime next week they're going to have the car towed back.'

Thorne hung up the phone. He decided that there was nothing more he could do today in New Hampshire. He might as well cut his trip short and head back home this afternoon. Tomorrow he'd have the Sawyers swear out a formal missing person's complaint so he could get assigned to the case. He'd get a search warrant – check the premises, the neighbours . . .

He stopped back at the cottage, hung around for a few hours, then packed his overnight bag. On the way home he kept playing Karen's conversation back in his mind. He did some quick arithmetic. If Jen were due on July 1, that meant she must have conceived in early October. About a month after her husband's death. What exactly had Karen said? Jen came out of it – but a month later, like it happened all over again, she went into a serious depression. That would have been just about the time she conceived. Could she have discovered she was pregnant and been upset over that? No, Karen was quite sure it was the knowledge of the pregnancy that 'pulled her out of it.' Out of what? Was she still feeling the pain of her husband's death? If so, no way she would have been sleeping with another guy . . .

Then as if a magnet had suctioned the pieces together, it dawned on him. The car swerved to the left. Thorne grabbed the wheel and righted it. He had been circling around the truth when all the time it had been staring him in the face. What the hell was the matter with him? There was only one possible answer that made any kind of sense.

Jen Sawyer had been raped.

CHAPTER FOURTEEN

BY EARLY AFTERNOON the sun slid behind the clouds and a dank, gloomy mist settled in. The weather matched the mood of the children, who moped around the cabin. After failing to interest them in games, Jen passed the time leafing through Seth's book of short stories. By three o'clock the cabin was cold.

'How about building a fire, Seth?' Jen suggested.

Seth looked at Matthew. 'Come on, son. You come with me. I'll cut some firewood, and you can help me bring it in.'

As soon as the door shut, Jen went to Margo, knelt in front of her and lifted her chin.

'Listen to me.'

Margo looked directly at her mother, but her eyes didn't focus.

Jen grabbed her by the shoulders and shook her.

'I said *listen*, Margo. It's important.

Margo's eyelids blinked as if she had just woken up.

'What is it, mama?' she said finally.

'I only have a few minutes to talk so I want you to listen carefully and pass on everything I tell you to your brother. Do you understand?'

Margo nodded.

'Seth has been keeping us apart on purpose. By doing that he's made us doubt ourselves and each other. We've lost control over our own lives, and it's overwhelmed us so much, we're all starting to give in to him, losing maybe the most important things we have going for us – our fighting spirit and our faith in one another. And without them, Margo, we'll never get out of here. Besides, what were they worth to begin with if the first time they're put to a test we all fall to pieces? Right now, you've turned yourself off like a zombie, and Matthew is so angry he can't see straight.'

'But what can we *do*, mama? It's so hopeless.'

'Not if you and Matthew dig down and get your acts together. I've never known you to lose your energy, your drive, and I've never known Matthew to lose his level head. You're both strong inside – each in your own special way. Now, if we're going to escape from this nightmare, I can't do it by myself. I need my fighters back.'

Tears slid out of Margo's eyes, and Jen reached up her hands and with her thumbs gently brushed them away.

'I have a plan, and I want you and your brother to be ready to carry it out. On the night of what Seth refers to as our wedding day, I'm going to ask you and Matthew to run the longest race you've ever run.'

'Where, mama?'

'The other day when you and your brother were out with Seth, I managed to get outdoors and do a little investigating on my own. The centre of town is that way.' She pointed south with her finger. 'When I tell you it's time, you and Matthew put on warm clothes, leave your bedroom, sneak downstairs and leave – heading in that direction.'

'Won't our door be locked?'

'That's my job . . . and I'll make sure it isn't.'

'But you'll be with us.'

'No, Margo, I'll be with Seth.'

'No, mama. We don't want to go without you. Please, you come with us.'

'I'm counting on both of you to bring back help. Besides, I'm not as fast as you two. I'd only slow you down.'

Margo's blue eyes seemed to darken. Her voice caught in her throat and squeaked when it came out.

'But, mama . . . he'll hurt you.'

'No, he won't, I can take care of myself. I'll be okay till you're back – so long as I'm sure you and Matthew are doing exactly what I tell you. Stick close together and run as fast as you can. It will be dark. I want you to stay on the left-hand side, the side where the woods are fairly level. Keep a little distance in from the road. Let the road be your guide – keep close enough so you don't lose your way, but not so close that you can be spotted by a car going by. It's a long way, Margo. I'd say maybe eight to ten miles. But it's the only road out of here.'

'Ten miles isn't so far.'

'If you come to a house before you reach town, stop at it and ask for help. Tell the people to call the police. If not, keep running until you reach town. *Don't* flag down a car, do you understand?'

'Why, mama? Will it be Seth out looking for us?'

Jen sighed, then reached out her hand, tucking Margo's hair behind her ears.

'Honey, I'm going to do everything I can to keep him here. But if he should find out you and Matthew are missing, and he does go out looking for you, I want to make sure there's no chance he'll find you.'

Margo nodded her head.

'And Margo, once you get to the police, tell them to contact a Lieutenant Mike Thorne from the Winfield police department. Can you remember all that?'

'Yes. But I'm scared, mama.'

Jen put her arms around her daughter.

'We can pull this off, honey. I know we can. What we *can't* do is let Seth win.'

Margo dug her fingers into Jen's shoulders.

'It's been so awful. And *I've* been so awful.'

Jen pulled herself away and blinked back a tear. 'We don't always react to things the way we'd like to. It's not just you – we all disappoint ourselves at times. But this time it's going to be different.'

Jen stood up and headed back to the chair just as she heard the back door slam shut. Seth and Matthew walked into the room, their arms piled high with logs for the fire. They set the freshly cut wood in front of the fireplace.

'You know,' Jen said, 'I already feel my insides beginning to warm.'

*   *   *

Back in Winfield before nightfall, Mike Thorne drove to Arden Road and parked in front of Number Two. He picked up the current mail, walked around to the side of the house, opened the foyer door and stacked it with the rest.

Back in his car, he rubbed his eyes and leaned his head forward against the steering wheel. He was tired. He couldn't remember the last time he'd been shocked by a crime, but knowing that Jen had been raped not only shocked him: it made him so angry he wanted to punch out at something, anything. Unless she had reported the attack at the time and he found that report, he couldn't substantiate his suspicions. Still, he knew.

He wondered how many women who found themselves pregnant through rape would go through with the pregnancy and bring up the kid. He didn't suppose there could be any statistics on something like that. He assumed most women would lie through their teeth about it. And what could they possibly tell their kid – how do you handle that?

He tried to push the subject aside; it wasn't getting him anywhere. He still didn't have a single clue to lead him to Jen. For that matter, he didn't have a clue as to what really happened or why. Had someone just up and taken the children? Certainly not a question of ransom. He looked at the neat modest house. A degenerate? Then where was she? She could have taken the kids off to New Hampshire and *then* met up with trouble.

It would just have to wait till morning. Right now, his mind wasn't functioning. He frowned. If Jen knew, would she mind being put on ice till morning. Shit. Why did he feel so damned involved?

Although Margo said little before bedtime, she stayed alert and took in every bit of conversation that passed her way, storing it for future use.

At nine o'clock Seth took the children to their rooms to oversee their preparation for bed. Margo pulled her arms out of her dress, put her nightgown over her head, letting it hang to her knees, then slid her dress to the floor. After washing and prayers, the children got right into bed. Before Seth left the room he crouched down at Margo's bedside. She stiffened, afraid he might be intending to kiss her. But if he had, he held back. He touched her tangled hair.

'Good night, honey.'

'Good night, Seth.'

He went over the Matthew's bed.

'We'll go hunting again, son. Maybe next time we'll bring us back a prize.'

As soon as Seth shut the door and headed down the steps, Matthew popped out of bed and tiptoed over to Margo.

'What happened?'

'What makes you think something happened?'

'Come on. You've been looking weird all night.'

She sat up and pushed her face close to his.

'We're going to get out of here, Matthew. We're going to escape.'

'Says who?'

'Mama.'

'What did she say?'

Margo told him everything Jen had said. He listened carefully, not saying a word till she finished.

'I don't like it, and I won't do it.'

'Why not? We could make it.'

'But what about mama? We can't just leave her here with him. Seth could do anything. If he finds us missing, he's going to go crazy, and she'll be the only one here for him to go after. I won't go without her.'

'Don't you think I'm worried about that, too?' Margo asked. 'It may not be the best plan in the world, but we don't have a better one. What should we do – stay here? Is that what you want? Mama says she'll be okay till we get back with help. Seth may not even realize we're gone. All I know is we can't just sit around here and do nothing. Mama's right: we're all acting like robots, doing what we're told and learning to hate each other.'

Matthew swallowed hard. 'Do you hate me and mama?'

'Not hate, Matthew. It's just that I keep thinking mama or you should be able to do something, and you can't.'

Suddenly tears spilled out of her eyes. She put her head down and pressed her face into the blankets. Matthew stared at her, not knowing what to say to make her stop. Finally, she caught her breath and looked up at him.

'Oh, Matthew, I feel so rotten. That's why I'm scared to think. I never knew a person could feel so bad inside. And now that I do know, all I want is for these feelings to stop.'

Matthew put his arm around her shoulder. He could feel tears forming at the corners of his own eyes. Embarrassed, he quickly wiped them away. She was right. He knew that. They'd have to take a chance.

'Okay, Margo, we'll do it. We'll go.'

CHAPTER FIFTEEN

JEN WENT THROUGH HER WARDROBE before she dressed that morning and chose a grey wool skirt and long-sleeved black knit pullover. She had scarcely used the makeup Seth had given her; now she applied just enough to accent her green eyes. She brushed her thick hair carefully, then hooked gold leaf drop earrings through her earlobes. Finally she stepped back and studied her reflection in the mirror.

'You look beautiful, Jennifer.'

Jen turned, startled to see Seth standing at the door.

'Thank you, Seth. I feel good, too.'

'And why is that?'

'Well now, we do have a wedding coming up. I don't look at that as a minor event in my life. I thought maybe we could sit down and discuss the arrangements after breakfast.' Jen could see his cheeks reddening.

'You've fixed yourself up like this – for me?' he said.

'Who else?'

He took her hand and led her downstairs, not once taking his eyes off her. After breakfast, he sent the children out to the backyard, and he and Jen sat on the sofa.

Jen smiled her most alluring smile.

'Seth, you know an awful lot about me, but not every-thing. There are some things I want to tell you.'

He started to speak, but she cut in. 'Please, let me finish first. I want you to understand because this is so important to me.' She went on. 'I've always wanted to give the children a father. In fact, I've always felt guilty that I hadn't – almost like I gypped them out of something they were entitled to. Of course, it wasn't easy for me to accept you, under the circumstances, and it even made me angry to think that after all these years you thought you had the right to break into our lives like you did.'

'But I've always wanted—'

'Please.' She stopped him again. 'Whatever your reasons were, you have to remember that I didn't know them. All I knew was that we had to get along by ourselves. I'm only telling you these things now, Seth, because I want you to understand how I felt – what it seemed like to me.'

She took a deep breath. 'Now I don't want to lie and tell you that I'm completely over being a little scared of all this. After all, it happened so fast – with no warning – and it's a lot all at once. But what I'm trying to tell you is that I want to try to make our marriage work. Not only for the children . . . but for me, too. I've been without a man for a long, long time.'

She could hear Seth's breathing. His mouth was open, as if he had forgotten to close it. She could tell he was sifting her words through his mind, trying to decide if he could believe her.

'If we're going to have any chance at making this a good marriage,' she said, 'we're going to have to learn to trust one another. Now I know that, up until now, I haven't given you much reason to trust me – and I'm sorry. In a way, the next few days will be our only opportunity to get close to each other before we become man and wife. I want you to try to trust me, just like we were starting all over again. I promise I'll do everything I can to be deserving of it.'

'It won't be easy, Jennifer. Not just because of you, either. I've never in my whole life been able to completely trust another person. Every time I put my faith in someone, I've been disappointed.'

'What about Dandy?' Jen asked. She nudged closer to Seth and put her hand on his shoulder, rubbing it gently.

Abruptly, Seth got up from the sofa and began pacing. Jen could see that he was agitated – in pain, almost. Why? Was it because she mentioned Dandy? The mention of his name seemed to ruin the moment she had struggled so hard to create. She had thought Dandy was Seth's one true friend. Then why was he so upset? She was confused.

'I'm going outside, Jennifer,' Seth said suddenly.

Jen nodded. 'Certainly, Seth. If that's what you want.'

The front door flew back on its hinges as Seth stepped outside, leaving Jen alone. Alone. Now, what *had* she done?

It was past noon by the time Clarence turned the last corner onto his street. The air was brisk – it was the kind of autumn day he relished the most and, as always, he came home feeling fresh and invigorated. Today he had a thin envelope tucked away in his pocket. Although Ashley had daily mail deliveries, Clarence had kept a post-office box of his own for years. Once a week, he'd stop down at the main post office to check on it. Often he found it empty, but when – like today – he did find something inside, it gave his whole day an added lift.

There were certain things Clarence wasn't good at, and he was the first to admit it. When it came to harping on a subject or digging into an opponent, he was at a loss. Faced with verbal battle, he was no match for Miriam – he just crumpled up and gave in; it was simpler and more efficient. But no one was going to tell him that any man with the slightest bit of gumption couldn't manage to keep a few things private from his wife, even a wife like Miriam. Clarence's post-office box gave him the added pleasure of knowing that Miriam didn't know every single thing about him like she thought she did. He knew perfectly well that she thought of him as an open-and-shut book – and a boring one at that. So be it – as long as he knew in his own mind that it wasn't true.

Since Lieutenant Thorne's visit on Friday night, Clarence had given a lot of thought to the business with Jennifer and the grandchildren. He tried not to let it get him too upset. After all, he had a lot of confidence in that girl; and while there was no doubt that she had a heap of responsibility for one person to handle, he'd always been impressed with the way she dealt with it. No news was good news, he told himself for the hundredth time. He suspected this detective fellow would let him know if there really were cause for worry. As closest living relatives, wouldn't he and the wife be the first to know if anything happened?

He twisted the brass knob and pulled open the back door leading to the kitchen. The dry heat inside hit him full force and fogged up his glasses. He pulled a clean, folded handkerchief from his back trouser pocket and carefully rubbed the lenses clear. He looked up to see Miriam sitting at the table, sipping at one of her endless cups of tea.

'You're later than usual, Clarence.'

He nodded. 'It's a fine day out there – perfect for stretching the legs.' He stepped to the hallway closet and placed the collar of his jacket over the hook.

'Someday, Clarence Sawyer, you're going to fall dead on the roadside from a heart attack, and no one is even going to know you're there. You're too old to be running around like a schoolboy. A man your age ought to be saving every last bit of energy he has.'

'I guess when I do that, I'll know for sure I'm dead.'

Miriam ignored the remark.

'You've got a message,' she said.

He cupped his hand over his ear. 'What's that?'

'You've got a message,' she repeated. 'What's the matter, your hearing going? It's not any fun for me to have to say things over and over.' She lifted a slip of paper from the table and shoved it into his hand. 'Here.'

'What is it?'

'Losing your eyesight, too?'

Clarence looked down to see Lieutenant Thorne's name and telephone number written in Miriam's heavy script.

'What's this for?'

'I'm assuming it's about Jennifer and the kids. He didn't tell me anything, just wanted you to give him a call. I don't suppose you'll know what it's about, either, until you do.'

Clarence studied the paper. He didn't like the sound of it. Here it was Monday morning, and they hadn't yet heard from Jennifer or been able to reach her themselves. Worst of all, here was this detective evidently still looking for her. No sir, he didn't like the sound of this one little bit. He lifted the receiver, dialled 617 and the numbers Miriam had written down.

At 12:30 p.m. Clarence Sawyer called in a missing person's complaint to the Winfield police department. Within ten minutes, Thorne was sitting across from Chief Ryan, a nervous slip of a man with horn-rimmed glasses that would not stay put on his nose.

Thorne tossed the complaint on the desk.

'I'd like to request assignment to this case.'

'Why?'

Thorne told him. When he finished, Ryan sat forward.

'You know you had no business investigating this on your own.'

'I was worried. I didn't see what harm it would do.'

'That's not the point. It seems to me you're already too involved. I don't know that you're objective enough about this.'

'What does that mean?'

'Just that you've been running around, snooping into this woman's life with no authority to do so. No complaint was filed. As far as you knew, no crime was committed. It might have been a simple case of a mother taking a few days off with her kids.' Ryan thrust out his finger and pushed up the rim of his glasses. 'And if it were, you can bet the department would take some heat.'

'Look, chief, the fact is that a complaint has now been filed. Someone's going to be assigned to this case. Why not me? At least I know the background.'

Ryan sighed. 'Okay, Thorne, on one condition. This isn't your only case, and I don't want you spending all your time on it. Your instincts are usually pretty good, but I still think you've got some emotional involvement here that might throw off your judgement. Watch it, will you?'

'I promise,' Thorne said and stood up. 'I'd like to go through the house and beauty shop. Can I get a search warrant?'

'Give me twenty minutes, but remember—'

'I know, I know.'

Thorne hurried back to his desk and called Rizzano in Ashley.

'I expected to hear from you earlier,' Rizzano said as soon as he recognized Thorne's voice.

'I need a favour. By the way, it's official now – we've got a missing person's complaint.'

Rizzano laughed. 'Since when does that make a difference to you? Okay, Thorne, what do you want?'

'I need to know if there was ever a rape report filed on Jennifer Sawyer – 1974'

'Your lady, again.'

'Yeah.'

'What would that have to do with her disappearance now? Rapists seldom return to their victims. And after twelve years . . . Do you think it's connected?'

'Maybe, maybe not. Probably not, but it never hurts to dig from both ends. Maybe I'll luck out and hit the middle.'

'You ought to put a patent on that piece of advice, Thorne.'

'You have my permission to write it down.'

'Listen, Supercop, I don't have time for chitchat, so I don't suppose you'll mind if I don't get caught up in a battle of wits. I'll get someone on the rape business right away.'

That afternoon Seth had done something he'd never done before – at least not to Jennifer. He had lied to her. He'd told her he needed to run errands when instead what he really needed was to come down to his workshop to think. And then, having told the lie, he didn't have any other choice but to lock Jennifer and the children in their rooms. To make matters worse, he hadn't allowed them to be together like he sometimes did.

The way she'd looked at him when he closed the door made his insides curl up. He was that ashamed. After all the talking she had done that morning about trust, and here he was lying and locking her up. Oh, she tried not to show her feelings, she'd kept that smile right in place. But he knew his Jennifer, and he could tell what that look in her eyes meant. She was disappointed in him. And could he really blame her? It was all for her own good, of course, but she didn't know that.

He thought about the way she'd poured her heart out to him that morning. It was almost sad – her telling him how much she'd needed someone to take care of her and the children, and waiting all these years for him to come to get them. He wanted to grab her, throw her down, and love her right then and there. But he hadn't done that. He had kept to his promise. He wasn't about to scare her – not now, not when she finally was saying all the things he'd always wanted to hear.

He thought back to their first time. No, Jennifer wasn't one of those tramps. He had tested her that night – long ago in the cemetery – and she had passed the test with flying colours. For a few seconds, though, she *had* made him doubt her – made him think that maybe he'd misjudged her. At first: the way her body arched back and loosened up almost as if she were enjoying it – that nearly destroyed him. What would he have done if she'd kept it up? Just the thought scared him. But she hadn't disappointed him one bit, and it *had* turned into something beautiful. Not once did he have to hurt her – at least not in the real sense, not out of anger and disgust. Only out of loving, and that was different. And the proof was the children, those two beautiful children who came out of that union.

But her actions today: what did they mean? She had sat close to him, touched him that way, and right after she said how much she wanted their marriage to work. Oh, he hadn't let it get to him; his body had stayed as tight and rigid as a ruler, but he knew what she was trying to do. It reminded him of his nightmares: the demons trying to take control. And that's what scared him. Never before today had he ever wanted to hurt Jennifer.

If she had been so forward with him, did that mean she had been forward with other men? Was she like one of those vultures who used men – drinking in their pleasures, only to spit them out in the wind? But how could that be? Hadn't he been watching, checking on her all these years?

Maybe she hadn't realized what she was doing. He sighed. Or maybe he was just kidding himself, making excuses for her. He put his head down on the workbench. God forgive him . . . he loved her. Even if he found out that she *was* that kind of woman, could he ever give her up? He knew the answer to that without even thinking: Never. And for that matter, why should he have to? With her loving him like she did, wouldn't he be able to teach her different? Once they were married, he'd have plenty of time to teach her . . .

Seth stood up, feeling better about things. He headed upstairs.

Anxious to get to Jennifer.

That afternoon, Thorne inspected the house at Two Arden Road as well as the beauty shop. Other than the batch of cookies, the unopened boxes of Chinese food, and a load of damp clothes in the washer, nothing was amiss. He walked over to the telephone and looked at the pad of paper and pen beside it. He picked up the pad – no writing, but he could distinguish an impression of letters on the top sheet. Taking it over to the window, he held it up to the light: the indentation clearly read *Post Road*.

So much for any idea of car theft – not that he had ever believed in it for a moment. Jen had driven herself there. Then what? He looked again at the modest furnishings. Definitely not a logical target for ransom. And a psychopath was unlikely to have contacted the family. Didn't that mean it was someone she knew?

For the next few hours Thorne made the rounds of neighbours as well as a number of customers whose names he had copied from her appointment book. When these efforts produced the names of two women friends who had been seen visiting occasionally, he interviewed both. Neighbours, customers, friends – they all confirmed what he already knew or had been told: she had not been seen or heard from since last Tuesday; she was a hard worker, well-liked, a good mother, well-behaved children, no boy-friends hanging around to anyone's knowledge. He studied the array of comments in his notebook. All in all, Jennifer Sawyer could have won first prize as the ideal neighbour who minded her own business.

He followed up by making some inquiries at the school. He learned that the boy had stayed after school for a few minutes on Tuesday afternoon, just long enough to get the results of a quiz. Thorne took down the names of the children's friends as well as those students in their classes who walked the same route. He went to each house and questioned the children. One boy – Danny – reaffirmed what he already knew: by 3:45 the children still hadn't arrived home from school.

When he returned to the station after five o'clock, he looked over the messages on his desk, singling out the one from the Ashley P.D.: no record of rape of Jennifer Sawyer in 1974. He closed his eyes and leaned back in his chair. He hadn't the faintest idea where to go next.

Schroeder turned to him. 'Still that lady?'

He nodded. 'The problem is, she kept so much to herself. Everyone describes her as pleasant, but she never confided in anyone I talked to – not even her girlfriends. Christ, I thought I tended to be private; next to her, I'm an open book. I haven't been able to hit upon one thing that leads anywhere.'

'She does have a past, doesn't she? Not too many people manage to get by without one.'

Thorne, still leaning back, closed his eyes even tighter.

'Oh, yes. She does have a past.'

'You've looked into it?'

Thorne nodded.

'Dead ends, mostly.'

'Come on, Mike, snap out of it. I was on the streets for quite a few years myself.' He gestured toward the computer. 'I haven't always been Lucy's partner, you know. I never once saw a past that didn't lead to a present. Some are just easier to dig out than others, and in some cases the link isn't always so apparent.'

Thorne sat forward and opened his eyes.

'I'm just so goddamned worried about them, Schroeder. While I'm out there inching my way along, sniffing out phantoms, who knows what's happening to them.'

'You're not getting any closer sitting here,' Schroeder said. 'Besides, who knows? Maybe your phantoms might turn out to be flesh and blood.'

Thorne squashed out his cigarette in the ashtray and stood up.

'Thanks, Schroeder. Every now and then you say something that makes sense. Something that doesn't sound like it came out of Lucy.'

Schroeder looked up, but Thorne was already headed for the door.

'Hey, Thorne,' he called out, 'what did I say?'

CHAPTER SIXTEEN

IT WASN'T UNTIL AFTER DINNER that Clarence finally had the opportunity to be by himself. As much as Miriam didn't like to admit it, she too was concerned about Jennifer and the children. Matthew was her favourite, of course. He reminded her of Jim when he was a boy. She paid scant attention to Margo, but he knew it wasn't because she disliked her. It was just that Miriam could never seem to care about more than one thing at a time, almost as if it took too much effort.

Her anxiety about the disappearance seemed to aggravate her aches and pains, and Clarence found himself busy applying heating pads, ice bags, and his home-prepared herbal lotions to her sore joints – anything to pick up her spirits. As soon as dinner was over and the kitchen put back in perfect order, Clarence promptly made Miriam as comfortable as possible. He propped her up on the sofa with pillows, tuned the television to a *Three's Company* rerun, and stacked the endtable with a neat pile of the latest movie magazines. That done, he beat a hasty retreat to his bedroom and closed the door behind him. He pulled the thin envelope that he'd been carrying around all day and ran a letter opener along the edge of the seal, neatly tearing it, then sat down in his one comfortable chair and began to read.

Dear Dandy,

I hope my letter finds you well. The weather chills early in these parts as you well know, but this time the anticipation of winter does not bring the gloom and depression I'm used to feeling. Even the nightmares which continue to disturb me don't upset me nearly as much, because I know that when morning finally comes, everything will be fine. In fact, I have never before looked forward to the winter season as I do now.

For many years now I have talked your ear off about my family, but due to circumstances you are well aware of and I still carry shame from, I have been unable to claim them as my own. But finally, if one prepares and has patience, as you've told me countless times, the good things do come. And that is my news, Dandy. I am no longer alone – finally I have the family I've always wanted. My two children and the woman I intend to make my bride are living with me. Although I might be jumping the gun on the wife part, and I know you've warned me never to do that, I plan to ask her soon to marry me, and I feel certain that she will accept.

I cannot help but think that without you, this day might never have come. Without your continued wisdom and caring, I might never have learned the patience necessary to put my life together. Even though there were times I wanted more from you than you could give, the fact is you were the only one who ever cared. You were there despite your responsibility to Jim and your sick wife. I never knew why God sent you to me or why you stuck by me even when I did those terrible things, but you did – always remaining the one person I could count on not to turn against me.

You may rest easy now, Dandy. My life is finally taking shape, finally heading in the right direction, and you should take most of the credit for this happening. I will, of course, keep in touch and bring you up to date.

As ever,
Seth

Clarence folded the letter, placed it on the bedside stand and settled comfortably into his chair, pleased that things were working out so well at last for the boy. As anxious as he'd been to read what Seth had to say, he'd been a little apprehensive: Seth's letters sometimes carried less-than-pleasant news. Clarence sighed. The boy had certainly got into a heap of trouble for one his years. Always that uncontrollable temper, even as a child. But once the boy got older, that volatile spirit really broke loose, hurting others.

Nevertheless Clarence had never for one second given up on the boy. After all, there was a lot of goodness there, too. Some just grow up slower than others – take a longer time to get that hellion out of them. Clarence couldn't even count the times he'd tried to pump some sense into Seth. Slow and easy, be patient – those were the things to keep in mind if he wanted to win back that girl he was always talking about. A couple of fine children she bore him, too. Left to his own devices, Clarence knew, Seth would have gone running after her a lot sooner. But for once he'd listened: prepared himself, worked on his self-control. And apparently it had paid off. Now he'd have a family of his own like he deserved. Clarence was happy for him.

If only this nasty business about Jennifer and the grand-children could get cleared up. Then he could truly rest easy.

Jen leaned back against the headboard, stroking an emery board across her nails with short upward movements as she thought back over the day's events. Things had been going so well until she made that one mistake. The rest of the morning Seth had not said one word, to any of them. Then after lunch he'd locked them up again – in separate rooms – and lied to her about going out. The car couldn't have gone down the driveway without her hearing it.

Whatever it was, though – whatever she had said or done – he had apparently worked it out in his mind. Once he came up and unlocked her door, he was fine – relaxed, friendly, even eager to talk about the wedding ceremony. There were times during the afternoon that she actually had to remind herself that they weren't the happy little family unit they seemed to be. She understood now how performers managed to get lost in their roles, sometimes at the expense of their own identities. As long as everyone followed the script with no mistakes, nothing to snap the actors back to reality, they stayed caught up in the act.

And that's how it had been when Seth brought the big rubber ball out into the backyard with them that afternoon and punched it over to Jen.

'You think *you* can send this flying,' she said, grabbing it out of the air. 'Watch this.' She swung her fist at the ball and sent it back to Seth.

'Watch this one.' Seth bashed his fist against the ball and sent it high in the air, almost reaching the upper branches of the trees. 'Catch it, kids,' he shouted.

Margo and Matthew both ran towards it, Margo reaching out and grabbing it first, then tossing it back to Seth.

'I bet none of you guys can do this one,' Seth shouted, placing the ball on his head and giving it a twirl. 'They call this the Anthony Headspin!'

Jen watched Seth, his arms far out at his sides, his eyes directed upward almost as if he expected to see the ball spinning around on his head. For that moment, she pictured him as he must have been as a child, almost as if she'd known him – playful, expectant, eager . . . or maybe he hadn't been like that at all; maybe he had never been able to really let himself go. And for that moment the anger and fear and hate she felt slipped away, just long enough for her to wish she could exorcise whatever it was that caused him so much pain.

She had to hold this moment – remember it – and make use of the feelings if she was to keep this act running. If she accomplished nothing else in the next few days, she had to keep this momentum flowing: he had to believe in her and, as much as Jen hated to think about it, he had to desire her. She was playing the oldest game in the book and she was asking him to buy it as if it were being marketed for the first time. She wanted to make him desire her so much that, when the moment came, nothing else but that moment would matter – not even the children.

Jen put the emery board back in the nightstand drawer and stared up at the ceiling. It was odd. Not all of what she had told Seth that morning was a lie. Maybe that's why she'd been able to convey it so well. She did feel guilty about not giving the children a father. But as much as Seth managed at times to look like the father she'd pictured Jim as being, the thought of telling the children who he was made her shudder. Would the children ever forgive her if she told them? Would they ever forgive her if she didn't?

She pressed the button on the bedside lamp, turned over onto her stomach, and closed her eyes, hoping that she wouldn't be awakened again tonight by Seth's cries. She wanted to turn her mind to something she could get pleasure from. She fell asleep thinking of Mike Thorne.

It was 8 a.m. and not many cars were headed north at this hour; the traffic was headed south towards Boston. Mike Thorne reached with his free hand into his pocket and pulled out the pocket watch. For some reason he hadn't turned it in yet.

He slipped it back into his pocket as he pulled up at the station in Ashley. He went straight into Rizzano's office. The chief looked up and pointed to a coffee pot on the corner table.

'Help yourself.'

Thorne poured himself a cup and sat down.

'There's some of that fake powder garbage over there, too.'

'Black's fine.'

Rizzano looked at his watch. 'Tell me, Thorne, they have you on an hourly wage over there? That how they get you to put in these kind of hours?'

'Double time before eight and after five. I'm raking it in so fast I don't know where to put it.'

Rizzano laughed. 'Okay. What can I do for you?'

'The only real lead I have in the Sawyer case is a suspicion that the lady was raped. According to your records, it was never reported. But if I'm right there's always the possibility that her attacker had raped other women, and there's always the possibility that he was caught.'

'Sounds to me like a lot of ifs.'

He shrugged. 'That's all I have right now.'

'Christ, you don't even have an M.O. You need at least a name before you can plug it into our terminal.'

'I know. That means I'll have to go through your card file, pull any assault and batteries, then run them through your computer.'

'That could take forever, you know. And besides, who's to say this rapist, if he exists, wasn't a one-timer, someone who knew the girl, someone with no other criminal history?'

'Any other suggestions?'

The older man shook his head. 'You got a thing for this girl?'

Thorne was getting tired of the question.

'Maybe I do.'

Rizzano leaned back and spread out his hands.

'What's mine is yours. Help yourself.'

Mike went into the file room and pulled out the first drawer, starting with 1970. He set it on the table, took off his jacket, and began to go through the cards one by one.

'I want the perfect wedding dress,' Jen told Seth, 'long and flowing and loaded with lace.'

Before Seth left the house, he took them all upstairs to the children's bedroom.

'I don't want you to think I don't trust you,' he said. 'Once you're my wife . . .'

'It's okay, Seth, I understand. I want you to feel sure of me. Soon, you will.'

She was not, in fact, upset that Seth had locked them in. As far as she could see, things were going along even better than she'd expected. Twice that morning he had gone to the basement, leaving both her and the children alone in the parlour for a few minutes. This time they were locked in, but they were alone together for the first time since the wedding announcement.

She spread out her arms and gathered the children close, pulling them down onto the floor with her.

'Come on . . . let's talk.' They sat in a tight circle on the floor.

'How will you get our door unlocked, mama?' Matthew asked immediately. 'He always carries the key ring in his pants pocket.'

The angry purple bruise on his face was beginning to fade, taking on tinges of different colours. Jen lifted her hand and touched his cheeks with her fingertips.

'That's my job, Matthew. I'll get the key.'

'Are you really going to go along with the wedding?' Margo asked.

'I'll have to. But remember, it's only a game – one that I have to pretend to play.'

'Will you be really married, though?'

'No, Margo. The ceremony will have no legal validity whatsoever.'

Jen looked at Matthew who was staring down at the floor, his teeth biting down on his lower lip.

'Please . . . don't worry about me. I'll be fine, Matthew.'

'But suppose Seth discovers us missing?'

Jen swallowed hard. She knew that there was a good chance he would. Her hope was that by the time he did, it would be too late to stop the children.

'Trust me to handle Seth. The only thing I want you to think about is getting to town as fast as you can.'

She held out her arms and both children moved in close, wrapping their arms around her. She kissed their heads, their faces. It had been so long.

'Oh, mama,' Margo said, 'we'll run the fastest we ever ran in our whole entire lives.'

Jen pulled back and looked at them.

'You two are the ones with the tough jobs. Mine is easy – I just sit and wait. Now, you've got to remember everything I told you. Stay on the left-hand side of the road. Follow it, but not so closely that you'll be seen by a car driving by. And don't forget to tell the police to contact Mike Thorne at the Winfield police department.'

Matthew gave his mother an extra hug, then moved back.

'You won't let Seth do anything to you – will you?'

Jen lifted his chin and looked in his eyes.

'No, honey. I won't let him do anything.'

When Seth returned, he sent the children downstairs and led Jen into her bedroom.

'Sit down,' he said, placing a large white box on the bed and slowly pulling off the cover. Carefully he lifted out a white floor-length dress.

Jen studied the puffed sleeves ending at the elbow, the scooped neckline outlined in beautifully worked lace. Lace-panelled peau de soie fell in soft folds from tiny tucks stitched in the bodice.

'Oh, Seth!'

'I knew you'd like it. You're going to make the most beautiful bride in the whole world, Jennifer.'

She stood up and flashed what she hoped was an ecstatic smile. 'Thank you,' she said.

Suddenly he grabbed her arm and pulled her over to him; his hands slid roughly across her body, then beneath her sweater. Her skin prickled as though hundreds of tiny insects were scrambling across her chest. She pressed her hands against his chest and pushed.

'No . . . please.'

He stumbled backward, looking bewildered.

'I want it to be perfect,' she said.

He nodded his head stupidly and shoved her away. She fell back down on the bed and watched him run from the room. The hall bathroom door slammed shut and she jumped. She felt like a player in a game of life and death that had no rules, no way of predicting what would happen next.

She lay her head down and closed her eyes. The house was quiet, except for the moans coming from the bathroom.

CHAPTER SEVENTEEN

IT WAS CLOSE TO SEVEN O'CLOCK when the name jumped out at Thorne from the cards. Seth Anthony. Of course it meant only that the man who had reported Jim Sawyer's accident had a criminal record. What of it? Nevertheless, he pulled the card and brought it right to the clerk.

'Can you run this through?'

Thorne watched over the clerk's shoulders as he punched the information in the terminal. Seth Anthony had a long string of minor offences – all in Ashley: trespassing, voyeurism, disorderly conduct. No convictions. But the last offence, in 1974, was serious enough to put him in prison: a five-year sentence for assault and battery with a deadly weapon. Thorne had the clerk pull Anthony's file; he took it back to the table and quickly leafed through it. The victim was a prostitute. According to the record, that was his last criminal offence.

Thorne wrote down the name of the prison where Anthony had done time, the name and address of the woman attacked, and the orphanage where he grew up.

He looked down at his watch. It was too late to follow up on any of this information today, but he did want to make one last stop at the Sawyers. Maybe something else had come to them in the last few days.

He slipped his notebook into his pocket. St Anthony's Children's Home. Was the similarity in names just another coincidence? As far as Thorne was concerned, most 'coincidences' weren't that at all. There was usually some logical reason why things turned up together more than once. He grabbed his jacket off the back of the chair and headed for the door. He would stay tonight at the cabin and get an early start in the morning.

Clarence had just walked into the parlour with a cup of tea for Miriam and himself.

'What in the world took you so long?' she asked.

He placed her cup on the endtable.

'Guess I didn't hear you the first time. I'm not up to par myself these days, worrying about the children like this.'

'You think it hasn't been preying on *my* mind? Where do you think that girl took them? And going off without telling us like that.'

Clarence sat down, folding a napkin in his lap and shaking his head.

'No, that doesn't sound like Jennifer. I'm inclined to agree with the lieutenant – maybe they met up with trouble. It's not so safe out there nowadays. There's a lot of crazies running around the streets. That's what worries me.'

Miriam stirred her tea. Hearing a car motor, she reached over and pulled aside the heavy drapes.

'There's that officer, now.'

Clarence set his cup on the table, went to the window and looked out over Miriam's shoulder, then headed for the front door and had it open by the time Thorne reached the steps.

'Any news, lieutenant?'

'Nothing yet. I thought I'd stop by to see if you or Mrs Sawyer remembered anything else – any other friends you might have thought of.'

'We haven't, though it's not for lack of trying. The wife and I have been talking about little else since your last visit, and neither of us can tell you one thing we haven't already told you.' He gestured for Thorne to come in. 'Will you join us for tea?'

'No, thanks. I want to get back to my cabin, get some rest. There's a few things I need to look into tomorrow.'

'You will keep us informed, won't you?'

Thorne looked at the old man, feeling sorry for him. He looked tired and frightened.

'Of course I will. There is one more thing—'

'Anything at all.'

'Your son, Jim. Did he have any close friends? Anyone who just might have been jealous, or angry? Maybe someone who knew your daughter-in-law?'

'He did have quite a few friends, mostly in the construction business like himself. None that I could say wished him any harm, though. They've mostly moved away from this area – building has slowed down around here.'

'Did your son ever know a fellow named Seth Anthony?'

'Now, why would you ask a thing like that?'

'I was looking through your son's accident report. Seems a fellow by that name reported the accident. I wondered if Jim knew him.'

'No. Jim never knew anyone by that name. Not to my knowledge.'

Thorne thanked him and headed back towards the car. Clarence stood in the doorway, puzzling over the question. Of course he knew it was Seth who had discovered Jim's car at the bottom of the cliff, but what of it? Why was the lieutenant trying to make that into something after all these years? Maybe Seth had a point when he complained that people just wouldn't leave him alone to live his life. How could Seth have anything to do with finding Jennifer and the children?

He closed the door, still upset. At least he hadn't lied to the lieutenant – he'd never do a thing like that. He'd told him the honest-to-goodness truth. Jim had never known Seth.

On the way to the diner the next morning, Thorne picked up a *Boston Globe* – it was the first newspaper he'd looked at in two days. He sat in a corner booth reading a page two article, his platter of bacon and eggs forgotten.

MISSING MOTHER AND CHILDREN FEARED DEAD

A car belonging to a Winfield woman missing with her two children was recovered Saturday by Ashley, New

Hampshire police. According to Winfield Police Chief Robert Ryan, the vehicle was found without registration papers or license plate in an uninhabited area of Ashley. Although no evidence has been found to lead police to the family, Ryan fears they have met with foul play.

The twin children, Margo and Matthew Sawyer, age 11, are sixth-grade students at Highland Elementary School and were last seen at 3 p.m. dismissal Tuesday, October 11. The mother, Jennifer Sawyer, proprietor of a Winfield beauty shop, reported the children missing and was last seen herself early Tuesday evening.

The car, a 1982 burgundy Toyota, was towed by the Winfield police to their laboratory for examination. A warrant was obtained from Judge Leonard Willis to search the house and business of Ms Sawyer. 'A detective has been assigned to the case,' says Ryan, 'and the department is making every effort to locate the family.' He asks that anyone having information pertaining to this case contact the Winfield police.

The missing person's complaint was filed by Clarence Sawyer of Ashley, New Hampshire after repeated unsuccessful attempts to reach his daughter-in-law by telephone.

Thorne put down the paper. The way he saw it, Ryan was now under pressure. Once the public got wind of it, phones would be ringing off the hooks – the police, city representatives. This type of thing brought out the paranoia. He looked at his watch: 8:15. Shoving the newspaper under his arm, he dropped a bill on the table and headed to the cashier to pay his check.

By the time Thorne reached the rotary at Blue Hills Avenue, it was close to 8:30 – just in time to get tied up in the traffic headed towards Northern Electric. By the look of it, the plant employed a good portion of the town and then some. He turned on the car radio and switched from station to station as the cars crawled towards the entrance to the plant lot. Finally past the bottleneck, he drove another three miles till he reached St Anthony's Children's Home. He swung his car into the driveway and parked, looking around at the building and grounds. The place reminded him of the elementary school he'd attended: red brick, three storeys, run-down, surrounded by asphalt.

After giving his name to the girl at the switchboard, he sat down on a wooden bench in the hall and waited. Ten minutes later he was escorted into a large sparsely furnished office where a tall, thin woman with snow-white hair stood up to greet him.

'I'm Sister Theresa. How do you do, lieutenant?' She motioned to a chair, then sat down behind her desk. 'Now, what can I do for you?'

'I'm from the Winfield, Massachusetts police.'

'So I understand.'

'I'm handling a missing-persons investigation and I thought you or another staff member might be able to help. In the course of my investigation, the name of someone who grew up here has come up twice.'

'What is the name, lieutenant?'

'Seth Anthony. According to the records I saw, he was here from 1953 to 1971.'

The woman rested her elbows on the desk.

'I do remember Seth,' she said. 'I remember him well. In fact I came here when he was very young, I'd say about four or five. He was one of the brightest children we've ever had here.' She sighed. 'Not that he did well in school – he didn't. He never lived up to his potential.'

'Do you have the names of his parents?'

'Lieutenant, most children here have no parents. St Anthony's is not a temporary facility. The children who come here have no other place to go.'

'Can you tell me how he got here to begin with?'

'I believe Seth was left here as a baby.' She held up her finger, walked to a file cabinet at the far end of the room and pulled open the bottom drawer. A few moments later, she returned to her desk and quickly leafed through a thin file.

'Yes. He was eleven months old.'

'Who brought him in?'

'When I said he was left here, lieutenant, I meant it literally. He was left on our doorstep with a tag giving only his first name, Seth, and his age. In fact we didn't even know his birth date. Of course, we assigned one as we do in these circumstances. In any event we have no idea who the parents were. Perhaps an unwed mother who could not give the child a home. In those days, remember, it was all but impossible for an unwed mother to bring up a child properly.'

'What can you tell me about Seth? What type of child was he?'

Sister Theresa frowned.

'Could you tell me what lies behind these questions, lieutenant? Is Seth under suspicion for a crime? Has something happened to him?'

'No. In fact, I'm not even certain how – or if – he's connected to the case I'm working on. But as I said, his name did pop up twice in my investigation and I'd be remiss if I didn't check him out. We're talking here about the disappearance of a woman and two children.'

'You think Seth may have taken them?'

'I don't know. It's too early to speculate on something like that. But it would help if I could learn something about his background. Even if only to rule out possibilities.'

She closed her eyes for a moment, then sighed.

'I really don't know quite what to tell you. Seth was a good boy in many ways. Quiet, obedient. However, he did have a temper that would flare up occasionally, usually prompted by incidents with the other children. Don't get me wrong – he was not a bully. In fact, as I recall, Seth was quite likely to be the boy getting pushed around by the others. It's difficult to explain, lieutenant. I don't know how familiar you are with children, but certain ones are accepted by their peers and others are not. Those that aren't can rarely do anything about it. It's as if the others have pegged them – put them into a particular category and denied them any opportunity to convince them otherwise.'

'What category would you say Seth was put into?'

She thought a moment. 'I'm not even sure it would be relevant or, for that matter, accurate. Children's decisions are not always justified.'

Thorne nodded. 'Well, justified or not – how did the other children see him?'

'I would say that for one thing he kept so much to himself that he may have given others the impression that he was better than they. And then, of course, the boasting didn't help.'

'What kind of boasting?'

'Seth had a good friend, an adult who came to visit him regularly. He'd bring him gifts and even take him out occasionally. It was somewhat like the Big Brother programme you hear about nowadays. It seemed that this man had taken a liking to Seth. He certainly gave him a lot of his time.'

'What was his name?'

She laughed. 'I only remember him as Dandy – that's what Seth called him, and it must have caught on. I believe he was a local resident. By the time I joined the staff, he was already a fixture around here.'

'Why Seth?'

'I beg your pardon?'

'Why did he single out Seth?'

She shrugged her shoulders. 'Why not Seth? He was a good-looking youngster. And very bright. Oh, Dandy was nice enough to the other children, but Seth was clearly his favourite, the one he really came to visit. Actually, lieutenant, it's not so unusual. We have volunteers and visitors who come here frequently – usually people who like children and enjoy spending time with them, perhaps making their lives and the children's lives a little richer. You have to realize, we do what we can here, but St Anthony's is still an institution. Better than most, but hardly comparable to a real home.'

'Was there any talk of adoption?'

'Actually that's what I was referring to when I mentioned Seth's bragging. Although to my knowledge this man never spoke to our administrators about adoption, he may have made some promises to the boy. At least, Seth saw it that way. He referred to Dandy as his guardian and would tell the other children Dandy would someday be his father and take him home with him. But children don't take kindly to that type of one-upmanship, particularly when they come to view it as an out-and-out lie. The fact was that as much as this man wanted to befriend Seth, his benevolence did not extend to any legal commitment. And though all of the children wanted a real home, I cannot recall one who wanted it more than Seth.'

'I see. Are you aware of the trouble Seth got into after leaving St Anthony's?'

'I know he was pulled into court on several occasions. And I know that he ultimately was convicted of a stabbing of some sort.'

'Do you know anything about him now? His where-abouts, in particular?'

She shook her head. 'Since he went to prison, I have not heard anything about him, good or bad.'

'Do the children here attend public school?'

'Yes, they do.'

'Did you ever hear the name Jim Sawyer? He would have been about the same age as Seth. Perhaps even the same year in school.'

Sister Theresa thought for a moment.

'I'm afraid not. Seth actually had no friends here. Of course, I wouldn't know about any school acquaintances.'

Thorne stood up. 'One other thing, sister. Is there any way you could get me the name of Seth's adult friend? Dandy, that is?'

'I'm afraid not – it isn't something we would have kept a record of. Of course, I could ask the rest of the staff, but none of them has been here as long as I have. The chance of anyone remembering him – let alone knowing his name – is remote.'

Thorne thanked her and walked out of the office. He stood for a moment in the hallway watching a thin boy with close-cropped hair hurrying along the corridor, his shoes clicking on the grey tile floor. An old woman bent over a pail, squeezing out a mop. When she stood up, he could see her wrinkled face, her sunken cheeks.

Thorne hurried out to the car. As he turned the ignition key, a minibus pulled up in front of the entrance. Watching the children file out, he remembered for a moment the scene at the school athletic field the other day. He sighed, pondering the latest coincidence to crop up in this case: the Anthony boy's name for his friend was only one letter away from 'Daddy.'

CHAPTER EIGHTEEN

MARGO AND MATTHEW RAN AROUND THE BACKYARD gathering bunches of leaves. Once they had amassed a huge pile, they took turns jumping from a low tree limb into the heap. From inside, Jen could hear the squeals as they landed. Then later, noticing the quiet, she stood up from the sofa, went to the window, and looked out: both children, weary from their game, sat talking in the middle of the scattered leaf pile. Pink cheeks and noses: alike, yet not alike. Her snowflakes. Would she ever be able to call them that again? She went to the kitchen and opened the back door – it was getting close to dark. She was about to call them in when she heard Margo talking to Matthew.

'Do you think mama would ever keep something from us, something real important?'

Jen stood there, her hand squeezed a little tighter around the knob. She listened.

'What are you talking about, Margo?'

'About Seth.'

'What about him?'

Jen could see her daughter's fingers plucking at the leaves in her lap. Then, suddenly, as if she were forcing out a piece of food stuck in her throat, she said what was on her mind.

'About Seth being our father.'

'You're crazy, Margo. She *told* us already, he isn't.'

'I don't think she really said that.'

'Of course she did. Don't you remember when she first came here? She answered us then.'

'I remember we asked, but the more I think about it, the more I remember she didn't give us a real answer.'

'Then what kind of answer *did* she give us?'

'A fake one. The kind people give when they don't want to talk about something. You know, they kind of answer another question instead of the one you asked in the first place. And mostly, you don't even know they're doing it until you try to remember the answer. Well, I tried to remember the answer, and I can't.'

Jen quietly closed the door and sank down into a chair. What *would* she tell the children? It was the last thing she wanted to think about. Even if her plan worked – and she *had* to believe that it would – she'd still have to deal with the issue sooner or later. But she was no closer now to knowing what to tell them than when she'd first learned about Seth.

Margo had already figured out that she had avoided the question rather than given a straight answer. Jen thought about it. She knew that both children loved her and trusted her: as for Matthew, she could do no wrong. Her daughter had somehow learned that her mother wasn't perfect. But her son had not. How had Margo gotten so old so fast?

Didn't she owe them the truth? Didn't children have a right to know who their parents were even though the truth might send them into a tailspin? She thought idly of the saying, 'What you don't know won't hurt you.' She wondered who'd made it up: was he sure of that, or was it just a rationalization – someone easing his own conscience, someone covering up his own secret guilt?

Seth was sitting in the parlour; she could feel his eyes on her, but she avoided looking up through the doorway. *You son of a bitch! Why couldn't you have just left us alone? What did we ever do to hurt you?* She took a deep breath, trying to clear her mind, to get rid of the anger. Then she tilted her head back until her eyes met Seth's and smiled at him. She stood up, walked to the door and threw it open. This time she called to the children immediately.

'Come on in. It's getting dark.'

The children stood up, brushed off their clothes, and ran to her. As Margo stepped over the threshold, Jen stooped down and put her hand to her cheek, looking into her eyes.

Margo reached up her hand, put it softly, gently, to Jen's face and smiled.

'Hi, mama.'

Jen pulled her close, reaching with her other arm for Matthew and burying her face in first one shoulder, then the other. Her daughter suspected her of lying, and her son was appalled at the very idea of it. But Margo would forgive her. What about Matthew?

Thorne called the prison and learned that Anthony had been an unruly prisoner, not getting along with either guards or inmates. While serving his time, he assaulted a female prison official with a knife and had another five years tacked onto his sentence. He was let out in December 1984. A check with the New Hampshire Registry of Motor Vehicles turned up nothing on him, which meant he didn't drive, was an unlicensed driver, or was licensed in another state. Thorne spent the next several hours trying to track down Anthony's victim. After following up several old addresses, he found the former prostitute working at a bar and grill on Ashley's main strip.

It was after five when he walked into the dimly lit restaurant and looked around – he was the only customer. He ordered a ginger ale; when the waitress brought it to his table, he flashed his I.D.

'You Diane Fleming?'

'What do you want?'

'I want to ask you a few questions.'

She paused, looked back to the bartender who was busy shaking mixes and lining them up on the shelf. She sighed, then sank down in a chair.

'What is it?'

'Look, relax. I'm not here to hassle you. What I need is some information on Seth Anthony.'

'Don't know him.'

'The guy who cut you up.'

She waited a few moments before she answered.

'I don't know anything about him,' she said finally. 'Last I saw him was ten years ago in a courtroom, and if I never see him again, that'll be too soon.'

Thorne rested his arms on the chequered tablecloth.

'I can understand your reluctance to talk about it, but he just might be mixed up in something that could land him back behind bars. You could really help me out if you'd tell me what happened.'

'I hope you don't expect me to show you. We've got a dress code here.'

Thorne smiled. 'Just tell me. I need to know what kind of person I'm dealing with.'

'There isn't really much to tell other than that he was a prize nut. I could tell you he wrecked my career, and it was a pretty damn good one at that. I made a bundle.' She laughed, but there was no smile on her lips. 'I do this now,' she said, gesturing around the darkened tavern, 'but I don't suppose that tugs at your heartstrings too much.'

'You haven't seen him since the trial?'

'If I had, you wouldn't have found me here. I'd have been off like a shot. As far as I'm concerned, they should have locked him up forever. But you know how the law is – wastes its time on big stuff like prostitution and gambling. It locks the psychopaths up for a little while, slaps them on the wrists, then gives them licence to go out and do it over again. I'm sure he's out there floating around. God help his neighbours.'

'Did you know him before the incident?'

She shook her head.

'Actually, he was clean cut, fairly well-dressed, a good-looking guy. I was damned fussy when I was in the business – turned down a hell of a lot of guys I pegged as creeps.'

'What set—'

'You know, lieutenant,' Diane cut in. 'You're not so bad yourself. You got a girl?'

Thorne raised an eyebrow.

'Waiting for me at my apartment right now.'

'Figures. What's her name?'

'Miranda.' Thorne leaned forward. 'Now, Miss Fleming, can you tell me what made him go after you?'

'He was kinky – you know what I mean, he wanted to play-act. I never minded going along with fantasies or weird hang-ups as long as they were harmless. This guy wanted to do the maternal bit. He was pretending to feed off me.'

'And?'

'I went along with it – nice and easy, like I was enjoying it, cuddling him and cooing like you would with a baby.'

'What went wrong?'

'Nothing was working, nothing was turning him on.' She stopped for a moment and took a deep breath. 'Then out of nowhere, he went berserk – crying, screaming, beating on me and finally running to the kitchen drawer, pulling out a knife and doing this.' She put her hand to her breasts. 'You know, I thought about it a lot. I guess I had enough time, sitting in the hospital all those weeks.'

Thorne stared at her.

'I wondered what he'd wanted from me. At first I thought maybe he just hated his old lady, getting me to play the part so he could act out his hate for her.'

'You don't think that now?'

She sighed. 'No. That was too easy. It was more than that.'

'What do you think he wanted?'

'Oh, I think he wanted me to play the part of his old lady, all right, but I didn't do it right.'

'What does that mean?'

'Guys like that are weird. Take it from me, I've seen a lot of them. What got them so screwed up to start with – what they hated the most – is often the only thing that turns them on.'

'You've lost me.'

'Well, look, I'm no psychologist but I think he didn't really know what he wanted – at least, he couldn't admit it to himself. What he needed was for his old lady to fight him, resist him. Maybe even beat up on him.'

'Why?'

'Because maybe that's what he remembers from when he was little. Maybe that's what she did.'

'I hate to burst your bubble, Miss Fleming, but Seth Anthony was an orphan. He didn't have a mother.'

'I hate to burst yours, lieutenant, but everyone has a mother.'

'Maybe you should have been a psychologist.'

Diane smiled. 'Laugh at me if you want, but I've met a lot of men and seen a lot of strange things. Psychiatrists sit in their little offices reading and listening about human behaviour. Prostitutes get out there and deal with it.'

Glad to get out into the fresh air, Thorne decided to call it a day. If Seth Anthony was the fellow he was looking for, he'd better have been picked up on another charge somewhere, or Thorne might never find him. And if Anthony was half as screwed up as Diane described, and Jen was with him . . .

Then again, he wasn't even sure he was after the right guy. Tomorrow he'd have Schroeder feed Anthony's name into Lucy. As he headed back to Massachusetts, he had the odd sensation that a storm was about to break, even though the skies couldn't have been clearer. The car's speedometer hit 75 most of the way.

That night Jen sat quietly beside Seth, focusing her thoughts on the next day. If the children escaped and brought back help, this night would be their last with Seth. She thought about the next day: tomorrow morning was the ceremony, tomorrow evening her wedding night.

'You're quiet tonight,' Seth said.

Jen looked up.

'Just thinking about tomorrow.'

'Don't be nervous,' he said lifting her hand in his. 'What's about to happen is right – it's meant to be. There's no reason to be scared.'

Jen studied Seth's expression. There were so many things she wondered about. Up till now she'd purposely kept away from any topic that might cause him distress and push him into a panic. Tonight, though, he seemed calm enough to risk it.

'Did you know anything at all about your parents or relatives, Seth?'

'Why do you ask?'

'Just wondering. For one thing, I was curious if there were any twins in your family.'

He looked at her, his eyes questioning, and she rushed on.

'Multiple births often run in families. There's no history of twins in mine – at least that I know of. Maybe there was in yours. It's something I always wondered about but never had the opportunity to ask.'

Seth's shoulders were hunched forward and he took his hand from hers.

'I can't tell you about things like that, Jennifer. I don't know.'

'Haven't you ever tried to find out more about your background? You know, search for your family?'

He shook his head. 'I don't want to know.'

'Why not?'

'Because now it's too late. For years I dreamed of the day my mother would come to get me. I made up all kinds of excuses why she'd go off and leave me like that. A kid's imagination can pose a lot of fancy possibilities. But in all those stories I concocted I counted on one thing – someday she'd be back to fetch me. Then one day it hit me: I'd been feeding myself a pack of lies, and that's when I hated her with all my might . . . You don't know how scary it can be to be left alone in the world, but I know. Sometimes it's just too late to make amends for a sin, even with God.'

Jen wondered how someone could live with that much hate – and why he had chosen her to take it out on.

'Seth, tell me how you know so much about me. You know my pet name for the children, you even know my favourite sachet of scent. How could you possibly have found out those things?'

'Well, Dandy told me some of it.'

Jen tried to keep her voice steady.

'I don't understand. Who is Dandy?'

'I told you, he's my best friend.'

'No, that's not what I mean. Do I know him? Does he know me? I've never heard that name before – how would he know those things?'

Seth touched her face lightly.

'Once we're married, Jennifer, then I'll tell you everything. It's not that I don't trust you now – I do. But once you're my wife, things will be different. I'll feel free to tell you everything, to bare my soul.'

Later, trying to sleep, Jen couldn't get the conversation out of her mind. Everyone she'd ever known – every innocent, friendly face she could recall – became ugly, evil, suspect. If she thought about it enough, if the right face came to mind, a bell would go off in her head and she'd recognize it instantly. Her thoughts raced in circles. How could anyone know those things? And why would anyone confide what he or she knew to Seth? It made no sense. How could she not have been aware of what was happening, whatever it was? Over and over came the questions, the faces – until, finally exhausted, she fell asleep.

Her dreams were filled with eyes, all peeping around corners, all watching her. No matter where she ran, she couldn't escape them. The eyes were all the same; they looked familiar, as if they belonged to a face she knew. But she couldn't quite place the face.

That night, after everyone else had gone to bed, Seth went to the hall closet and pulled a large white box off the shelf. He carried it to the sofa and opened it, taking out the midnight blue tuxedo. He hadn't told Jennifer about it; he wanted to surprise her when she came walking down the stairs. He had never worn one, but he'd seen the way men who wore them looked in the movies.

He picked up the vest, slipped it on and risked a glance at himself in the mirror on the inside of the closet door. Then he took a deep breath, relaxing inside. He liked the way he looked tonight – maybe because he was so happy. He wished he could keep on looking like this, but he knew he wouldn't. He was the type of person whose looks changed from time to time. Sometimes he'd look so different that he'd almost scare himself. Sometimes he'd stand in front of a mirror with his eyes squeezed shut, then open them only a little bit at a time. That way he could get used to the person looking back at him, get used to parts of his body being smaller or larger than he remembered them. It wasn't so bad as long as he was ready and knew what to expect.

That was one of the nice things about Jennifer – she never looked different. Except for that one time, the time she'd tried to take control of him. But when he thought about it now, he wondered why he'd been so worried. Not once since then had she done anything to make him suspicious, to make him want to hurt her. Even on that day he'd gotten carried away – almost forgetting his promise to himself – she had been the one to push him away.

Thinking back to their conversation this evening, he was glad he'd soon be able to tell Jennifer all about Dandy. There were other things that he ached to tell – those times he'd gone to Massachusetts just to be near her, all those times he'd walked right into her house, and her leaving the door unlocked for him almost as if she'd known he was coming. It wasn't true that he completely deserted her all those years. When she'd accused him the other day, he'd wanted to scream out the truth then, but he hadn't. She'd just have wanted to know why it was he didn't pick her and the kids up there and then and take them home with him. And what could he have said to her? 'I was working on patience, on staying in control, so I'd never, ever hurt you like I did the others'? He could never say that.

Seth reached in his pocket, took out a little velvet box and opened it. He lifted out the two matching gold bands – one for Jennifer, one for himself – then sat down on the sofa and examined the glittering circles, wondering if he really had a right to be this happy. Some things he was used to, but happiness wasn't one of them. Still, when he thought about it, he knew God wouldn't have given him all this unless He'd wanted him to have it. He dropped to his knees beside the sofa, clasped his hands together and prayed out loud.

'Let me not hurt her, God. Please, dear God, let me not hurt Jennifer . . .'

CHAPTER NINETEEN

EVEN BEFORE JEN OPENED HER EYES, she could feel the fear tunnel its way in. She sat up, crossing her arms over her chest: today was her wedding day.

She got out of bed and showered, then sat in front of the mirror studying her face, wondering if a person could change permanently in such a short time. A mask seemed to cover her face, making it look pinched, plastic. Maybe it was just her expression. She forced a smile to her lips, but even to her it looked unnatural, as if someone were standing behind, pulling her lips upward. She lifted her mascara from the dressing table and began to sweep the tiny bristles through her eyelashes.

What would she do if her plans backfired? Suddenly they seemed foolish, ill conceived. Seth was so much more clever than she'd been willing to give him credit for. He seemed to have an extra sense that told him what others were thinking, signalling him which button to press to make *them* jump instead of himself. She leaned her elbows on the dressing table and lowered her head onto her hands. The plan had to work: this would be their last chance. She knew, beyond any doubt, that she had only enough energy left to get through today. She had to free Margo and Matthew from those strings Seth had them dangling from. Or tomorrow she'd wake up and be the woman in the mirror, and the children would be those people she didn't know.

She walked to the closet and lifted the hanger holding her gown off the bar, then laid it across her bed, admiring it. Ever since she was a little girl she'd dreamed of getting married in a dress like this, yet Jim and she had stood before a justice of the peace, wearing simple street clothes. Today she would put on this beautiful dress – the most beautiful dress she'd ever seen – and float down the stairwell. To Seth.

Although the children had been up talking since daybreak, they now lay quietly in their beds, thinking. Matthew had never in his whole life felt quite like he did at this moment: so many different feelings racing around, all at the same time. As much as he wanted more than anything else in the world to get out of this house, he didn't want to leave. Not without mama.

The plan had so many ifs. Would she be able to get their door unlocked without Seth seeing? More important, would she be safe with Seth while they were gone? What if he discovered them missing – what then? Would he get angry and go after her? The thought scared Matthew so much, he could feel a thin line of sweat form over his lips. With the back of his hand, he wiped it away. If anything happened to mama, he'd want to just go off somewhere and die. Suddenly he remembered the rifle in the cellar cabinet and the handguns. He jerked up in bed.

Margo sat up and looked at him.

'What's wrong?' she asked.

He turned away from her, staring at a knot in the wood that looked like a target with a bullet hole through the centre. It was the same knot he looked at when he was trying to fall asleep at night.

'Tell me, Matthew.'

He still didn't look at Margo.

'Suppose he hurts her,' he said finally.

Now it was her turn not to look.

'We can't think that way,' she said. 'Not if we want the plan to work. Even you said so. Remember what happened in the woods? You warned me beforehand that the plan wouldn't work if I let myself be scared for you. And you were right.'

'But this is different, Margo.'

'Why?'

His teeth bit into his lower lip; it hurt, but he dug his teeth in deeper anyway. Then he turned and looked at his sister.

'For one thing, it's mama we're talking about.'

Matthew lay back down and rested his head on the pillow, ending the conversation. He knew Margo was right – he couldn't let himself think that way. He'd mess up everything. But still – all he could think about now were the guns . . .

Seth too had been awake since early morning. The day before he'd gone down to the basement, dusted off the victrola, and tried it out. It hadn't been used in years. Now he set it in the corner on the floor, plugged it in and put a 45-rpm record on the spindle. He lugged the same table he'd used for Sunday services back up from the cellar and arranged two straight-back chairs to face the table – the children's seats – then went to the kitchen and checked the time: eight o'clock, two hours to go.

He opened the closet, took out his tuxedo and put it on, careful not to look at himself till he was done. Finally he turned towards the mirror: this time his reflection *was* different, but not the bad kind of different he was used to. He looked dashing, confident, just like the bridegrooms in the movies. Then his stare travelled down to his feet, startling him: he seemed to be floating, almost like someone had strung him up a few inches from the ground. He tried to stretch his toes inside the black shiny shoes, but his feet wouldn't go down to meet the floor. He bent over, then straightened back up, relieved. It was only an illusion, the mirror playing tricks.

He closed the closet door, went to the sofa and sat down. Everything was done, all he had to do now was wait. He could already hear footsteps upstairs – everyone was busy getting ready. A few minutes before ten, he'd unlock her door, place the white Bible at the threshold, then bring Matthew downstairs with him. He didn't want to see Jennifer one minute before-hand. He knew that was supposed to bring bad luck.

Thorne got to the station early and busied himself with the paperwork stacked on his desk. On the dot of nine, Schroeder walked in and saluted.

'You still work here?'

Thorne smiled. 'I'm hanging in. That is, unless you know something I don't.'

'Ryan was after your ass for a while for neglecting the warehouse burglary investigation, but once the press got hold of the Sawyer story, you got off the hook. Right now I'd say he'd auction off his Wilson driver – the one that he sunk the hole-in-one with – if you crack this case and get everyone off his back.' Schroeder sat down at his desk, clearing a space for his mug. 'So what have you got? Anything?'

'I do have a name I'd like you to punch in—'

'Hold it. Before you tell me you need the information in three minutes, I'm going to drink my coffee. Urgency doesn't register well with my system until I've lined it good with caffeine.' He lifted the cup to his lips and sipped. 'So tell me, how's it been going?'

'Lousy. I've got one suspect, and I've all but lost his scent. I was hoping you could pick up something on Lucy – see if he's been picked up on anything in Massachusetts. I haven't been able to get one thing on him – not a driver's licence, a credit card number, a car loan. Nothing.' Thorne lit a cigarette, then tipped his chair back. 'I don't even know if I'm headed in the right direction, but he's all I've got. You tell me, Schroeder, how three people manage to disappear without a trace.'

'You checked the lady's friends, relatives in New Hampshire?'

'Yeah, and I can count them all on one hand with fingers to spare.'

'What about up this way? Just because you found the car in New Hampshire doesn't mean we're not dealing with some local nut.'

'It's just a feeling. For some reason I think if I'm going to find anything it's going to be there, not here.' Thorne looked up. 'Any information phoned in here?'

'After the article ran we had maybe eight, nine calls. We screened them all out – curiosity seekers, do-gooders, and

202

one of those mystical types claiming to have seen the three of them during some sort of religious experience. Not one had any hard information.'

'Where did he say he saw them?'

'Who?'

'The mystic.'

'Jesus Christ, Mike, you *must* be desperate.'

'Where?'

Schroeder sighed. 'Buried in a fifty-foot ditch in the White Mountains.'

Thorne was silent.

'Come on, Mike, you're not going to let that kind of garbage get to you, are you?'

'Unless something shows up on a readout of my suspect or something in my head clicks off, I've got nothing.' He stood up and tossed a piece of paper with Anthony's background onto Schroeder's desk, then turned around and drove his fist against the filing cabinet.

'Shit! You've been a cop long enough, Schroeder, you see what goes on out there. For all we know, that nut may be right – she and the kids might already be dead. Or close to it.'

Schroeder got up quickly and went over to Thorne. He stood now with his arms folded on the filing cabinet, his head resting on his arms. Schroeder laid his hand on his shoulder.

'Come on, Mike,' he said quietly. 'Sit down, take it easy for a few minutes.'

Thorne went back to his desk. Schroeder poured a cup of coffee and took it over to him, then sat on the edge of his desk facing him.

'Look, Mike, all kidding aside. I know how involved you are in this one. But you know as well as I do, anger isn't going to get you anywhere. It's only going to mess up your head. You're the best detective we've got on the force; there's not a guy here that comes near you. So calm down and let that brain of yours do its work. If anybody can find them, you can.'

Thorne looked up at Schroeder for the first time since he started talking.

'Thanks, Henry. Guess I got a little out of control there.'

Schroeder picked up the slip of paper on his desk, then pushed his coffee mug aside.

'Who brewed this sludge anyway? Tastes like hell. I'm going to do one better for you, Mike. If I don't come up with anything here, I'm going to have this fellow checked out through the whole New England area.'

With one finger he was already punching in Seth Anthony's name.

CHAPTER TWENTY

THE ROOM WAS SO QUIET that when Seth placed the arm of the record player onto the record and the tinny version of 'O Promise Me' blasted forth, Matthew jumped. He looked down at his hands: he was holding a little red velvet box: inside were Mama and Seth's wedding rings. Margo, in a lacy high-collared dress that Matthew knew she hated, appeared at the top of the staircase. Then, one step at a time, she walked downstairs holding a bouquet of yellow daisies tightly in her fist. Once she reached the bottom step, she came and sat down beside him. He looked over at Seth all dressed up in a blue tuxedo.

Then just by the look on Seth's face, Matthew could tell she was coming. He turned back towards the staircase and for a moment he almost couldn't breathe. Mama's long, dark blonde hair was pinned up, with just a few short strands of hair falling and curling at her ears. She looked more beautiful than he'd ever seen her look in his whole, entire life. Not at all like a mother. She walked downstairs carrying a small, white Bible in her hands. Small, slow steps, like Margo. But when *she* reached the bottom, she went over and stood beside Seth. Seth turned toward her, waiting for the music to end. Once it did, he took a sheet of paper from his pocket, opened it, and started to read.

'I, Seth, take Jennifer as my wife, and standing here before God I promise to love, to cherish, and to protect her from this day forward for all eternity. Even in death.'

Seth turned over the sheet of paper and put it into mama's hands.

'Your vows,' he said. 'Read them.'

Mama looked at Matthew and Margo, looked at the paper, then began to read.

'I, Jennifer, take Seth as my husband, and standing here before God I promise to love, to honour . . .' She stopped.

Seth nudged her.

'Go ahead . . . read it.'

Her voice came out shaky.

'To obey, to respect, to be faithful to him . . . the father of my children . . .'

Matthew sucked in his breath, remembering what Margo had said out in the yard. But it couldn't be – mama would never lie, not about that. She had showed them pictures of their real father, lots of times. He looked again at the paper she was holding in her hand. Seth had made the words all up and was making her say them. It didn't mean anything, just like it didn't mean anything when Seth called him 'son' or pretended he was his father. Matthew sat still and tried to listen to the rest of the ceremony, but one word ran into another. It didn't matter, anyhow – all the words were just a bunch of lies. When mama was through, Seth beckoned to Matthew.

He stood up, walked to Seth and handed him the box. Seth slid the band onto mama's finger, then she slid the larger band onto his. Seth reached out his arms to her . . . Matthew quickly looked down at the floor, staring at a black speck in the carpet. As he looked at it, it seemed to get bigger.

'Come on, everyone,' Mama called out. 'Breakfast.'

Matthew looked up. It was over.

They all filed into the kitchen and soon mama was piling food onto the table: waffles, maple syrup, thick slices of ham, cocoa and hot cross buns, Matthew's favourite. He looked out of the window, wishing he and Margo could go out, but it was cold and rainy. He always wanted to go out in the rain, and mama would never let him go. But tonight she would have to . . .

'How are the buns, Matthew? I baked them last night.'

He looked down at the bun on his plate, then picked it up and bit into it.

'Good, mama. Real good.'

'I was thinking,' she said, looking around the table, 'Seth brought up a stack of old records from the basement. Maybe we could have a singalong after breakfast.'

'Sounds good to me,' Seth said.

Matthew and Margo just looked at each other and smiled.

'Hold on there, you two,' mama said, pointing her finger at both of them. 'I have a suspicion you're trying to tell me something. Could it by chance have anything to do with my singing? Because if so, your only hope will be to sing loud enough to drown me out.'

Right then she went over to the record player, put on a record, then turned up the volume so loud, the music filled the whole house: *You are my sunshine, my only sunshine . . .*

While they were all singing, Matthew turned and looked at Seth's face. He looked happier than Matthew had ever seen him.

Matthew wondered how the very same thing could make one person feel so happy and another person feel so sick. He stared at his lips as the words came out: *Please don't take my sunshine away . . .*

The computers in several states turned up nothing on Anthony, and for the better part of the afternoon Thorne worked hard at other assignments, hoping to distract himself for just a few hours.

Now, driving back to the department, his mind wandered back to the case. It was as if the guy had been released from prison, crawled into a hole and stayed there, which didn't make sense at all. From what Thorne knew about his background, he'd have thought Anthony would have been picked up again on other charges. The guy was sick and that kind of sick didn't cure easily. For that matter, it usually got worse. Of course, Anthony could have made a new start . . .

Thorne slowed down as he neared the centre of town and its late-afternoon shopping traffic; he sat back and waited for the light to change and the long line of vehicles sitting bumper to bumper to move. Almost as bad as the tie-up the other day in Ashley. At Northern Electric. He pictured the huge silver letters standing on the building, the *N* and *E* twice as tall as the other letters. If this traffic kept up, he wouldn't get to the station until nearly 4:30. Damn. He looked at his watch, at the digital face. If he didn't make progress soon, Schroeder would be gone by the time he got back. Thorne thought of Northern Electric again and then suddenly clutched the steering wheel. *The watch he had found.* He pulled it out of his pocket and turned it over, staring at the 50. Fifty years. Then at the initials *N.E.* A coincidence again? Maybe not.

A horn blasted from behind; the traffic was moving. He quickly turned the steering wheel, guiding the car to the right lane, passing the cars in front of him. Instead of taking a right turn to the station, he continued straight for three blocks, then climbed the ramp onto Route 93.

It was 4:45 by the time Thorne pulled up in the Northern Electric parking lot. He'd have just enough time to find out what he wanted to know.

John Quinn was just about to leave when Thorne walked through the swinging doors into the large first-floor suite and demanded to see the personnel director. Quinn ushered him into his office. As soon as Thorne introduced himself, he pulled out the watch from his pocket and dangled it in front of him.

'Does this look familiar?'

'I beg your pardon?'

'My question is, do you people give out watches to your employees when they retire – and if so, would this be one of them?'

'We do. What is this all about?'

Thorne handed him the watch.

'Please, just answer my question.'

Quinn examined the watch, turning it over and reading the inscription.

'I can't verify that we gave out this particular watch, but it certainly looks like one of ours – including, of course, the inscription.'

'May I see a list of those employees who retired in, say, the last twenty-five years? Those who received gold watches?'

'I don't see why not.' Quinn pressed a buzzer on his intercom and asked his secretary to get a list of the names. 'Only those completing fifty years of service,' he added.

Suddenly Thorne felt a chill as if someone had just opened a window.

'Could you ask her to hurry that up?'

Quinn complied. Thorne thanked him and went out to the adjoining office to wait. Within fifteen minutes, he had the list, containing more than a hundred names. When he hit the 1982s, he saw it.

The son of a bitch. What on earth did Clarence Sawyer have to do with Jen's disappearance?

At five o'clock Jen went into the kitchen to prepare dinner. As much as the afternoon seemed to drag on interminably, as much as she wanted the time to go faster, now that night was falling she felt as though each tick of the clock were bringing her closer to a stick of dynamite, already lit. She would put the children to bed at eight o'clock, then she and Seth would retire to the bedroom. If she couldn't easily persuade him to leave the children's door unlocked, she'd wait until he undressed, send him to fetch something downstairs, get the key from his pocket and open the door herself. These plans she felt relatively confident about.

What she wasn't at all sure of was just how long she could keep Seth occupied, or how safe the children would be outside. She looked out the kitchen window: it was still cold and rainy. She'd have to make sure they dressed warm. She felt her face heat up at the thought of being with Seth in bed while the children ran to safety. It was important that she prolong the act as long as possible – the longer it took, the longer they'd have. She was counting on some help from the wine she'd asked Seth to pick up the day before.

She took a head of lettuce from the refrigerator and began

to tear it apart. She could see the children sitting on the floor in the parlour playing rummy with cards Seth had hunted up for them. Seth sat on the sofa watching them, his eyes glistening. Jen picked up a small paring knife and sliced a tomato, anxious to get dinner made and over with. She looked up at the clock: only two hours to go.

CHAPTER TWENTY-ONE

ALL THE WAY TO THE PARKING LOT, Thorne kicked himself for not showing the watch to the old man earlier. He wasn't sure what he had hoped to get from Northern Electric – maybe just a bunch of names, potential suspects. He hadn't expected to find Anthony's name – he was too young to get a retirement watch – and he certainly hadn't expected to find Sawyer's.

It was possible that the old man had given the watch to Jen, but a man's pocket watch was hardly a gift one gave to a daughter-in-law. Maybe a grandson . . . But the boy was only eleven and a chunk of gold like that had to be worth hundreds of dollars. Even if it were a gift for the boy, surely his mother wouldn't let him carry it around with him.

Thorne steered the car around the corner into Sawyer's street, hoping that the watch would finally enable him to locate Jen and the children. He didn't know how, but he was willing to bet that the old man knew more than he was telling.

Sawyer opened the door a few seconds after Thorne's knock.

'Come in, lieutenant. You have news?'

Thorne put off answering his question while he followed him into the kitchen.

'The wife and I were just about to begin supper. Will you join us?'

Thorne nodded to Miriam who was sitting at the table. 'No thanks.' He slid his hand into his pocket, pulled out the watch and held it up to Clarence. 'Is this yours?'

'Why, that's your retirement watch, Clarence,' Miriam said. 'What did you do – go off and lose it?'

Clarence looked at his wife, then back at Thorne.

'Where did you find that?'

'In your daughter-in-law's car.'

'I don't understand. How did it get there?'

'I was hoping you could tell me.'

'Well, now, I . . . I don't know.'

'When did you last see the watch, Mr Sawyer?'

'Why, I . . .'

'Mr Sawyer, I suggest you level with me. We're talking now about the lives of your grandchildren. I don't know exactly how this watch is connected, but I know it is. Now, you apparently didn't give the watch to Jen or the children. I need to know how it ended up in your daughter-in-law's car.'

'For godsake, old man,' Miriam shouted, 'have you gone dumb as well as deaf? Tell the lieutenant what he wants to know.'

Clarence slumped down in his chair and stared at the table.

'I gave it to Seth,' he said finally.

'Seth?' Miriam cried out.

Thorne looked at the old lady and raised his hand to quiet her, then turned to face Clarence. Suddenly he knew at least part of the truth: he was looking at Dandy.

'Suppose you start at the beginning. First I want to know all about your relationship with Seth Anthony.'

The old man's words came out so muffled that Thorne had to read his lips to understand.

'His name's not Anthony – it's Sawyer. Seth is my son.'

Thorne ignored the moan he heard coming from Miriam.

'What do you mean, your son?'

'Seth was Jim's brother. His twin brother.'

Miriam sank down in her chair, the top of her body swaying as if she were about to fall. Thorne reached out to steady her; but he kept his eyes fixed on her husband.

'Go on,' he said.

Clarence avoided his wife's eyes, looking only at Thorne.

'When Miriam became pregnant, it was quite a shock. Neither of us were youngsters at the time, we were well into our forties. We'd given up any thought of having children by then.'

Thorne stared at him, unable to believe what he was hearing. What could he possibly say to justify giving away his child?

'Miriam was never a well woman, lieutenant. When we found out she was expecting, it darn well threw us into a panic. And when we learned she was going to have twins, it was twice the shock. Now, I wasn't that upset myself – I kind of liked the idea. I'd always wanted kids. But Miriam came near to having a nervous breakdown. You see, there was a history of mental illness in her family – the mother, the sister, the grandmother – and I was afraid she might develop the same kind of problems.' His eyes searched Thorne's, trying to enlist his understanding. 'So I promised her I'd help out, do anything to make it easier, and I did. You can ask her yourself.'

Miriam sat whimpering in her chair. Thorne wasn't about to ask her anything.

'Those first months,' Clarence went on, 'I was up at dawn, changing diapers, washing clothes, and when I'd get home from work, I'd take over the care of the youngsters while she rested. But as it turned out, it wasn't Miriam I should of been worrying about . . .'

'Go on, Mr Sawyer.'

'You see,' he said finally, 'the boys didn't look much alike – more like brothers than twins. And for sure they didn't act alike. Miriam fed both of them at the breast. One day I came home to find things in a bad way. Real bad. When Seth was feeding, he hurt the wife – bit down hard on her, so hard I had to take her to the doctor. She had gotten mad. After all, when something hurts you, surprising you like that . . .'

Thorne sighed. 'She beat the baby. All right, go on.'

'It was only the one time, it never happened again, and it wasn't a bad beating – nothing broken, nothing like that. But after that she wouldn't put the boy to the breast. That she was adamant about: only Jim would she feed that way. Finally I had to face facts: it just wasn't going to work. The boy refused the bottle though both Miriam and myself sat with him for hours trying to get him to take it. He'd cry and scream all day long. Always angry. Once even going after his own brother in the playpen. He had a temper, that one. Whenever I'd come home, I'd find them all crying and carrying on until finally I had to do something.'

'So you gave him up.'

Clarence took a deep breath, then went on.

'I made inquiries. Found a good orphanage, close by.'

Miriam, who had been hunched over in her chair, sobbing, now jerked her head up. 'You didn't! You told me you found the boy a good home – a childless couple who wanted to take him in like their own, adopt him. Not an orphanage!'

'I thought you'd maybe get stronger.' His pale eyes confronted hers. 'I thought someday we'd be able to take him back home with us – adopt him, legal-like. But you never did get stronger. Even with just taking care of the one child, and him as sweet-tempered a baby as God ever made, you whined and complained.'

'For godsake, Clarence. Where did you finally leave him?'

'I took the boy to St Anthony's here in town.'

'You *left* him there?'

'I visited him regular – every day. I wanted to give him all the caring and attention we gave his brother.'

Thorne looked back and forth from Miriam to Clarence, both of whom had forgotten he was there.

'Did he know who you were?' he asked Clarence softly.

'No, he never knew. I was Dandy to him – a friend, that's all. Oh, of course I wanted to be more than that, and he wanted it too. God knows how I ached to bring him back home. But I couldn't.' He pointed at his wife and shouted at the top of his voice. 'And you, old lady – may God damn you forever – you're the reason why.'

Thorne held up his hand. 'Stop it.' They both looked up at him, as if startled to find him still seated in their kitchen. 'Mr Sawyer, did Seth know either Jim or Jennifer?'

Clarence shook his head. 'Only from what I told him. He was always asking questions about my family, and I'd tell him – it made him a part of things. Now, he might of known who Jim was from school. I wouldn't know about that.'

Thorne was having trouble digesting it all – he had never heard anything like it. Who would give away his child in real life?

'Where is Seth now?' he asked.

'At the cabin.'

'*Where?*'

Sawyer looked again at his wife, as if there were still something left to tell.

'I gave him the folks' cabin in Maine. He's been living there now almost two years... I help him out with expenses. I wanted him to have all the advantages—'

'Then you know where he is now?' Thorne cut in.

'Well, of course I do. I got a letter from him just the other day. He's doing all right for himself – got a couple of youngsters and a good woman he's about to marry. He's had a rough time of it over the years, but he's straightened out—'

'Get me the letter.'

The old man stood up and scuttled out of the room, leaving Thorne and Miriam staring at each other, not speaking, until he returned.

Thorne read the letter, then looked up.

'Don't you understand, Sawyer? He's talking about Jennifer and the children. I want you to take me there.'

Clarence nodded but didn't move.

'Now!'

'I'll get my jacket,' Clarence said.

Miriam stood up, grabbing onto the back of the chair to steady herself.

'I'm going, too. Just give me a minute to get dressed.'

Just before eight o'clock, Jen cornered Seth alone in the kitchen.

'Now that we're a family,' she said, 'I think we should act like one.'

He looked at her, his expression wounded.

'The children, Seth. It's not natural to lock kids in their room at night – it frightens them. You're my husband now.

You're their father. Of all people, you ought to be able to understand.'

He thought about it, then nodded.

'All right, but I want you to warn them not to leave their room.' He smiled shyly. 'After all, Jennifer, tonight is special. We don't want any interruptions.'

She smiled back at him.

'Okay, kids,' she called out, 'time for bed. Let's get moving.'

Margo and Matthew jumped up as if she'd rung a bell and headed upstairs. Once in their room, Jen pulled them near the window, and they huddled together.

'When I go down, you get dressed. You have no pants, Margo, so I want you to wear your brother's clothes. Both of you put on long johns, cords, and heavy flannel shirts. Now, it's cold out there. Don't forget to zip up your jackets and wear a hat.'

They nodded.

'As soon as you hear Seth and me close the door to our room, you wait five minutes, then tiptoe out of your room and downstairs. Don't forget to close the bedroom door when you leave, and don't even whisper until you're away from the house. And remember, if you hear a car, run into the woods till it passes.'

She grabbed both of them and hugged them tightly.

'Now, I'm counting on you. I'm cheering for you like I cheer for you at the meets. And ... I love you.' They all hugged each other until Jen pushed away, afraid she'd start to cry.

A few moments later she closed their door and stood at the top of the landing, taking enough deep breaths to calm herself. Then, with slow, even steps, she descended the stairs to meet Seth for the second time that day. He was waiting for her on the sofa: she sat down next to him, lightly touching his arm.

'I've fixed us a tray of cheese and crackers,' she said. 'Suppose we take that along with glasses and the bottle of wine to our room?'

Seth carried the tray up to the bedroom. Once inside, Jen shut the door, took the tray from him and set it on the end table. He put his arms around her from behind, hugging her and nuzzling her neck.

Gently she disengaged his arms, then turned to face him.

'Please, Seth, I'm a little bit nervous.' She giggled; it sounded false to her ear, but Seth was smiling. 'A glass or two of wine will help me relax,' she said. 'And then it will be even more wonderful.'

She poured the wine into each of the glasses, her hands almost steady. Setting the bottle down, she handed him a glass.

'To us. To our family.'

They sat on the edge of their bed and touched glasses.

Down the hall, Margo and Matthew had already put on their warm clothes. Margo edged her way to the door.

'Is it time, Matthew?'

'Not yet. Mama said five minutes.'

They waited, breathing heavily as if they were already running. Finally Matthew nodded to Margo, carefully cracked open the door and peeked out. There was no one in the hallway, but he could hear mama talking: her voice was real low, kind of out of breath. He hesitated a few moments, then grabbed Margo's hand and tugged at it. Slowly, they tiptoed out of the room. Matthew shut the door very carefully, then put his finger to his lips. He reached for the bannister with his other hand, wincing in anticipation of a creak from the staircase. He lowered one foot down – only a faint squeak – then the other foot. Margo followed along until they were both on the first floor.

Margo headed right towards the front door, but as she passed the cellar stairs, Matthew grabbed her arm.

'Wait.' He opened the door; she stood still as Matthew turned on the light and went down the cellar steps. He held his breath so he wouldn't have to smell the awful stink, then headed for the workbench. He searched the cabinet shelves, then the drawers, stopping his search at the bottom drawer when he saw the long wooden box. He lifted it out. Heavy. He tried to open it, but it was locked. Holding it up, he shook the box – the handguns were in there – then set it on the floor and pushed it way back through the narrow space under the workbench. Matthew stood up, pulled the rifle off the shelf, and went upstairs.

Before Margo could say anything he put his hand over her mouth and nodded for her to follow him. Together they tiptoed out of the house, carefully closing the front door behind them. They ran from the yard to the road, then turned left in the direction of town. They had only gone a few hundred yards when Margo put her hand on Matthew's arm, stopping him.

'Why'd you take the rifle?'

'Because I don't want him to be able to use it. Come on, let's get moving.'

'What if it goes off?'

'It's got a safety guard. Seth showed me how to use it.' He hitched the black strap up on his shoulder. 'Come on.'

Then together they began to run: little by little, pacing themselves, increasing their rhythm; their bodies like a machine, one piece setting another into motion. They passed clumps of trees as if the trees themselves were moving to meet them. Faster, then faster.

They were running for their lives now – and for mama's as well.

Clarence had been holding the pocket watch in his hand for the past two hours, watching the second hand creep round and round. It was 8:15. Though the lieutenant was driving at a good speed, it was rainy and foggy and the mountainous roads weren't easy to make time on at night. They had an hour to go yet.

No one had said much during the trip, not even Miriam. It was as if they were silently conversing with themselves – himself most of all, Clarence supposed. What had he done to make things turn out so badly? How could he have known that all this time Seth's interest in Jennifer and the children was anything more than just a lonely boy's curiosity about his friend's family? The boy always loved to hear about Jim, and even Miriam.

And then once the grandchildren were born, Seth never missed a time asking about them and Jennifer. Once he'd even sent a pair of hand-carved lovebirds he'd made himself for Clarence to send to them. And Clarence had sent it along in the mail pretending it was from the wife and himself. He just couldn't understand why Seth would want to do a thing like this. After all, the boy cared about them as if they were his own family – he'd told Clarence that himself. All this time he'd been telling Clarence about *his* sweetheart, *his* children. They were Jim's, not his. But all this time, the boy had been fooling himself into thinking they were.

Clarence sighed. There was just no point in blaming Miriam for all of this trouble, even though she'd been the one who forced him to give up his own flesh and blood in the first place. The more he thought about it, the more he could see the truth – he'd mishandled the whole thing right from the start.

Thorne spoke to him for the first time in over an hour

'I don't know if now's the time to bring this up, but I suppose it's as good a time as any. Didn't you think it was quite a coincidence that Seth should be the one to find Jim and report his death?'

Miriam spoke up quietly from the back seat.

'Why, I never even knew that.'

Clarence shook his head.

'I suppose it was, but I never made much of it. Are you saying that it was more than just a coincidence? That Jim's death wasn't an accident?'

'I'm saying that Seth wanted to be your son and he always believed he would be – at least, it sounds that way from the conversation I had at the orphanage. Under those circumstances, he could easily resent his brother.'

'But Seth never knew Jim was his brother.'

'That may be true, but he did know Jim was your son, and he might have looked at him like he'd taken something that

219

belonged to him – namely, you. I'm no psychiatrist, but I'd guess he must have hated Jim.'

Clarence put his head down into his hands, covering his face but not even trying to muffle the little cries coming out of him. Miriam sat forward on the back seat and put her hand on his shoulder. It was the first time in years that she'd shown any sign of affection for him, and it made him even sadder. He lifted his arm and grabbed onto her hand, holding it tightly.

God help them – what had they done?

CHAPTER TWENTY-TWO

JEN WAS STILL NURSING HER FIRST GLASS of wine when Seth put down his glass, stood up and extended his hand to pull her to him. She looked up and smiled playfully.

'Come on, Seth, just one more little sip.'

Seth laid his hand over hers, slipped the glass from her fingers, and placed it on the table.

'That's enough, Jennifer.'

She put her hand into his and let him pull her up.

'Seth, you've got to give me some time to get ready.' Her voice got lower. 'I want to look beautiful for you.'

He squeezed her hand.

'First let's go look in on our children.'

'But this is our time, Seth. Besides, I'm sure they're fast asleep by now.'

'That may be, but I'd feel better looking in on them. I want to check – make sure they're covered up, nice and warm.'

'Why don't I just go and take a peek myself? It'll only take me a minute.'

'You're forgetting something, Jennifer. I'm their daddy now.'

Jen watched as Seth headed for the door. She leaned down and grabbed the wineglass from the table, kicked off her shoes and followed him out to the hallway, her mind searching for the right words, the words that would stop him. But the words all seemed to swim around in her head, not lighting long enough so she could find just the ones she needed.

Seth put his finger to his lips.

'We'll be very quiet.' He reached down to turn the knob and Jen looked down at her glass. The moment her eyes saw it, she loosened her fingers from around the stem, letting it fall to the floor. The glass shattered on the landing, sending a puddle of wine down the stairs. Wincing, she ground her foot into a piece of glass.

'Ow!' she cried.

'Are you all right, Jennifer?'

'I think I've got glass in my foot.'

'Lean against the wall and let me see.' Jen backed up toward the wall and raised her foot, letting Seth pull out the chip of glass.

'Oh, I've made such a mess. It was so clumsy of me.'

'It's okay, Jennifer – it was only an accident. As long as you're all right, that's all that counts. Now, there's not much blood, nothing that can't be fixed up with a Band-aid. I'll go get one, you wait right here.'

As he headed into the bathroom, Jen took a step to the children's door, quietly cracking it open.

'Now, you two get right back to sleep. We didn't mean to wake you. It was my fault, I dropped a glass.' She waited a moment, then went on. 'No, no, everything is just fine. Cover up and get back to sleep, now. Daddy is taking care of everything.'

She closed the door and turned around to see Seth watching her from the bathroom doorway, a Band-aid in his hand, a huge smile lighting his face. He came to her, lifted her foot and, bending over, tore the backing off the adhesive strip and pressed it to the bottom of her foot.

'Let's go back to our room,' he said, his eyes moving over her body. 'Now, we'll get ready.'

She followed him back to the bedroom and opened the top dresser drawer, lifting out a filmy black nightgown. She hurried into the master bathroom. It had been at least twenty minutes since they'd come upstairs, which meant the children were well on their way. She undressed, folding her clothes in a neat pile on the toilet tank, then slipped the gown over her head. It fell around her body in soft pleats. Jen wrapped her arms around herself, feeling chilled, and lifted her face to look in the mirror. She'd lived through the rape: she'd live through this. The important thing was to buy as much time as possible by keeping Seth happy. She paused, and a shudder went through her. *Would* this make him happy? Did she really know what would make him happy?

She could hear his footsteps outside the door – he was pacing. She took a deep breath, lifted her chin, then turned the doorknob and pushed the door open.

Seth stood naked in the centre of the room, his arms folded tightly over his chest, a granite statue looking down at her. She lifted her feet – chunks of clay moving toward him. It was then that she saw the tattoo on his arm – her name carved in granite. She stared at the letters, unable to look away, feeling as though she'd somehow been robbed. First he'd taken her name then he'd taken her. He had always known, hadn't he? He had known all along that this night would happen. She turned her eyes away . . .

Now she stood in front of him, their bodies almost touching – but the statue didn't move. She waited, her eyes half-closed, her jaws clamped shut, until she felt his hand on her arm, leading her to the bed. He pulled the gown over her head and eased her down onto the mattress. She swallowed hard and focused her mind on the children: *Right now they were running. To safety . . . She had to give them more time.* Lifting her arms, she placed her hands gently on the back of his head, her fingers stroking his hair. He reached out to pull her hands away. She moved her lips to his, but he drew back, his features stiff, his expression forbidding. She lay there waiting. *More time . . . give them more time.* Then he looked down at her breasts and his eyes grew moist and glistening. His head sank down, his mouth at her breast. She let her arms lay limply at her sides, not daring to touch.

Then she felt his teeth – pain rocketed through her body. Her hands squeezed into tight balls, but she held them at her sides. *More time . . . more time.* And then she heard his cries. Like echoes of the past breaking through the barrier in her brain, she remembered. She remembered the cemetery.

'Mama ... Mama ... MaaaMaaa!' The high-pitched wail screeched in her eardrums like a drill boring into her head.

Obscenities – anything, but not this. Now she fought, her body writhing and twisting, legs kicking, fists pounding against his back, his head. But with each blow Seth's excitement grew, then mounted as if her blows were caresses. His hot trembling body, slick with sweat, was now all over her, his cries filling the room. She tasted blood in her mouth. Then her body jerked backward, and her head crashed against the headboard ...

Seth leaned over her, gently fingering the lump on the base of her skull. 'Jennifer?'

She lay there, not moving.

'Jennifer, talk to me.'

Still she didn't answer.

He ran to the bathroom, soaked down a washcloth with cold water, came back and held it on the swelling. 'It'll be okay, Jennifer, I promise you.' With his other hand, he stroked her hair, and then he smiled down at her. 'You were so wonderful, Jennifer. Do you know that? Sweet and beautiful and ladylike. Just like I knew you'd be. And it's only the beginning ... The kids and—' He stopped. Shouldn't he check up on the kids? The noise might have awakened them. He adjusted the cloth on her head, then pulled the covers up around her and headed to the children's room.

The moment he turned the knob, he felt it: like a hot coal had begun to sizzle in his chest. He threw open the door and looked around the room. The children were gone.

First he got her clothes, then he grasped his hands on her shoulders and pulled her up. 'They're gone, Jennifer. The children are gone!'

Silence.

'Let's go look for them,' he said. With one hand he held her in a sitting position and with the other he tried to pull her arm through the blouse sleeve. She didn't move, her eyes stayed shut. He threw the blouse on the floor. What now? He couldn't just leave her here like this – he couldn't do that.

It only took him a few moments to decide. He gently lifted

her, careful not to disturb her sleep, and carried her down to the cellar. He would find the children and bring them back before she even woke up. It was a good thing she'd banged her head and fallen off like this – what would she do if she knew they had run off? He didn't think she'd even heard when he'd told her, which was just as well: she'd only worry and cry sad tears, and he didn't think he could stand that. Here he was, a husband promising her a good life, a family – and now the kids were trying to spoil it all. Once he got hold of them, he'd really teach them a lesson. How could they do a thing like this, especially to Jennifer? There wasn't a better mother in the whole world. Maybe she'd been a little too light on them, a little too lenient, but one thing he'd learned if nothing else: kids need daddies to keep them in line.

He pulled down the latch and opened the chamber, placing her carefully on the dank floor and sliding a soft duffle bag under her head. Then he stood up and looked down at her. She looked so peaceful, so beautiful he hated to leave her here, but he didn't have much choice. Where else would she be this safe? It was his duty to take care of her, and he wasn't about to forget that, not after tonight. Not after she'd made him so happy.

'I'll bring them back, don't you worry,' he whispered, closing the wall panel from the outside. He ran over to the work bench and slid open the cabinet, searching with his hands for the rifle. Gone! He looked around in a panic, then crouched down, pulled open the drawer and groped for the flat wooden box. He couldn't find it. He stood up, fists balled at his sides, a storm beginning to rage in his head. *Easy . . . calm . . . easy . . . calm.* He recited the words in his head just like Dandy had taught him. And just like Dandy had promised, saying them cleared his mind, helped him to think.

He hurried back to the chamber, pushed the shelving aside again and reached down for Jen's suitcase. He unzipped the little bag and pulled out the revolver. *She must have known all along, she must have known someday we'd need it.* He closed the compartment once more, locked it, stuck the revolver in his belt, then ran as fast as he could out to the car. They couldn't have gotten that far – and even if they had, he'd find them. After all, they were only kids.

The two of them had been running for forty-five minutes at a steady pace when Margo reached out and tapped Matthew's shoulder to stop him.

'You okay?' he asked.

It took her a few moments to catch her breath.

'Yes, but I need a break.'

He pulled the rifle off his shoulder and they both sat down on the wet grass under a huge tree. There was just enough moonlight for them to make each other out.

'How much longer do you think we have to go, Matthew?'

He looked around.

'I don't know for sure, but we must of gone more than five miles by now. Mama said it would be eight, maybe ten, so we must be more than halfway.'

'Do you think she's all right?'

'We've got to believe she is, just like you said, or else all this is wasted.' He touched the rifle in his lap. 'And remember, we've got his gun.'

'What about the other gun? The one he used that day in the woods?'

Matthew smiled. 'It was locked in a box and I hid it.'

Margo decided not to say anything about mama bringing daddy's old gun with her in the suitcase. There was no use in worrying him more – besides, Seth probably never even found it. Still, just the thought of the gun made her jumpy. She stood up.

'Let's get moving, Matthew.'

Just as Matthew stood up and slid the rifle strap over his shoulder, they heard the car cruising along the road. He grabbed Margo's arm and pulled her behind the thick tree trunk. They fell to their knees and peeked around the tree. The car had slowed to a stop.

'Is it Seth?'

'Shush.' Matthew squinted, trying to make out the car, but he couldn't. It sat at the side of the road about two hundred yards away from them. They waited several minutes, but nothing happened: then the car door opened and they could see a figure walk across the road headed in their direction. They still couldn't make out who it was, but they knew it was Seth.

Margo pulled at her brother's sleeve.

'We better run, Matthew.'

'No,' he whispered, watching the figure headed in their direction. It was still a good distance away.

'He'll see us for sure, Margo. Stay on your hands and knees and follow me.'

Matthew began to crawl, slowly, quietly leading the way. Pine needles and pebbles stuck in their hands and knees, but neither made a sound. Finally, Matthew stopped and pointed ahead to a ditch. Once they reached it, he leaned down and inspected it, then looked at his sister. 'Come on.'

They both let themselves down carefully, all the way to the bottom. Margo sat up, wiping her face with the back of her hand.

'Matthew, do you think he saw us?'

'Why else would he of stopped here?'

'Oh God, we've got to get out of here – we've got to get help.'

'What we've got to do, Margo, is listen so we'll know when his car pulls away and it's safe for us to climb out.' Then they heard the voice call out to them.

'Matthew . . . Margo. Come on out wherever you are. I'm going to take you home to mama. She's looking for you. She wants you home.'

'I'm scared,' Margo whispered.

Matthew put his arm around his sister and pulled her close to him. Margo could feel his breath on her face. They sat huddled together, listening.

CHAPTER TWENTY-THREE

JEN OPENED HER EYES – to darkness. She sat up instantly feeling the sharp pain course through her head . . . her breasts and down her body. She raised her hand, wincing as her fingers touched the lump, then twisting her head from side to side, she looked around, but couldn't see a thing. Her breathing was laboured; she hung her head down for a moment, taking long, deep breaths. And that's when she recognized the smell: the cellar. Oh, God, why was she here? She had to get upstairs; she had to get out of the suffocating darkness.

She tried to stand up, but her legs buckled beneath her and she toppled onto the floor. She slid herself forward, inching along the damp cement floor, trying to find the wall. Her eyes had adjusted to the darkness, enough so she could make out vague oblong images in her path. Her hand touched something furry . . . it moved . . . scooting away from beneath her fingers. She jerked her hand back, shuddering and wrapped her arms around her naked body, hugging herself.

She sat still, listening, not daring to move; she could almost hear the silence. Then, slowly lifting her head and squinting, she looked around the room. The cellar looked different than she remembered it – smaller – and she could make out the whitewashed walls around her. She reached out, yanking a cloth from a table, and threw it across her shoulders. Then, standing, she groped for a light, waving her arms back and forth in the air over her head. For a brief second her hand touched a string, then lost it. Finally she caught it and tugged at the cord. The light was dim, but bright enough to see that there was no door. Jen realized that she was in some kind of secret room off the main cellar.

Now Jen noticed the two long wooden benches topped with glass. Each one stretched from wall to wall; each one was delicately hand-carved with animals, birds, and butterflies on the sides. Had Seth made these? She walked over and looked through the glass tops. When she saw the remains of the dead animals, she bolted to the other corner of the room; a spasm wrenched her stomach and she vomited, spattering the walls. Finally she dragged herself away from the mess and stood in the centre of the room.

The smell was making her dizzy: her legs threatened to buckle. She tried to breathe through her mouth, but it felt as though her throat were closing up and she would soon choke. Then, looking down, she realized that the cloth draped over her had not come from a table. A big wooden box, three feet high, stood on the cement floor in front of her. She stared at it, hesitating, wondering if she dared. More dead animals? Gingerly she reached down and very slowly lifted the lid. Suddenly she heard screams, echoing through the chamber, louder and louder. She slammed her hands over her ears, not even realizing that the screams were coming from her. '*Stop! Make it stop!*'

The box lid was up and she was staring inside. The thin gold plaque on the edge of the lid read: James B. Sawyer.

Jen was still shrieking when Thorne threw open the front door to the cabin. He froze for a moment, looking, listening, trying to figure out where the sounds were coming from. Downstairs. He headed for the first door he saw, flipped the light switch and ran down the stairs. He looked around, feeling at the walls as he did.

'Dammit! Where is it coming from?'

Clarence, behind him on the stairs, pointed towards the shelving.

'There's a sliding panel. The latch is under the shelf.'

Thorne pulled the latch and pushed the shelving aside. Jen was standing over the coffin, naked, her hands over her ears, her eyes squeezed shut, screaming her head off. A shroud lay on the floor at her feet. Thorne flinched when he saw her bruised, bleeding body. He grabbed the cloth and tried to swing it around her: she pushed him away, beating at his chest with her fists.

The Sawyers, holding on to one another as if they were scared to let go, crept up slowly behind him and looked into the coffin. Thorne looked too, then shut his eyes and closed the lid. He dropped the shroud and reached down for Jen, lifting her in his arms.

'Get upstairs,' he told the Sawyers as he ran up carrying Jen. Once there, he grabbed the throw cover from the couch and wrapped it around her, then stretched her out and knelt beside her on the floor.

'Can you hear me?' His voice was choked.

Her eyes opened and focused on him.

'Mike . . .'

Tears ran down her cheeks. Thorne pulled a handkerchief from his pants pocket and wiped at the tears.

'Good girl. Cry.'

Suddenly she stopped and tried to sit up, her hands pushing against the sofa pillows.

'The children, Mike. He's out there looking for them.'

Thorne ran his thumbs in outward strokes along her cheeks.

'We'll find them – don't worry. Tell me where they went.'

'To get help.'

'Where can I find some blankets, Jen.'

She pointed to the closet. Thorne got the blankets, came back, and bundled Jen in the covers.

'Are you warm enough?' She nodded and he lifted her up. 'Then let's get the hell out of here.'

Clarence and Miriam stood backed against the wall, their white faces a stark contrast against the wood.

'Get in the car,' Thorne said. 'We're going to find your grandchildren.'

Clarence scurried along, pulling Miriam at his side, and climbed into the back seat. Thorne put Jen on the front seat next to him, then rolled down the window at her side.

'Breathe in – deep.'

She took a deep breath, holding the fresh air in her lungs a long time before letting it out.

'All right, now.' He turned the key in the ignition. 'Which way do we go? Further up the mountain or down?'

'Down,' she said. 'Towards the village.'

They had travelled five miles before they spotted the car. Thorne turned off his lights and engine, coasting the last few hundred yards until they reached the blue Ford. He got out, feeling for his gun at his belt.

'You stay here,' he said. 'All of you.'

To Thorne's surprise, Clarence opened the rear door.

'Let me out,' he said. 'He'll listen to me.'

Thorne paused for a moment, debating with himself.

'All right, you come.' He looked at Miriam, sitting silently in the back seat. 'You stay here and help your daughter-in-law. You might start by explaining to her who Seth is.' Finally, he looked down at Jen.

'Lock the door after me. If you see anything, turn the key and lean on the horn.'

Seth had been searching the area with a lantern for more than forty-five minutes without catching a glimpse of the children. He knew they were here – he'd caught sight of them as he was coming down the mountain. At first he'd thought it was only an animal darting around a tree, but the more he thought about it, the more sure he was. Certain feelings he had learned to trust. And now – they had disappeared into nowhere. If they had run off, he would have seen or heard something, but he hadn't. He wasn't about to leave this area; he knew they were still here.

All the time he was behind the wheel, all the time he was searching in the woods, he had been carrying around a picture of Jennifer in his head like she was sitting right there inside him, where God sometimes sat. And just like God sometimes looked, her face was angry. Why shouldn't she be? He hadn't kept his promise, he hadn't taken care of the children properly like he swore he would. By the look in her eyes he knew she blamed him – even though he also knew that she couldn't possibly be mad at him yet, that she hadn't even woken up yet from her sleep. Was this the picture of what was to come? Jennifer's *hate?* And if it was, would he have a chance to change it? Or was everything going to happen because it was meant to happen?

Thoughts like that always made him feel like a bug with a pin stuck in his back, wiggling to get free. If things were destined to happen right from the start of conception, then what were his chances of ever really being happy, of ever making his life the way he wanted it to be? What were dreams but vicious tricks that your mind played on you, like giving a winning lottery ticket to a dying man?

He tried to push the fear out of his mind as he patrolled the area. He had tried shouting to the children, but they wouldn't answer. He still didn't understand how they could do a thing like this to their own mother. There he was, thinking his children were perfect – and now this. Had both he and Jennifer been wrong about them, had Jennifer maybe been in danger all this time while she'd been living alone with them? If they had this flaw, and if it had sprouted from his seed, no one else but he would know how to handle them. They needed his restraint, his protection, as much as Jennifer needed protection against them.

He could feel an aching fullness in his bladder, but he didn't dare unzip his fly and relieve himself. If he did that, who knew what else would leave him in the process? No, he could no longer afford any mistakes. He needed everything in his power, everything inside him, to behave rationally and do what was necessary. *Easy, calm, easy, calm.* This time the words weren't helping. No matter how many times he said them, his muscles still twitched and jerked . . .

He squatted down in the bushes, holding his gun ready to fire if anyone dared to hurt or take his children. He would never abandon them. Never. Suddenly he felt a peculiar thickness in the air, closing in closer and closer to his body. Then he knew. The something that always threatened to take him in his sleep was now hovering over him, watching, waiting. He mustn't let down his guard now, not for a split second.

He put the lantern on the ground and crouched in the bushes. His two hands grasped the gun tightly, trying to keep it from shaking. He was almost in control.

Thorne had quietly searched the area, but found nothing.

'Let me call to him,' Clarence pleaded. 'There's no need for guns, lieutenant. I know he'll come to me.'

Thorne looked around the forest, then back at Sawyer.

'Okay, give it a try. But stand right here with me, behind the bushes.'

Clarence cupped his hands around his mouth.

'Seth! It's me, Dandy.' They listened. Nothing. 'Seth, I'm here to help you. Please answer me.' Still nothing. 'I know you're here, Seth, and I'm not leaving until you come out. Do you hear?'

This time they heard a voice call out – a child's voice.

'Dandy . . .'

As Thorne turned his head, trying to figure out where the voice was coming from, Clarence scooted out from behind the bushes and headed towards the centre clearing. Thorne pulled out his gun.

'Get back here,' he called out, but Clarence kept walking.

'Come on out, Seth,' he said again. 'You know I won't let yone hurt you. Come here to Dandy.'

It was then that the spotlight went on and Thorne saw Seth standing behind the thick brush, holding a gun pointed at him.

'Drop that gun, and put your hands over your head,' he said. 'Then come close, close enough so I can keep an eye on you. Don't do something that's not going to leave me with any choices. I don't want to have to hurt anyone. Please don't make me.'

Thorne raised his hands over his head and moved out of the brush towards Seth. He stopped a little distance behind Clarence, then dropped his gun.

'Get back,' Thorne warned Clarence. But the old man kept walking until he was no more than ten feet from Seth.

'Stop right there, Dandy.'

Clarence spread his hands.

'It's okay, son, no one's going to hurt you. Throw that gun away and come over here to me. I've got something important to tell you – something I've wanted to tell you for a long, long time.'

'I don't want to hear it. I know why you're here and why he's here – with the gun.' He gestured towards Thorne. 'And I'm not letting you do it.'

'Do what, Seth?' What is it you think we want?'

'You want to take Jennifer and the children away from me. You want to give them back to Jim.'

'Why, that's not true at all, son. Jim's dead – remember, Seth? Jim's dead.'

'You're just saying that to trick me, Dandy. If Jim were dead, you would have made *me* your son. Your sick wife would have been able to handle another little boy to take his place.'

'No, Seth, you're not thinking clearly. Try to be calm, try to remember. You've told me yourself, you went to visit him at the cemetery,'

Seth stood there a moment, thinking. 'You mean the creepy, crawly bugs?'

'That's right, son. Now you remember.'

Seth looked at Thorne, then back again at Clarence. 'I took him away from the bugs, Dandy. So you wouldn't have to worry about him anymore. It was my duty to do that.'

'I understand, you did it for me.'

'But I'm not going to do this for you. I'm not going to let you take my family away from me. You don't understand. The children are sick. I have to protect them, watch over them. I promised Jennifer.'

'If the children are ill, Seth, you've got to bring them home, let us get them to a doctor.'

'Oh no, that's not the kind of sick they are. Guess what, Dandy?'

'You're not listening, son.'

'But I've got something to tell you. Something important.'

'Okay, Seth, you tell me first.'

'Today I made Jennifer my wife. She loves me, Dandy. It's finally *me* she loves, not Jim.'

'Why, that's fine news, boy. All the more reason why you've got to respect her wishes. She wants the children back. She told me that herself.'

'You couldn't have talked to Jennifer, Dandy, you must have been mistaken. She's fast asleep back at the cabin, waiting for me and the children. Why don't you go back home to take care of Jim, and let me get on with what I have to do. If I don't hurry, Jennifer's going to be mad at me. Real mad.'

Hearing a sound, Thorne jerked his head in time to see a small figure scurrying behind a bush. Seth and Clarence twisted around at the same time. Seth flashed the light on the bush.

'Margo,' he called. 'Come on out – I see you. Come here to Daddy.'

No answer. The girl crouched near the ground, her body partially covered by branches.

'Do you hear me?' Seth shouted. 'Get over here, now.'

Still no answer.

'Now son,' Clarence said. 'There's no point in shouting like that. You're just scaring the youngster. I've told you time and time again, you can't just demand things like that.'

Seth's voice softened to almost a whisper.

'But Dandy, I just want to see her – talk to her. That's all I want.'

Clarence looked at Seth for a few moments, then sighed.

'I'll tell you what. If you promise to behave, if you promise to let the children go back where they belong, I'll get Margo over here myself. Now, first you give me your word.'

Seth glanced again at Thorne, then back at Clarence.

'I promise.' He set the lantern on the ground and tilted the light upward.

Sawyer slowly crept up to the bush as Seth's eyes travelled back and forth from Thorne to Clarence.

'Margo, honey,' Clarence called softly. 'It's me, grandpa. You can come on out now. There's nothing to be scared of. Grandpa's going to take care of things. You just come with me.'

He reached in his hand. Slowly, hesitantly, a little hand reached out and Clarence took hold of it. Margo stood up, letting him pull her away from the bush. He put his arm around her shoulder and hugged her. 'Now don't you be frightened, honey. Everything's going to be just fine.'

Margo hung onto his arm as he led her into the clearing. As he walked her towards Seth, she stopped, pulling Clarence to a stop with her.

'Now, it's okay, honey. Come with grandpa.'

Seth finally took his eyes away from Thorne as Clarence came forward pulling Margo closer and closer. It was then that Thorne dived to the ground. As he swept the pistol up and grabbed it with both hands, Seth lunged out from the bushes, grabbing Margo from Sawyer and pulling her to him. Thorne's hands froze instantly.

'Drop it!' Seth shouted.

Thorne looked at Seth, then at the girl pulled tightly against him. He dropped the gun and slowly raised his hands.

'Stand up and kick the gun away.'

Thorne stood up and shoved it forward with his foot. 'Let the girl go,' he said. 'Then we'll all go together to find Jennifer.'

'No, you don't understand. This is my little girl, *I'm* going to take her to Jennifer.' Seth looked down at Margo, whose body was as stiff as a plank of wood. 'Right, honey?'

Clarence started to object, but Seth paid no attention. He rocked Margo as if she were a baby while his one hand still held his gun. 'Daddy has you now.'

Suddenly she began to fight: her feet kicked back at Seth's legs, her fists beat against his arms.

'Let me go!' she screamed. But he held on. Then, turning her head, she bit down on his arm.

Seth jumped back, enraged. He lifted his arm, balled his hand into a fist and swung.

He never completed his swing. They all heard the gunshot: Seth's arms flew upwards, his gun dropping from his hands as his fingers spread apart, clutching for air. His cry of anguish rang through the forest; his body snapped forward and sank to the ground.

Thorne leaped forward and grabbed Margo, then looked up. Behind Seth – with both legs spread apart and both feet firmly planted on the ground to steady himself – stood Matthew, the rifle clenched tightly in his hands.

Clarence knelt beside Seth, rubbing his hands over his chest, crying. Thorne carried Margo to her brother and sat her down next to him. Gently he pulled the boy's stiff fingers from the trigger, then took the rifle from his hands.

'It's okay, Matthew. It's over now. Your mother is waiting for you and your sister in the car.'

The boy slowly forced his eyes from Seth to Thorne. Thorne took Matthew gently by the hand and then reached for Margo, leading both in the direction of the car.

Both children clung tightly to the man as they made their way back. A minute later they saw Jen. One hand was holding the covers around her; the other was waving in the air. She was running, barefoot – a smile on her face and tears on her cheeks.

EPILOGUE

IT WAS ONE WEEK LATER, and Number Two Arden Road in Winfield was once again brightly lit. Jen had just tucked in the children and tiptoed out of their rooms, leaving the night lights on. Matthew now had frequent nightmares and Margo had wet her bed several times. It would take time, she knew – it would take a while for the wounds to heal.

As for Jen, she found herself hovering over the children a little too much, worrying about them when they went out. But she was making an effort to watch herself, to keep the children from realizing how nervous she still was. It was up to her now to quieten their fears, not reinforce them . . .

But the truth was, the fear had not yet left her. It was still hard for her to believe that Seth was Jim's twin – all those years and Jim never knowing he'd had a brother or, for that matter, Seth never knowing that the boy he'd envied for so long was his own flesh and blood. Had Seth had anything to do with Jim's accident? They would never know; they could only wonder. And there she was – not once suspecting that the man who'd raped her even knew who she was when, in fact, Clarence had told him everything. Had Seth been watching her himself, too? Just another thing she'd never know for certain. But she had taken to locking her doors – no need to invite trouble. She shivered and tried to push the thoughts away; it was not good to dwell on them.

She still hadn't spoken to Clarence or Miriam since the night Mike and she dropped them off on their way home. She would call eventually, of course. Margo and Matthew really *were* their son's children, although they would never know which son. With both their boys dead, she couldn't deprive them of grandchildren, too. After all, who was she to judge them? They'd be living with their mistakes and lies for the rest of their lives.

And what about her own lie? Even if she had wanted to tell the children who Seth was, she couldn't do it now. It was enough that Matthew would have to deal with knowing he'd killed someone; she could never let him know that he had killed his own father. It was a decision she'd made, and she'd just have to live with it. Lies were not easy, but sometimes the alternatives were even worse than the lies themselves.

She walked to the front door and flicked on the front porch light – she was expecting Mike. She hugged her arms around herself, smiling. He was fun and gentle – she liked him. And it was even more than that... She wondered how long it would be before she'd jump when a man tried to touch her. Mike was probably the most patient man she'd ever met in her entire life. Though the children still didn't say much, she could tell by the way they acted that they liked him too.

Tomorrow was the children's track meet. They were all going together. In fact, Mike said he was even bringing along a friend – someone he wanted them all to meet. The name, he had told her, was Miranda.

THE END

WELCOME TO THE DUNGEON

It is a fog where time twists minds and voices call out from a swallowing darkness.

It is a jungle in which finned creatures dwell and torment all that pass through its vines.

It is a maze whose tunnels trap the daring and whose creatures challenge the brave.

It is a chamber in which proportions are lost and fortitude is one's only weapon.

From the veldt of the dinosaurs to the gates of Tawn, this is the quest of Clive Folliot, explorer and hero.

Ask your bookseller for Volumes 1 and 2 of
Philip José Farmer's THE DUNGEON:

The Black Tower
The Dark Abyss